PENGUIN BOOKS

THE CHILD'S CHILD

Barbara Vine is the pen-name of bestselling crime writer Ruth Rendell. This is the fourteenth novel written under the Vine name. Ruth Rendell sits in the House of Lords as a Labour peer, and lives in Essex and in Maida Vale, London.

The Child's Child

BARBARA VINE

PENGUIN BOOKS

PENGUIN BOOKS

Published by the Penguin Group
Penguin Books Ltd, 80 Strand, London WC2R ORL, England
Penguin Group (USA) Inc., 375 Hudson Street, New York, New York 10014, USA
Penguin Group (Canada), 90 Eglinton Avenue East, Suite 700, Toronto, Ontario, Canada M4P 2Y3
(a division of Pearson Penguin Canada Inc.)
Penguin Ireland, 25 St Stephen's Green, Dublin 2, Ireland (a division of Penguin Books Ltd)
Penguin Group (Australia), 707 Collins Street, Melbourne, Victoria 3008, Australia
(a division of Pearson Australia Group Pty Ltd)
Penguin Books India Pvt Ltd, 11 Community Centre, Panchsheel Park, New Delhi – 110 017, India
Penguin Group (NZ), 67 Apollo Drive, Rosedale, Auckland 0632, New Zealand
(a division of Pearson New Zealand Ltd)
Penguin Books (South Africa) (Pty) Ltd, Block D, Rosebank Office Park, 181 Jan Smuts Avenue,
Parktown North, Gauteng 2193, South Africa

Penguin Books Ltd, Registered Offices: 80 Strand, London WC2R ORL, England

www.penguin.com

First published by Viking 2013
Published in Penguin Books 2014
002

Copyright © Kingsmarkham Enterprises Ltd, 2013
All rights reserved

The moral right of the author has been asserted

Typeset by Palimpsest Book Production Limited, Falkirk, Stirlingshire
Printed in Great Britain by Clays Ltd, St Ives plc

ISBN: 978-0-241-96357-9

www.greenpenguin.co.uk

Penguin Books is committed to a sustainable
future for our business, our readers and our planet.
This book is made from Forest Stewardship
Council™ certified paper.

2011

The book was on the table in front of us, along with the teapot, the two cups and a plate of mince pies. It *was* a book and not the manuscript I had expected and, if I'm honest, feared.

'Privately printed, as you see,' Toby Greenwell said.

'Your father had that done himself?'

'Oh, yes.'

He picked it up and handed it to me. Like many such books, it had no jacket but a shiny cover with a picture of a young girl with pigtails and wearing a gymslip. She was standing in a green meadow and the title of the novel had been amateurishly done in black letters by someone who was no expert in the art of Times Roman.

'When we spoke,' I said, 'you told me your father had mentioned this book to you but you never saw it till after he and your mother were dead. He was quite a distinguished novelist. He'd had – how many books published?'

'Twelve. They weren't bestsellers but they were – well, I think "widely acclaimed" would be the phrase, don't you?'

Toby is not a writer himself and never has been. He is an architect, retired now, and living with his wife and the one remaining child still at home in a house he designed himself in the Surrey Hills. We met in the Highgate house he'd inherited from his mother six months before, Victorian Gothic and not much admired by him, though he grew up there. Martin and Edith Greenwell lived there from some time in the 1930s, a few years before Toby was born, until Martin and then Edith died. It was there, while going through the contents of the house, all of which now belonged to Toby, that in a bookcase in Martin's study he found the privately printed novel. I asked him if he could remember what his father had said about

The Child's Child and the reasons he gave for its having never been published.

'My dad told me the title,' Toby said, 'and that's how I knew what it was. He hadn't said he'd had it printed and bound and – well, as you see it now. I was surprised, to say the least. Less so when I remembered what he'd told me about it. You have to know that my mother was quite vehemently opposed to any attempts to have it published. I know that from him, not her. Apparently, she would never discuss it.'

I asked Toby if he had spoken to her about it.

'Oh, yes. After he was dead. I didn't know about the bound book then. I thought it was somewhere among his papers in manuscript. My mother's comments were memorable. Perhaps you have to remember that she was born in the last years of the First World War, which made her very old when we spoke about the book.'

'What did she say?'

'That she had read it but was too disgusted to finish it. I think it was partly the fact that it was a true story or based on a true story, someone my father knew. If it were published, none of the people they knew would speak to them again, but she was sure no one would publish it. And she was right. He did try with the company that your brother works for – they had published all his previous books, there were nine by then – and his editor suggested he make certain changes. The character of Bertie could be made into a woman, for instance. Maud might be three years older than she is in the novel. But it was the homosexual element that they objected to. This was 1951, sixteen years before the act that made homosexual activity between consenting adults in private legal.'

'I take it your father didn't agree to modify the book?'

'No, and when you read it you can see why he wouldn't. I'm no literary critic, but I can see that you have to try and get into the sort of climate that existed then to understand perhaps why he wanted to write it and why he wouldn't change it. Hence, private printing. You see, it was not only about getting understanding for homosexuals

4

that he was very keen on, but also about changing the attitude to illegitimacy and what he called "unmarried mothers". What would you call them now?'

That made me smile. Toby had his naive moments. '"Single parents", I should think,' I said.

'But that's fathers as well.'

'I know. It's called equality. It's also called political correctness.'

'Anyway, that's the other theme of the novel. Would "theme" be the word?'

'I expect so,' I said. 'Why not?'

'One theme, then, is the injustice with which gay people were treated in the thirties and forties, and the other the injustice with which – er, single parents and their offspring were treated. There's a brother who's gay – that's the man my father knew – and his sister who has an illegitimate baby –'

I interrupted him. 'Don't go on. Let me read it.' I had another glance at the book before putting it in my bag. 'I'm not an agent, you know. You know I'm a university lecturer, working for a PhD that happens to be more or less about one of the themes in this book.'

'As you know, it was your brother who suggested you might be the right person to read it. I thought he'd read it, but as he reminded me, though he's in publishing, it's in marketing, not editorial.' Toby spoke almost humbly. 'I just want you to tell me if you think it will find a publisher. I think I listened to my mother too much and in my head I still hear the things she said.'

I told him that of course I would read it but it might take me a bit of time.

'I think my dad would have liked you to look at it. He wanted it published, but as it stands, not expurgated, not neutralized to suit a narrow-minded readership.'

'I'm not sure that "narrow-minded" is the term,' I said. 'They were of their time. They were the society of the day. Whatever I think of your father's book, I can guarantee no one is going to want to expurgate it. We live in an entirely different climate of morality and sexual behaviour, a whole world of difference.' I looked at him, guessing that he was thinking of his mother's disapproval. 'As you know, young people today, many of them or even most of them, wouldn't understand what you and I have been talking about.'

'That's true. My own children wouldn't.' In a burst of confidence, he said, 'My mother is dead. It couldn't have been published during her lifetime, but it could now. I keep telling myself that and feeling more and more guilty about what I'm doing.'

'Time enough to feel guilty if and when it's published. Let me read it first.'

I took *The Child's Child* home with me, where my grandmother had all twelve of Martin Greenwell's novels in hardcover. They were first editions, all with their original jackets, each one a little work of art and all a world away in taste and design from the pigtailed child in the green field. I looked inside, but of course *The Child's Child* wasn't listed among Greenwell's previous works. It occurred to me then that a friend's mother had once told me how she'd smuggled a copy of Henry Miller's *Sexus* through Customs when coming home by sea from France some time in the 1950s. A world away from today's contraband, when it would be drugs, not a book.

2

While teaching at a university in west London, I had been working for a PhD on a subject with which no one among my family and friends seemed to have any connection: single parents or, in the phrase Toby Greenwell had used, unmarried mothers. As my supervisor remarked after I chose the subject (and she reluctantly approved), it would be a bit absurd in a climate where nearly half of women remain unwed. So 'Single Parents'. Such women in English literature was the idea, but I was still asking myself – and Carla, my supervisor – if this should be extended into life. Into reality. Would this make it too much like a social-science tract?

When my grandmother died, I had already begun reading every English novel I could find that dealt with illegitimacy or with the mothers of illegitimate children. I was living in a flat in west London that I shared with two other women and a man, a not unusual configuration in overcrowded noughties London. The day before her death I had visited her in hospital, where she had been for just a week. A stroke had incapacitated her without disfiguring her, but she could no longer speak. I held her hand and talked to her. She had been a great reader and knew all those works of Hardy and Elizabeth Gaskell and a host of others that I was reading for my thesis. But when I named them she gave no sign of having heard, though just before I left I felt a light pressure on my hand from hers. The phone call from my mother came next morning. My grandmother, her mother, had died that night.

She was eighty-five. A good age, as they say. No one ever says 'a bad age', but I suppose that would be mine, twenty-eight, or my brother's, thirty. We were just the age when people tire of sharing flats with two or three others or crippling themselves with a huge mortgage for two or three rooms, but at the time of our grandmother's death we could see no end to it. We mourned her. We went to the funeral, both of us in black, I because it is chic, Andrew because as a fashion-conscious gay man, he possessed a slender black suit. My mother wore a grey dress and cried all the time, unusual for her in any circumstances. Next day we heard from my grandmother's solicitors that she had left her house in Hampstead jointly to my brother and me.

I have been honest about why we wore black, so I may as well keep up the honesty and say we expected something. Verity Stewart – we had always called her Verity – had a son and a daughter to leave her considerable fortune to (and she did leave it to them), but as we were the only grandchildren I thought we might get a bit each, enough, say, to help start on what's called the property ladder. Instead we got the property itself, a fine big house near the Heath.

Fay, my mother, and her partner, Malcolm, thought we would do the sensible thing, the practical thing: sell it and divide the proceeds. Instead, we did the unwise thing and kept it. Surely a house with four living rooms, six bedrooms and three bathrooms (and about three thousand books) was big enough for a man and a woman who had always got on with each other. We failed to take into account that there was only one kitchen, one staircase and one front door, congratulating ourselves that neither of us played loud music or was likely to have a party to which the other was not invited. There was one thing we never thought about, though why not I don't know. We were both young, and if we had none now, each had had several partners and one of us, perhaps both, was likely to have a lover move in sooner or later

In Andrew's case that happened quite soon.

James Derain is a novelist, his books published by Andrew's firm, as were Martin Greenwell's, which is how Andrew knew about his literary output. They met at a publisher's party. The occasion can't have been the anniversary of Oscar Wilde's birth or, come to that, his death, it was too late for that, but it was something to do with Wilde, a hero of James Derain's. At that party James told Andrew about Martin Greenwell and a book he'd written but never published that was based on the life of James's great-uncle. That party was the start of their friendship. It led to a relationship – and soon a falling in love, which they celebrated with a trip to Paris for the weekend. They went to look at Wilde's newly refurbished tomb. It had been restored to Epstein's original pristine whiteness before its surface was damaged by the lipstick of all the women who had come to kiss it over the years. Who would have supposed lipstick could scar marble? Andrew was happy about the lip imprints, saying it almost made up for all the women who spat at Wilde in the street after his downfall.

Andrew and I had made a rough division of the house, the rooms on the left-hand side, upstairs and down, mine, and those on the right, his. That was all very well: I got one bathroom, he got two; I got three bedrooms and Verity's study, he got my grandfather Christopher's study and three bedrooms. But we had to share the kitchen, which was enormous and on my side of the house.

'How many places have you lived in,' Andrew asked, 'where you've had to share the kitchen with two or three other people?'

I thought about it, tried counting. 'Four. It seems different in a place this size.'

'Let's give it a go. If we can't stand it we'll have another kitchen put in.'

It didn't much concern me. The house was marvellous to live in – in those first weeks – and like my grandmother I spent most of my time blissfully reading. It was spring and warm and I sat reading out in the garden, comfortable in a cane chair with a stack of books on the table in front of me, all of them fictional accounts of unwanted pregnancies and illegitimate births. Sometimes I raised my eyes to 'look upon verdure', as Jane Austen has it. Only one such birth in her works, only one 'natural child', and that one Harriet Smith, for whom Emma attempts the hopeless task of encouraging a clergyman, and therefore a gentleman, to marry her. Harriet may be the daughter of a gentleman, but somehow her illegitimacy negates that and makes her fit to marry a farmer but no one higher up the social scale.

One book I didn't look at was *The Child's Child*, and I wasn't conscience-stricken, not then, though I did mention it to Andrew, who came out into the garden before going to work. He hadn't exactly forgotten about the book but seemed to drag it up out of the depths of memory before light dawned.

'It's been lying in a cupboard for half a century,' he said. 'No harm done if it hangs about for a bit longer.'

Something happened that afternoon which was to have great importance in my life, as much as it has had in Andrew's. I met James Derain.

3

The first thing anyone would notice about James was how handsome he was. Not like an actor, because actors aren't necessarily
good-looking the way they once were. Or film stars once were.
Andrew had amassed a huge collection of DVDs of thirties and forties films, and the male stars, Clark Gable and Cary Grant and James
Stewart and Gregory Peck, were all stunningly handsome and,
when amalgamated, looked like James. Or he looked like them.
Maybe more like Cary Grant than the others. I've heard that Cary
Grant wasn't very bright. If that's so, the resemblance didn't extend
to his brains, for James was very bright indeed. He was – well, *is* –
tall, slim, dark and seems to have a permanent, perfectly natural
tan. His eyes are dark blue; his teeth are like Americans' teeth and
have apparently been looked after by a dentist from Boston. He's a
flawless man with perfect, long-fingered hands, and his feet, which I
saw bare in the garden on a hot day, are strong and sinewy but as
unblemished as a child's.

I've described him as if I found him attractive and I did, but only
as one finds a man in a painting or a photograph desirable. Even if I
had leanings that way, I'd have tried to suppress them because he
was Andrew's and because I know how pointless it is for a woman
to have sexual feelings for a gay man. I rather disliked him and I
worked on suppressing that too.

I encountered them in the hall. They had just come into the
house and Andrew introduced us. James said a cool 'Hi' and walked
off ahead of Andrew towards the right, having already been told, I
suppose, that the right-hand side of the house was Andrew's and
the left-hand side mine.

So I worked on it, telling myself that he might be shy or just awkward with women. He stayed the night but not, as far as I could tell,

the following night. I found myself listening for his departure next morning, and when I heard Andrew seeing him off and from the study window saw him walking down the street, I felt relief. This I crushed down, telling myself I shouldn't judge someone on an isolated meeting, and when he came back after a week or so, I concentrated on feeling how good this was for Andrew, who looked happy the minute James appeared.

He began to be at Dinmont House much more often than he had been at first. That's normal in a love affair, of course. If it isn't going to fizzle out it's going to grow stronger. I realized I was thinking about it far too much, speculating about it, even watching them together for what signs I could spot that they were thinking of themselves as a couple rather than an 'item' – stupid word but expressive of the start of something that might never become a relationship. Was this going to be that? The worst possible outcome, as far as I was concerned, was that they intended to live together. In other words, that James would come and live here. I could have asked Andrew, but I told myself that I didn't want to put ideas into his head. Stupid of me, because who could be made to live with a lover because his sister suggested it?

In the interests of observing signs I invited them in for coffee one Saturday morning. James had been staying here since Thursday evening. We went into my favourite room, Verity's study. Like the drawing room (Verity's name for it) and the unused dining room and several bedrooms, it is full of books. Books on the shelves, books in the cabinets, stuffed in treble in places, one row pushed to the back and another two in front of it. James picked up *Adam Bede*, which was lying face-downwards on the table, glanced at it, turned a few pages and said he wouldn't have the patience to read anything like this.

'The way he goes on and on, paragraph after paragraph and page after page. Description and dialect – bores you to tears.'

I said, 'He was a woman.' I was shocked, because I thought

everyone knew that, and James is a published author himself. But shocked at myself too, for speaking so scornfully. I was still trying hard to like him.

'Why call himself George, then?'

'Because she was more likely to get published than if she used her own name.'

'Wasn't that dishonest?'

In spite of the way I spoke, I didn't want to quarrel with him, so all I said was that that was an original way of looking at it and had they had breakfast? Would they like something to eat?

'No, thanks, Sis,' Andrew said. He had taken up this unusual and old-fashioned usage when we were children. 'We've both got hangovers. Coffee is fine.'

James stared. '*Sis?* That's amazing. I've never heard anyone say that before.'

I managed a broad smile, but my eyes, I fear, remained cold. Still, I was determined to like him come what may and, once they had gone, returned to the novel James Derain, the *novelist*, thought was written by a man. Verity, quoting from somewhere in the Bible, used to tell me not to sit in the seat of the scornful, so I resolved not to be scornful or scathing even in my thoughts. So back to *Adam Bede* (telling myself that James's mistake was one even an intellectual might make), and it occurred to me as I read that nowhere does George Eliot actually say that seventeen-year-old Hetty Sorrel is going to have a baby. Hetty has been seduced by Arthur Donnithorne, and this we also must assume. All we have been shown happening between them is a kiss. Hints are dropped, a great sorrow weighing on poor Hetty is talked of, but that she might be pregnant is never mentioned. No doubt James would call this dishonest, but those of us who know anything about Victorian prudery are aware that the author dared not refer directly to the unmarried Hetty's pregnancy if she wanted her novel to be published. We know of the baby's existence only when Adam is told it is dead and Hetty is on trial for murder.

We are supposed to be in 1799, and although George Eliot was writing in the 1850s, moral attitudes hadn't changed much, if at all. Before I started on *Adam Bede* I had been reading a paper about a school in Cheshire started specially for young mothers aged fifteen or younger where they could take their babies with them while they worked for their GCSEs. It was a world away from Hetty Sorrel. The concept of disgrace and shame has utterly gone. In George Eliot's day, unmarried pregnancy was all about disgrace and shame, as it still was halfway through the twentieth century. About punishment and endless retribution also. I started checking on detail in *Adam Bede* once more, and I was wondering if Hetty even knew she was pregnant, if living on a farm hadn't taught her that what happened between her and Arthur might have this outcome. But, no, if girls weren't told how they might get pregnant, would they make any connection between themselves and a cow coupling with a bull in a field?

At least all this had distracted me from Andrew and James. I picked up *Adam Bede*. Only George Eliot could make me – or anyone else, I should think – actually approve of a man such as Adam Bede marrying a Methodist woman preacher. We don't dislike and despise him for it; we certainly don't cast up our eyes because he's married this woman who is also the choice of his difficult, old mother. There is even some guilty relief that now he can't marry poor little Hetty because she has been transported for her crime. I wondered what Trollope would have made of it all. He has at least one illegitimate child in his fiction, but she is a rich, well-connected woman whose life led to a happy ending. I have moved on now to Fanny Robin in Hardy's *Far from the Madding Crowd*, another poor girl whose impending 'confinement' drives her to some sort of sanctuary in the workhouse; she nearly gets married but goes to the wrong church by mistake. But it is she that Sergeant Troy loves, not Bathsheba Everdene, whom he marries. And a fat lot of good that love does Fanny when she dies, alone and wretched, in childbirth.

I made a calculation of when the condemnation of 'unmarried

mothers' ended. Easy to know when it began: the distant past, since for ever, since marriage came into being – marriage that men did their best to avoid and women dreamt of and struggled for. But when did society stop ostracizing these girls, even praising them and encouraging them to go back to school with their babies and plan for their futures? The conservative Christian culture of the fifties kept many women from premarital sex, but this changed with the coming of contraception that worked: with the pill. I fix on the mid- to late sixties, much the same time as homosexual activity ceased to be a crime.

My saying this, quite innocently, because we had been talking about the possibility of civil-partnership legislation being extended to same-gender couples, led to a row between James and me, that quarrel I was determined to avoid. I hadn't foreseen this – why should I? Besides, I was trying to like him, to step down from the seat of the scornful. I had a little fantasy about that, seeing it as a cumbersome armchair that I put up for sale on eBay, nasty old antique that it was. So, having got that out of the way and hoping to establish a friendship between him and me, I invited them to dinner. I was quite a good cook in that I dared to make things that are supposed to be culinary challenges, and tonight we had a cheese soufflé followed by a lamb dish with aubergines, vaguely Greek, which I knew Andrew enjoyed. James ate his without comment. They had brought the wine, a bottle of white and a bottle of red, and I resolved to drink it or drink one glass of it, supermarket plonk that it was. That the wine wasn't very good didn't surprise me because that was what they drank all the time. Not for want of cash. James was rich, independent of his book sales. I think he had a wealthy father.

I showed them *The Child's Child*, which Andrew had, of course, seen before and James knew all about through the connection with his great-uncle, and because they were particularly apposite, I told them about its two themes. That one of those was close to the subject of my thesis was a useful coincidence and we had moved along to the cheese when James asked me, quite pleasantly, how my research was coming along. That led me to tell him about fixing a date for when unmarried motherhood ceased to be shameful and how that date was roughly coincidental with when homosexuality in private stopped being illegal.

James said, quite roughly, his tone changed, 'There's no comparison. Sending men to prison for being gay was outrageous, an affront to their human rights. Your girls just got looked down on by a bunch of old women.'

I said no one had ever heard of human rights in 1967, and as for 'my' girls, they suffered comparably. If gay men killed themselves from fear of discovery so did young women dreading disgrace.

'No girl went to jail for having a baby,' he said.

'But they did,' I told him. 'Or the equivalent. They were sectioned and put in mental hospitals, called lunatic asylums then, for nothing more than having a child without being married. Some remained in them for years.'

'I've never heard that. That can't be true. It may happen in these novels you read, but not in real life. Tell her about Wilde in chains on Clapham Junction station, And.'

So that was what he called my brother. 'He's told me,' I said. 'Anyway, I knew. Believe me, I'm not saying gay men didn't suffer terribly, I know they did. I'm only saying that women did too.'

'No, you're not.' James filled his glass so full of Pinot Noir that it overflowed. 'You're doing what women always do, claiming an unfair share of the world's ills. Victims, as usual.'

'James,' said Andrew quietly.

'No, it's not "James". You needn't defend her, she can look after herself. Those girls of hers had only to put on a wedding ring and they'd be all right. Men were ostracized, attacked, killed. My great-uncle – the one the book's based on – was blackmailed, outlawed. He lived in daily fear of discovery.' He was looking at me now, ceasing to talk as if I were not there. 'That thesis of yours, in making some sort of tie-up between the Act of 1967 and women taking the pill, is an insult to all the men who suffered. Plenty of them are still alive, they'll only be in their sixties. It's an outrage to them. Luckily, it'll never be published, or not where any of them are likely to read it.'

Andrew had got up, fetched a cloth and mopped up James's spilt wine. He is more sensitive than I am, maybe I should say more tender, and his face had gone red. The hand that held the cloth was trembling. He was in love with this man, he must be, and I was appalled.

'Perhaps we should change the subject,' I said for my brother's sake.

The seat of the scornful hadn't been sold but had become a throne for James. 'Obviously, you would like that. You've got yourself into a corner and this is your only way of getting out of it. Change the subject. What else can you do?'

I said that I could leave the room and would. Andrew said, 'No, Sis, no. I don't know how we got into this. It's ridiculous. Please stay.'

In a mocking, rather high-pitched tone, James said, 'Please, Sis, stay. Please don't go.'

He sounded like a kid of five, not a grown man. His face had gone purple and I realized it was with rage. This meant an awful lot to him. But I shrugged and went. Down the passage and into the kitchen. I put plates in the dishwasher and washed up Verity's silver by hand, listening for sounds from the dining room. What I was really listening for was footsteps crossing the hall and making for Andrew's living room or his staircase. It must have been years since I'd had a falling-out with my brother. I thought the last time was when we were children. After a while I heard those footsteps and laughter. It was James's laughter, only James's. A door slammed and I decided this was the last I would see or hear of them for the night.

I cleared the dining table and started the dishwasher. That was when I remembered the last time Andrew and I had had a row. A table in another house, the house we grew up in, and Fay had gone to answer the phone, leaving the remains of all sorts of delicacies behind. Andrew started picking at them, hunks of cheese and

17

half-eaten pots of crème brûlée, slices of pineapple, and I was hissing at him to leave them, not to touch – other guests were in another room – and I grabbed his hand, the hand that clutched a spoonful of some exotica, damson cheese I think it was. Twelve-year-old Andrew started to cry and Fay came back, exasperated, shaking her head.

That was eighteen years ago and he didn't cry any more, though he was still a lot more vulnerable than I was. But tonight I was the one who was tender and sensitive, partly because I felt that quarrels, if they must happen, should be about personal matters, not near-political things. It made me think that this one might have been deliberately engineered. It was a fine evening, a nearly full moon shining. A walk round the garden might have done me good, made me feel calm and taken away my resentment. Like all the gardens around, ours was large and dense with trees and shrubs, a lawn like a green island in the midst of them. And because the walls between were overgrown with ivy and creeper and clematis, they were not like separate gardens but formed one great estate, the grounds perhaps of a big country house.

I wouldn't need a coat, it was still too warm for that. I walked down the passage to the single glass door that led to the garden – Andrew's part had French windows – and as I put the key in the lock I saw him and James walk from under the trees on to the lawn. The moon was quite bright enough to show them to me. James had his arm round Andrew's waist, and as I watched he placed his hand round Andrew's head, drew it to him and kissed him deeply. Abruptly I turned away. I went to the furthest point in the house from the garden, the study, where all those books were. Somehow I knew, and I didn't like it but was powerless to do anything about it, that Andrew would bring James here to live with him.

By my age I ought to have known the truism that things always look different in the morning. As the night comes on and the deeper it gets, the more mad we are, the more prone to dreadful fears and fantasies. In the morning, not when we first wake up but gradually, things begin to look different from how they looked at eleven, at midnight. I don't suppose this rule applies in the case of a terrible shock or a tragedy striking, but nothing like that had ever happened to me. I didn't have presentiments either, I didn't have a sense that something bad would happen later in the day or something good. But I could replay the events or sights or words uttered that had so upset me and look at them in a new way. I had, after all, no reason apart from a kiss to believe that Andrew would ask James to live here with him, and I couldn't even know for certain that he was in love with James.

Next morning I was due to see my supervisor to talk to her about the progress of the thesis, see what she would say about including real cases in the nineteenth century of women giving birth outside marriage or if she thought I should concentrate solely on contemporary fiction.

Andrew came in, looking not so much awkward as sad. 'I'm sorry about last night, Sis,' he said. 'I'd have done anything to avoid it.'

I said that I knew he would, and his face was just as it had been eighteen years ago when I grabbed his arm and the lump of damson cheese flopped on to a white lace table mat. He was not crying, of course, not quite.

'You see, James feels very intensely about what gay people went through. He feels it personally. He had this uncle, or great-uncle maybe, whose friend hanged himself because he was gay, and he's got a friend, a very old man now, who was sent to a mental home for aversion therapy. They showed him pictures of gay porn and gave him electric shocks if he reacted – well, if he got excited by them.'

This only reminded me of those poor girls sent to penitentiaries and put to harsh domestic work for nothing more than being pregnant outside marriage. But there was no point in saying it aloud. 'It's all right,' I said, though it was not. 'It's over.' And then I asked, because I really had to know, 'Is James going to come here and live with you?'

'Would you mind if he did?'

'Your half of the house is yours and my half is mine. You must please yourself.'

'You'd hate it, though, wouldn't you?'

He did that a lot, told people how they felt when he didn't really know. He did it to me, to our mother, Fay, and her partner, Malcolm, and no doubt he did it to James. I told him I wouldn't hate it (not true) but that he should think carefully before he asked James, and then I felt I'd gone too far. I was not his mother or the wife he would never have.

'I've done that, I've thought carefully,' he said, but he didn't tell me the outcome of these thoughts of his. He had to leave for work if he was to get in by ten. He'd scarcely gone when I heard James's footfalls pounding on the staircase and the front door slamming as he went out. He slammed it so hard that the whole house seemed to shake.

Carla, my supervisor, cautioned me against letting too much reality creep in. If I could find a case that closely paralleled, say, the experience of Fanny Robin when she goes to All Souls' Church instead of All Saints', where Sergeant Troy is waiting to marry her, I could use that or briefly refer to it. There was probably a case Hardy had heard of and I might try finding it. Otherwise, I should go easy on the social work and the case histories.

My head, rather against my will, was full of James Derain. Although we both knew it was a possibility, we had never, Andrew and I, talked about lovers moving in with us. The house was left to us, and we were a brother and a sister who got on well together. We were so excited about it, so pleased, that we shifted our stuff in without thinking much, without considering the possible pros and cons. We had both had boyfriends, but Andrew had never shared his flat with anyone. I had shared a single room once, but only for a few months; it had not been a serious relationship. If James was going to live in the other half of Dinmont House I knew I must make a superhuman effort to get on with him. If I examined my behaviour I could honestly say that I had done very little, if anything, to antagonize him, and it looked to me as if he was one of those gay men who dislike women, *all* women. I had never met one before, but I had heard of them. I knew they existed. They were the antithesis of those whose closest and best friend is a woman and of whom they are often fonder than they are of their current lover.

I delayed going home. The sun was shining, it was lovely in Regent's Park and I thought of walking all the way home by way of Primrose Hill. When I was a child I used to think of Primrose Hill as being the seaside. I was standing in the sea or just on the sand and looking across the hill itself, the green rise such as English coastal resorts have, with beyond it that long terrace of tall houses like Brighton or Eastbourne. But I wasn't standing in the sea, I was sitting on a seat on the Outer Circle. It would take me a long time to walk home and it would be uphill all the way, and I knew I was putting it off in case James Derain was there. I had heard him go out, but that was three hours ago and he might have come back, Andrew might have given him a key. I told myself that I couldn't live like this, that yesterday I was happy, or at least content, and now I was letting myself be driven out of my own home by a friend of my brother's I hardly knew.

Instead of walking across Primrose Hill, I went to the 24 bus stop and was turning into our street when I saw James in the distance. My instinct was to hide from him, cross the street, even just bend down to take a stone out of my sandal, but of course I did none of this. I advanced on him and he advanced on me, and he was charming, all smiles and how was I and wasn't the sun wonderful. Then he said he was sorry for last night, he always got aggressive when he drank too much, it was a problem he had to 'address'. He and Andrew had been drinking before they came and that was something he would have to stop. Could I forgive him?

Of course. What else could I say? I had a shred of hope that he was making for Hampstead tube station, not Dinmont House, but no, he was going home, he said, and by that he plainly meant my home and Andrew's. When I went back into the house after posting a letter, I waited in the hall, listening. James was a writer so he didn't go out to work, he worked at home. Writing by hand? On a type-writer, if anyone still does? Or on a computer, as I would expect? And was he at home in any permanent sense? It was most likely that he was only staying here with Andrew for a few days or a week, and at the end of it he would go back to wherever he lived.

It was no good loitering there like a lost soul. I went into the study, looked through all the files of notes I had accumulated and finally came upon an account I had got from somewhere of a young woman executed for infanticide in 1801. This story of terror and despair, of a homeless, destitute girl with nowhere to turn, her cry-ing, distraught child a heavy drag on her, I had found upsetting the first time I read it and found it doubly so now. Perhaps because I was in an anxious, uncertain state. It might be that the newspaper in which this account appeared was seen by George Eliot and gave her the germ of an idea for *Adam Bede*. But she wasn't born until 1819, so she could not have seen it until some forty years at least after it had appeared. Perhaps I should have abandoned this attempt at an analogy and seen instead what I could find of instances of brides going to the wrong church, as Fanny Robin does. And then, out of nowhere, I was reconstructing in my mind's eye James Derain as he looked when we encountered each other in the street half an hour ago.

He was carrying a 'man bag', a black-canvas-and-tan-leather thing on a long strap, exactly the size of an average laptop. He was carrying a computer. It was plain what had happened. When I heard his footsteps on the stairs this morning he was going home to wher-ever his home was to fetch his laptop. So that he could work on his new book here in this house. Andrew would very likely give him a little bedroom on the top floor to write in. He would work up there in the peace and quiet of an upper room in Dinmont House, with its view of gardens, of trees, of a sea of leaves, and beyond them in the thin mist that hangs over London, the river and the tall blurred towers . . .

I stopped myself there and suggested I pull myself together out of wild imaginings. James had probably come only for the weekend and was one of those obsessive writers, compelled irresistibly to a keyboard as they once were to a pen and ink.

Apart from *Mary Barton*, I had never been very happy with the works of Elizabeth Gaskell. Carla told me that everyone used to call her 'Mrs Gaskell' until feminism intervened and dropped the honorific. Her novels all have axes to grind. They aim to set the world right, as many Victorian novels do, but many try to disguise this, which hers do not. I sat on the sofa in the study to begin *Ruth*, very much aware that I would have been outside in the garden in the swing seat but for the thought of James Derain watching me from the other study. This was pure paranoia, for I had no reason to believe that he would watch me or cared at all what I did. If I was not out there it was because I knew I couldn't settle to my book just under that upper window, in the eyeline of anyone sitting at the desk.

Ruth isn't a slow read, it's almost a compulsive read, and I raced through the early chapters. What struck me was that while those other novels are about other things as well, have subplots and interwoven stories, *Ruth* is concerned entirely with seduction and illegitimacy. Hardy's *Tess* has the courtship of Angel Clare and marriage to him; Wilkie Collins's *No Name* and *The Woman in White* are much more involved with the legal aspects; Hetty Sorrel's history is important but still subservient to Dinah's work and religion and to the Bede family's way of life. So here I was in Verity's study learning what it was really like to know one is pregnant by a faithless lover, to put on a wedding ring and call oneself 'Mrs', yet ultimately deceive no one. Every character believes Ruth has committed a terrible sin, even the sympathetic ones, the kindly ones who take her in and share what little they have with her, even they speak in hushed voices of her sin and her 'crime'. The Bensons' old servant Sally forcibly cuts off Ruth's hair so that she may 'sham decently in a widow's cap tomorrow', and Ruth submits without protest, for she too believes she has sinned and her punishment is justified.

This was where I laid down the book for the time being, rather surprised that I who have read *Tess* and *Oliver Twist* without feeling more than pity and wonder could be so affected by a novel written 150 years ago. There was no doubt in my mind, so persuasively honest is Gaskell's writing, that the social scene was really like this, this was the fate of the 'fallen woman'. She is thought to have based the character on a real woman called only Pasley, whose life of rejection and banishment to a penitentiary seems to have been worse than anything Gaskell allowed to happen to the fictional Ruth.

That evening I was going out with friends, just a meeting in a pub. I certainly wouldn't change out of jeans and T-shirt and I wouldn't keep my eye on my watch, checking that I was not late, as I had sometimes done in the past. I would even put on trainers instead of my newish, rather nice sandals, because I meant to walk across the Heath to Highgate. These trainers were in a cupboard in a spare room on the top floor. They were up there because I still hadn't emptied the wardrobe and cupboard in my bedroom of Verity's clothes. I told myself and told Fay, who offered to do the emptying for me, that as a busy solicitor she shouldn't take on that and I didn't mind them being there. But the truth was that I liked them in the house, they reminded me of Verity, and sometimes I opened the wardrobe and put my cheek against silk or delicate wool and smelt the Coty L'Aimant she always wore.

Upstairs, I found my trainers and was putting them on when I heard a sound that made me jump. It was coming from the other side of the wall in Andrew's part of the house and it was the five-note signature of Windows starting up or logging off. A little phrase, but not much like Proust's. So James Derain was working here and in the study. Well, what had I expected? I knew it already and it was stupid of me to mind. I directed my thoughts and my eyes back to single parents, and real ones this time, not the fictional kind.

Mary Wollstonecraft had an illegitimate child by a man called Imlay and would have had another had not the philosopher William Godwin married her five months before the birth of the girl who became Mary Shelley. That was in 1797. Rebecca West had a child by

H. G. Wells, Dorothy L. Sayers had a child by a man called Bill White. Both these births were in the teens of the twentieth century and the writers had the children as a gesture of defiance. But they put no illegitimate children into their fiction, though Sayers has a 'fallen' woman in *Strong Poison*. The date of this novel's publication was 1930, a few years after Verity's own birth. Harriet Vane is tried for murder, and at her trial her history comes out: she has cohabited with a man without marriage for a year, and if she is not ostracized by the people she knows, this is because they are an arty, bohemian crowd. Others deeply disapprove of her, but things have moved on a bit. No one talks about her crime or her sin. She is not sent to Coventry or cast into outer darkness, and eventually, many books later, she is considered sufficiently redeemed so as to be able to marry Lord Peter Wimsey. Of course she doesn't have a baby – not, that is, until she comes to have several in wedlock.

Sayers's child was born in 1924. She seems to have made no attempt to look after John Anthony herself. No doubt she wasn't prepared to call herself 'Mrs' or wear a wedding ring. The baby was fostered by Sayers's cousin Ivy and called Sayers 'Cousin Dorothy'. Even when the novelist married Atherton Fleming in 1926, John Anthony continued to live with Ivy. Sayers's parents deeply disapproved of her marrying in a registrar's office and never knew they had a grandson. She wrote once more about marital irregularities and touched on illegitimacy in *The Nine Tailors*, in which a couple marry in the belief that the woman is free while in fact her husband is still alive. Their children are illegitimate and must remain so even though the Thodays marry as soon as they legally can. This is more of a typically Victorian situation, the kind of thing Wilkie Collins wrote about, than a subject for a novel published in 1934. It shows, though, that the desperate need for respectability was still going strong long years after Verity was born.

While I was learning all this, someone tapped at the study door. I knew who it was because Andrew and I had never knocked on doors when the other of us was inside. We just walked in. This had to be James. He was carrying a book, an oldish paperback of *The Picture of Dorian Gray*. Determined to be nice, I told him untruthfully that I was just about to make tea and asked if he would like a cup. He would, so I made two mugs of tea and carried them into the study. All the time he was talking about Wilde's novel, how it was banned when it first appeared in 1891, then issued in an expurgated edition – though it's difficult, as James said, to understand what could possibly have offended. Apparently, some reviewer or commentator of the time said no innocent woman should be allowed to read it, and this reminded me of Toby Greenwell's prudish mother. James had bought Wilde's new (or original) version. He couldn't see much difference between the two, a word here, a phrase there. He drank his tea and at last came to the reason for his visit. It was an olive-branch call. His apology when we met in the street wasn't enough and he needed, apparently, to underline it. He asked if there was any more tea.

While you have boiling water and tea bags there is always more tea, and I reluctantly produced it. James was now telling me an anecdote or story about contemporaries of Wilde's, two men called Raffaelovich and Gray who were in love with each other, and how Raffaelovich gave up everything to follow Gray and live near him when he went into a monastery. It was interesting and quite romantic, but I had to go out quite soon. I was already late starting, but when I told James that I had to go out and had to leave now, he obviously didn't believe me.

I recognized that I was contending with someone who was quick to take offence. He had come into my life without my having anything to do with it, he had been *brought* in. Taking his cue from Andrew, he thought he could just knock on one of my doors whenever he felt like it and come in and stay and stay. Andrew probably said to him, 'Oh, I never knock on doors, she's my sister, but perhaps you'd better the first time.' When I started imagining him just walking in any time he liked and then suggesting we all live together and I could cook for them and make them tea whenever they liked, I knew I was letting the whole thing assume gigantic (and hysterical) proportions. Of course that wouldn't happen.

By this time I was in Wedderburn Road and nearly there. Damian and Louise were already in the King of Bohemia, sitting at a table sharing the *Evening Standard*. When I came in they jumped up and kissed me and I realized how much I'd missed them.

4

More olive branches next day, this time on my part. I asked my brother and James in for supper.

'Not this time, Sis,' Andrew said. He gave me an unexpected kiss, a gesture which made James's lip curl as if we had been involved in some incestuous obscenity. A creature of moods, James had changed once more, becoming unnecessarily critical and scornful, refusing the meal I offered. I said that was fine and anyway I had work to do, suddenly feeling not so much angry as close to tears. A slug of vodka was what I wanted, but I settled for a cup of tea instead. I ate some bread and cheese while imagining all kinds of unwelcome things: James moving in, avoiding me when he could, calling me 'she' instead of by my name, and encouraging Andrew to have less to do with me, walking into my part of the house when he wanted something, even taking over rooms and playing terrible music, though I had no evidence for any of these last.

After a long time, reclining on the sofa with my feet up, no lights on, I listened to the silence of the house. Houses like this one, large, standing alone in their gardens, even places in the suburbs of a city, are silent in the evenings. The utter quietness seemed to confirm my fears, though of course it did nothing of the sort. This was an opportunity to start on Greenwell's book, but I'd promised myself not to read anything but books for the thesis at least until I'd started to write it, so I averted my eyes and made my way into the study, turning on lights as I went. I worked on the thesis for a couple of hours, concentrating on the unbelievable guilt and dread of discovery felt by Lady Dedlock over giving birth to Esther Summerson. But you don't have to believe Dickens, that's not what he's about. If I describe him as 'the father of magic realism' in my thesis will my supervisor call me presumptuous? Probably. So I went to bed thinking, as I often did, about how these women felt when they knew they were pregnant, the disbelief, the realization, the horror, shame, fear and wish for death.

It would probably have been good for me to run next morning, but Hampstead isn't the best place in the world to go jogging unless you're on the Heath. I was walking in the other direction and hadn't the right shoes on. I picked up the *Evening Standard* in Heath Street and went into a café to look at it while I had a cappuccino. The front-page lead was a murder in Soho last night, the stabbing of a young gay man outside a club in Old Compton Street. When you're in my circumstances and you read something like that your heart does miss a beat. But it wasn't Andrew, it wasn't James, it was some-one called Bashir al Khalifa. His picture, taken a couple of years back, showed a handsome young man from somewhere in the Mid-dle East. Perhaps he came here because he believed no one would persecute him for his sexual orientation, and they didn't persecute him. They killed him.

I stayed out a long time, going down to the West End on the 24 bus and calling in at the London Library to pick up a couple of Vic-torian novels I needed and Verity didn't have on her shelves. Neither she nor my grandfather had catalogued their books, and I wondered if I should catalogue them. It would be quite a task but one I think I would enjoy. Must finish the thesis first and read Greenwell too, of course. On the bus going home – walking to Hampstead is uphill all the way – I thought about phones and realized I'd scarcely known a time when the mobile didn't exist. Fay had a big, brick-shaped, black thing when I was a small child and it never worked well. Before that, like everyone else, we just had a landline, and a telephone actually with a dial that had letters on it as well as numbers, so that once upon a time you could phone exchanges called Ambassador and Primrose and Riverside. And you could get away from the phone bell. You just went out. You weren't imprisoned by the phone as you are now. Of course (as an observer from another planet might say) you could leave your phone at home, but the point of a mobile is that it's mobile. It is almost as if it's inside you, living in your head, never letting you be alone. Turn it off, says the ethereal visitor, only you seldom do. Light in weight as it is, what's the point of carrying it if it's turned off?

As if it wanted to prove to me how useful it is, a call came in while I was on the bus. It was from Sara, to say that she was almost certain she was pregnant and if she was she would be very, very happy. Could we meet for lunch soon, say tomorrow? I came into the house to find the door to Andrew's living room was wide open and the music coming out was Bob Dylan's 'The Times They Are a-Changin''.

Andrew called out, 'Come in here, Sis. You're laughing, so you can cheer us up. We need cheering up.'

Bob Dylan was coming from an iPod speaker. Andrew turned it off and came up to me and hugged me.

'What's all this, then?'

'Oh, don't say that,' said James, whose voice was quite different from the day before, who even looked different, worn and older. 'You sound like a comic cop, and we've had enough of cops for ever, haven't we, And?'

Bashir al Khalifa had been their friend and they were with him in that Soho club. A bunch of thugs who were something to do with the English Defence League had set about him at three in the morning, when they all emerged from the club. They called him all the names people like that use to insult gay men, and perhaps they abused him rather than Andrew or James because my brother and his friend didn't have stripes of purple and white running through their hair and weren't wearing white suits. But they too were surrounded by the EDL men and friends who joined them out of the gathering crowd. They punched Bashir to the ground, kicking him, and one of them pulled a knife out of his pocket and stabbed him. When Andrew and James struggled with them in an attempt to pull them off, they too were thrown to the ground and might have suffered Bashir's fate if the police hadn't arrived.

'We're covered with bruises and sore all over, but nothing's

30

broken.' Andrew made a face and rubbed his left shoulder. 'I've never been kicked before. It's worse than being punched.'

'I don't know,' said James. 'It depends on the size and probably the youth of one's assailant and what size boots he takes. We spent the rest of the night and some of the morning in a police station telling them what we could.'

'It wasn't much.' Andrew shook his head. 'We knew him and we liked him, didn't we, James? But all we really knew was that he was gay and an actor.'

They had to go back to the police station later on. I sat about all the afternoon, reading *The Vicar of Wrexhill* and thinking Frances Trollope wasn't a patch on her son Anthony. How oppressive it must have been for those English nineteenth-century writers who weren't *allowed* to write about sex at all; how nice, good babies apparently came simply as the result of a wedding ceremony, while wicked, bad babies came because of an unnamed sin. And how they harped on marriage, how they clung to it, even the greatest of them, even Dickens. I've already said that we don't expect reality from him, and perhaps we understand how, in satisfying his public, he makes sure that in *Great Expectations* Estella's parents are securely married, though it's most unlikely that a convict and a slum woman would have been. Back in those days my friend Sara's baby would be one of the good ones, because Sara is married, while Damian's girl-friend's baby would be bad, stigmatized for ever, because Fay has told me that, though the law has now changed, in those days, even if the mother and father of an illegitimate child got married after the birth, the marriage wouldn't legitimize it.

Andrew phoned to say he and James had to pick out one of the men who attacked Bashir, at an identity parade. They did it separately and both picked out the man called Kevin Drake. Later, from another line-up, they're going to see if they can pick out the one who kicked Bashir in the head. Both of them hated doing this, though they know that the man they have to identify killed some-one for no reason other than that he was homosexual.

They failed to identify the man called Gary Summers and were relieved they had failed, but were now responsible for a man being charged with murder, and James particularly dreaded having to be a witness in court. That wouldn't happen when Kevin Drake came up before the magistrate this morning. He would plead not guilty and be committed for trial to the Crown Court. Both Andrew and James would probably be required then, and though Andrew said he was sure that when the time came he could face it without too much angst, James, who has more imagination than my usually cheerful brother, said that if he was cross-examined, if for instance some barrister asked him if his testimony had been influenced by 'the kind of books he writes', he might find himself unable to speak or else burst into tears.

'I know what you're thinking, Sis,' Andrew said to me. 'You're thinking that if he does, the judge will feel that these queers are all the same. Crying, struck dumb, they're all the same.'

'I wasn't thinking that. Don't you ever think that since your guesses about what's going on in other people's heads are always wrong, you might stop guessing?'

I was having lunch with Sara that day. She was just back from her honeymoon and now she knew she was pregnant. She'd had the test. Of course she knew this or was pretty sure before her wedding, but now it had been confirmed and she and Geoff were overjoyed. Both of them had got an idea in their heads that they couldn't have children.

I asked her why she thought this, and she said because they had both had relationships before 'without issue', as she put it, giggling.

'But you were on the pill, weren't you? And no doubt Geoff and his previous girlfriends were using something.'

'Oh, yes, I know. And as soon as I stopped I got pregnant. But I suppose I don't really trust those things.'

'You will now,' I said.

In Verity's day there were pregnancy tests, she once told me. I was amazed. I thought early detection had come about in my own lifetime. But, no, the woman who thought she might be pregnant had a sample of her blood injected into a rabbit, and if she was right, the rabbit died. I think that's how it was. Doctors didn't much like having this done, and one woman Verity knew was told to wait and see because 'you wouldn't want to kill a poor little rabbit, would you?' There was still a long time to go before you could buy a home pregnancy test over the counter.

Talking to the police, being questioned and facing the possibility of a court appearance had a bad effect on James. He couldn't write. He was starting a new novel and was pleased with it, but now he had a kind of writer's block, something that had never happened to him before. When he closed his eyes he saw the killing of Bashir all over again. He heard the man's desperate cries and saw the blood spouting from a stab wound. Things were very different for Andrew, who was coming to accept what had happened. It was terrible, it was senseless, but it was in the past now and they had to get over it.

James said, 'How long, O Lord, how long?' meaning when will people accept homosexuality, all of them, as just another lifestyle, and I told him – unnecessarily and pointlessly – that prejudice targets others who differ from the norm, ethnic minorities and the disabled, members of certain religious bodies, the overweight and even redheads.

'It's not the same,' James said. 'When did you last hear of a woman who hasn't got a husband being set upon by thugs because she's had a baby? When? It never happens.'

I couldn't argue with that because he was right. I *had* never heard of a single mother being attacked because she was unmarried, though maybe they were seventy or eighty years ago. But James was off in telling me I should find a worthier cause to support than 'little bastards and their mums', God knew there were plenty. I didn't support them, I told him, they didn't need anyone's support, they were not persecuted. Ever optimistic, Andrew started laughing at us, telling us – he had got hold of statistics from somewhere – that homophobic attacks were becoming less frequent. The assault on and murder of Bashir were the first for a long time. Still, he was sympathetic to James in his way, though I was not sure that telling a

33

fiction writer he had too much imagination for his own good was the best way to go about it. For his part, once they'd got past the trial, Andrew would teach himself to forget the whole affair.

Meanwhile, I had begun to write. There was more reading to do, but the writing had to begin and I was asking myself if, considering the subject I had chosen, it was possible not to get emotionally involved. How to convey the hope, the dread, the panic and the horror and finally the absolute, beyond-a-doubt confirmation. This was the point at which so many young girls decided that they preferred death to disgrace and drowned themselves. Of course, I'm not writing fiction, I am writing about fiction. I should be detached, I should be objective. It was easier for a man. He could stand outside the issue because he could only experience an unwanted pregnancy vicariously and often not even then, but I am not a man.

I had told myself that this was the point at which, the research virtually finished, I would begin *The Child's Child*. It was weeks now, a couple of months, since I had brought the book home from Martin Greenwell's house and I was starting to feel guilty about it. Lying on this table or that in this big house, it seemed to reproach me as I came into the room where it was, its bright, tasteless cover eyeing me and telling me I was neglecting it. So I sat down and wrote a letter to Toby Greenwell – the first letter as against an email I had written for years – apologizing to him for not as yet having started on the book and pleading pressure of work. No reply came from him, and that made me feel worse. Andrew, who came in briefly to tell me how unhappy James was at the prospect of appearing in court, said I should remember that I wasn't an agent, I wasn't being paid for doing this – what was wrong with me?

5

In the end I tucked the book under a cushion on Verity's chaise longue so that it was out of sight. There it remained while I worked on the thesis in solitude. It really was solitude, for I had hardly seen anything of Andrew and James since the day my brother told me about the Bashir al Khalifa murder. That they were there I knew from the faint hum of the television from Andrew's living room across the hall, a sighting of him turning at the top of the stairs to wave to me. As a result I had lost my fear of James's coming to live at Dinmont House and of our all being unable to share without constantly bumping into each other. I might almost have been the sole occupant for all I saw of them.

Until that evening it hadn't been important. I assumed that by this time Andrew had cured James of his fears and all was now well. In which case we could perhaps all meet and have that supper together which had been refused last time. I didn't just walk in; I thought discretion might be better and knocked on the door.

Instead of calling to me to come in, my brother opened the door and said, 'I thought you were the ghost.'

'The ghost?'

'James says there is one. It knocks on doors.'

James was half sitting, half lying in an armchair, staring at the ceiling. I could tell by just looking at him that his fears were still with him. He didn't speak but turned to me with a small, rueful smile and that in itself seemed very unlike him. Andrew said he was going to get the two of them something to eat and did I want to join them? James didn't move.

For the first time I was glad our circumstances made us share a kitchen. Andrew got smoked salmon and cream cheese and a loaf out of the fridge while he talked. While he was resigned to appearing in court and answering searching questions put to him by Kevin Drake's counsel, for James this had become not just an unpleasant prospect but a kind of doom. He could see nothing beyond it. The date of the trial, set for November, had become his death date. It was an absolute finality. He had become ill, couldn't write and scarcely went out.

He sat, Andrew said, or more likely lay down, upstairs and he barely ate. Andrew had to go to work but he said that he devoted more time to James than to work.

'I've never before come across anyone so imprisoned – for that's what it is – in fear.'

These words were so uncharacteristic of my brother that I found myself turning away from the pain in his face. He truly loved James, I could see that. 'I won't join you,' I said. 'Better not.'

He gave me one of those uncharacteristic kisses. 'Goodnight, Sis.'

Next day, when his lover was in a sedative-induced sleep, Andrew told me how James had become humble and curiously meek. He constantly apologized. Over and over he said he was sorry, but he couldn't help himself. Andrew said that in the days before witnessing the murder, James never spoke like that. Andrew had never known him to say he was sorry. James was a different person, he said, the smoothness, the sophistication and the sexiness (Andrew's words) all gone. Sometimes, when James had taken one of the doctor's sleeping pills and I was taking a break from the thesis, Andrew and I talked it over in my living room or Verity's study. What were we to do? How could James ever actually be got to court? Could he somehow, by legitimate means, avoid this ordeal? Was there some let-out? There are all sorts of reasons for getting out of being a juror; do the same rules apply for avoiding being a witness in a murder case? Our mother, Fay, said not when she looked in later, and she should

36

know. She didn't understand what was wrong with James and put it down to what she called 'affectation'. No one was going to be unkind to him. Counsel might and very likely would say that he was mistaken and try to show that he was not a reliable witness, but he wouldn't be called a liar.

'Ah, diddums,' she said when Andrew was out of the room checking on James. 'No one's going to make him cry.' She had read James's first novel and said she couldn't understand how anyone who could describe such vicious acts and write such penetrating dialogue could be so feeble.

'You know what he's most scared of?' Andrew said when he came back. 'One of the things. He's afraid counsel for the defence will ask him about gay men's lifestyle. What were two highly educated men like him and me doing in a club like that in the early hours of the morning?'

'He or she may ask that,' Fay said.

'Would *you*?'

'I don't know. I'm not likely to be in that situation. But I'll tell you one thing. I'd ask a similar question of a comparable man and a girl in a similar club at the same sort of time.'

'James will never see it like that. He'll see it as being singled out because he's gay. The trial of Oscar Wilde may have been more than a hundred years ago, but he says things haven't changed that much. The public may tolerate gay people, but they don't want to know what we do, and if their attention is drawn to it, as the jury's will be, they'll all be disgusted. I'm telling you what James believes, not necessarily what I think.'

'*Necessarily?*' said Fay.

'Not what I think, then.'

'That fantasy of his is meaningless. Things have changed enormously. The law has changed. Ask him if he thinks you could have discussed this subject with your *mother* even fifty years ago.'

When Fay left, Andrew told me he was afraid that James might kill himself before the trial. He talked about this relative of his, his grandfather's brother, whose friend committed suicide, the people *The Child's Child* is based on. Andrew thought it was because they found out the man was gay and abused him for it. I asked Andrew what James felt about Kevin Drake. I mean, James picked him out from a line of men and had no doubt about it, this was the man he saw repeatedly stab his friend Bashir. Did he have no feeling of the rightness of bearing witness against Drake for Bashir's sake?

'I don't know. I've tried that argument with him, but he says he doesn't want to talk about it, yet this case and the trial and Drake and the other man are all we ever do talk about. You'll say try to steer him on to another subject, and I've tried, God knows I've tried, but he never will, or if he does say a few words about something else he'll bring it straight back to this. D'you know what he calls it? "My doom," is what he calls it. "Kevin Drake is my doom," he says.'

I asked if James was serious.

'Dead serious. He's got no religion, as you know, but he talks about Kevin Drake being sent to be his doom. Drake was sent to kill Bashir because he was gay, and James says we were sent to witness the killing and that's his doom.'

I asked about this ghost James had invented which knocked on doors. It seemed in the same league with dooms.

'It's so absurd,' said Andrew, 'that it's funny. Or it would be if the whole business wasn't so wretched.' He took a great swig of the whisky he'd fetched. 'I'm drinking too much, as you've no doubt noticed. It's what keeps me going. I dread he'll kill himself, and of course I do my best to stop that.'

He couldn't kill himself, I said, if he never went out and he hadn't got the means in the house.

'What makes you think he never goes out? He goes out when we're out. I'm sure he watches us and goes out. He used to use the hard stuff – not heroin, never that, and he stopped before he met me, but it's prescription drugs now, mainly oxycodone. He's collecting it now from this dealer he knows. It's for his doom, to make his doom happen.'

My thesis progressed – for good or ill. Good, I hoped. I was concentrating now on how the culture has changed out of all recognition, not the physical facts. None of those young women in the nineteenth-century novels went near a doctor, still less a hospital, when pregnant. Their periods stopped, I supposed, so they knew the worst had happened. But even if these girls had asked a doctor to examine them, what could he have found? Perhaps that the foetus was alive, but not much more than that. No scans in the middle of the nineteenth century, none in the middle of the twentieth, come to that. No means of measuring blood pressure. The interesting thing here, though, is that all of them belonged to the working class. They were all servants.

Are we to take this as showing that middle-class or upper-class girls never had babies outside marriage? Surely not. It has to be that the working-class ones were more often the victims of middle- or upper-class men because they were maids or children's nurses or even governesses in landed families. Also that servants abounded in their thousands in cities and the country. The middle-class young women were accorded respect and in any case never left alone with a man. Impossible to imagine an Anne Elliot or a Dorothea Brooke ever putting herself in a position to be seduced. It seems that only in cases (such as in Trollope's *Lady Anna* and *Dr Wortle's School*) where a women finds herself bigamously married through no fault of her own can a middle-class woman have a child which turns out to be illegitimate. In fact, of all Victorian novelists, Trollope is the most rigidly on the side of married virtue. He seems to shock even himself with his invention of Mr Scarborough, the landowner who has two sons; though both were born while he was married, he forges documents to prove his perfectly legal marriage, which took place before the birth of his elder son, in fact happened after it, then contrives to marry his wife again before the birth of the younger. And all this to enable him to bypass an entail in the event his first son is a bad lot and his second a pillar of virtue. One wonders what he would have done if the latter had been a girl.

But in reality unmarried middle-class women did have babies. I thought of the two I know of, Rebecca West and Dorothy L. Sayers, giving birth respectively in 1914 and 1924. In reality too, away from fiction, Fay said that many people of her age have an aunt or a great-aunt who had a child outside marriage which was brought up by its grandmother as her own. So were West and Sayers unusual only in that they were middle class? Carla would remind me not to get emotionally involved if she knew what I was thinking about, the terrible unhappiness of these women, forced by society to hear their children call a grandmother or an aunt 'mother'.

6

Something happened that I never foresaw and wouldn't have believed possible. Two things really, because the first and the minor happening was the ghost. It was in the very early morning, I suppose about four. I only say 'about four' because my bedroom was in total darkness when there should have been pale green light on the bedside table. My digital clock had gone out. I reached for the switch on the bed lamp, but before my forefinger touched it, there came a soft knock on the door. Now, I should have realized that this was a power cut and that either Andrew or James had knocked on my door because there was a power cut. But I who don't believe in ghosts, of course I don't, thought of what Andrew had told me and lay in bed, rigid and, for some mad reason, terrified. The clock suddenly leapt into life, its blinding lime-green digits flashing on and off. I got up to reset it, put on the central light to check all was well and at last opened the bedroom door. No one was there. But it must have been ten minutes since the knock, so, ghost or man, there hardly would have been.

The other thing, of far greater significance, of earth-shaking moment you might say, happened the next day in the afternoon. I had heard Andrew go to work at about eight, closing the front door infinitely quietly as was his new habit. I went off to the university, which all my students call 'uni', to take some of them for a tutorial, the ones who had bothered to produce essays. They knew quite a lot about nineteenth-century women's fiction and women's poetry but nothing, it seemed to me, of nineteenth-century social history. One of them thought it was quite usual to possess a car in the 1890s and another that divorce was much as it is now, easily and quickly obtained and the wife having custody of the children.

I came back into the house expecting to find it empty and

planning on going online to find some nineteenth-century social-history websites and recommend them to my students. Instead I encountered James crouching on the floor in our hallway, waiting for Andrew.

Or so I supposed, but in fact he was waiting for me. And he was a sight, misery itself, the tears running down his cheeks, his back hunched, his hands fidgeting, wringing and twisting in front of him.

'I hoped you'd come,' he said. 'I longed for you to come. I can't stand being alone any longer.'

So I knelt on the floor beside him and put my arms round him, half expecting to be shoved away. But he held me more tightly than I held him, his face pressed into my shoulder. I don't know how long we stayed like that, several minutes certainly. Then we both got up, simultaneously it seemed, and I told him I was going to make us a cup of tea. He followed me into the kitchen, saying he couldn't write, he'd tried but he had what he called 'the grandmother of all writer's blocks'. He could use the Internet for emails and research, or he could if he had anyone to send emails to or anything to discover, but he hadn't. If he tried to write the novel he was halfway through, all that appeared was what happened in Old Compton Street that night, his friend attacked, stabbed and kicked to the ground. He could describe Kevin Drake's blue-and-silver trainers, soon to be splashed with blood, his bare bony ankles and his frayed jeans. He could write the words that Drake and the other man, Gary, had used when they'd egged each other on, and describe the distortion of their faces, red with meaningless, unprovoked rage. But the novel that he wanted to write, all that was lost and gone. He told me this as we walked into the study, carrying our mugs of tea. In the weeks since that night in Soho he had grown thin, his once-handsome face like a skull, the tendons on his neck ropes stretched taut.

'Even if I were capable of doing anything,' he said, 'I've nothing to do. All I've done for years is write and now I can't. I've no outside interests, I don't care for sport and I've no hobbies. Do people have hobbies any more? Train sets and stamp collections? Maybe they do, but I don't.'

This was when I had an idea. I asked him if he would help me with the social-history websites, expecting a blunt no.

But he said, 'You mean find some websites and go into them and see what they say?'

'I'd like someone from the outside to look at this stuff from a fresh perspective,' I said. Give him something to get interested in he'd never thought about before. This plan was just a stage in my amateur therapy. Let him do something, *instruct* someone even, all in the good cause of distracting him from those disproportionate fears. 'What I'd like,' I went on, lying, 'is if you could sit beside me and tell me what you think. Would you do that?'

He would try, he said. He knew nothing about the Victorians or their social history. I fetched more tea for us, thinking that this might be the therapy Andrew was hoping for. I hated to think that my brother might stop loving him just when he obviously needed love so much.

I sat down at the computer and James drew up a chair beside mine. I was told something I'd known for years, how to use a search engine. I told him the language defeated me. I was a purist when it came to language, and among other solecisms I didn't care to use 'access' as a verb. He told me I didn't have to do it 'in the great world' offline. Think of it as a foreign language you're learning, he said, and then it will be all right. A few websites were found and I told him I didn't want to have to go online every time I needed to refer to them. Print them out, he said, and I pretended never to have printed anything out, so he told me how, and soon we had a whole stack of quite useless sheets of paper that I didn't need for my students and would never look at again.

But 'helping' me like that did James a world of good. He already looked much better, said he would give me another lesson in using the Internet whenever I liked. I had a bottle of sherry in the cupboard that was here when we moved in. It's an old-fashioned drink, but I suddenly had a fancy for it, so James and I each had a glass and he told me I had saved his life. The oxycodone was what I thought of, whether he was still using it and if it might take the life I was supposed to have saved. I hadn't yet thanked him but now I did, and he said it was nothing, as people do, and then he asked if I would hold him in my arms again as I did when I found him in the hallway.

He was gay. I had never had any doubt about that, but doubt came quickly then. The kiss he gave me was a lover's kiss and the hands that began touching me were a lover's. Why didn't I stop him? Why didn't I just say no gently and kindly, take my mouth away from his, slide away from under him and remind him who and what we were? Andrew's lover and Andrew's sister. Trusted absolutely because trust was taken for granted, trust wasn't even necessary to think about. So why didn't I? Maybe because, skeletal though he had become, he was attractive. I'd noticed before, but I'd made myself not be affected by his attractions because he was gay and because he was Andrew's. I forgot all that, yielded in silence and participated in silence. No arguing, no protest, no words at all, but a simple and intensely pleasurable giving and receiving.

We were on Verity's sofa in Verity's study, and because we made no sound but for a faint sigh, a quiet gasp, we came to a mutual climax on a deep, long sigh. He held me afterwards with a tenderness I took for gratitude and that surprised me. I moved away from him, expecting remorse, but none came, and I thought to myself, it must have been the sherry, that unfamiliar, old drink that may have been Verity's favoured tipple. The date would be right.

Still silent, we got back into those clothes we'd taken off and at last I said something. I said what was bound to be said sooner or later. 'I thought you were entirely gay.'

'So did I.'

'But?'

'I was married once, so I suppose you could say I'm bisexual, but I haven't been since my divorce and I never think of myself that way. Grace – what a lovely name that is – Andrew must never know.'

Perhaps he wouldn't mind. After all, it was over and we were not going to do it again. That I was sure of and sure too that Andrew would mind very much. 'It won't happen again. We should tell him it happened once.'

'No, Grace, no.'

'We must tell him, but we can take two days and a night to think about how we'll do it.'

And that was what we were doing. Apart, of course, for I was in my part of the house, my living room, and James was in Andrew's part with Andrew. At about eight I heard them go out. I heard them talking as they crossed the hall where James had sat hunched up in despair and then I heard him laugh, a carefree happy laugh, the like of which hadn't been heard since the murder of Bashir.

7

Whatever conclusion James might have come to, if he had thought about it at all, I knew we had to tell Andrew or our failure to tell him would hang over all my relations with my brother and spoil them. He had to be told, whatever came of it. This was what I would tell James in the morning after Andrew had left for work. And in thinking this way I saw that I was already on the path to deception, for I had never before thought of keeping a secret from Andrew. And such a secret.

But for the time being they had gone out and were having a happy time, if James's laugh was anything to go by. This was the first time I'd heard him laugh for weeks. I had planned to use this evening reading at least the beginning of *The Child's Child*, wondering if it might possibly be of use to me in my thesis, and anyway I wanted to know what happens. But as I went into the study a strange thing occurred, or perhaps not strange at all. My thoughts went back to what had taken place there a few hours ago, not with sentimentality or any enhanced view of my feelings for James, but with guilt and a degree of shame. What it came down to was, I shouldn't have done it. I could have said no to him and sat up and hugged him again. Now I have forgotten why I did do it, but not forgotten that I did. One single act of sex can have a profound effect on one's life and now I had a quite reasonless fear that what James and I had done was one of those acts and the result would be cataclysmic.

I went into the drawing room and contemplated the books on the shelves in there. But not for long. My eyes turned to the big window from which the garden could be seen. It began to rain, and not just to rain but to come down in floods, beating on the glass and bouncing off the stones. Through it, the shuddering veil of it, the lawn and trees and bushes were a dense mass of varying greens. Lightning struck while I watched, lighting up glittering slate roofs and tossing treetops. I told myself what I sometimes tell my students in a comment on what I have found in their essays: do not subscribe to the pathetic fallacy. James and I had nothing to do with the weather and the weather nothing to do with us. The thunder came so long after the lightning that it made me jump.

I wondered if James, in spite of what he said, was even now confessing to Andrew. Would he tell me if he were? I went up to bed but couldn't sleep and came down again in my dressing gown. This time I did pick up *The Child's Child* and started to read the first page again, but I got no further than the first line: *He knew it was wrong of him, but his life today was so full of wrong actions that it seemed to him one long sin.* It reminded me of me. Except for the sin part. 'Sin' is a word that has gone out of our vocabulary, except, I suppose, for Catholics in the confessional.

I had started leafing through it, passing the point I had reached, looking for a date, when I heard the front door close softly. I did a stupid thing. I switched off the light. No one could have been deceived because anyone coming to the front of the house would have seen it, but I left it off, sitting there feeling like a fool and waiting for one or both of them to come in. To walk through the drawing room and maybe burst into the study. Neither of them did. The porch light went out, the hall light went out, and I wasn't just sitting in the dark, I was in the profoundest, deepest blackness. I don't know why I felt for the window and then for the curtains. Pulling them back revealed the half-lit street, a cat as grey as the night sky emerging from under a car and streaking into the dense foliage of a garden.

As far as I could tell, the whole house was now in darkness. My green digital clock told me it was half-past midnight.

In the morning, after Andrew had gone to work, James came down to talk to me. Like the ghost, he knocked on the drawing-room door, something he had seldom done before. He sat down, picked up *The Child's Child* and said, 'Here's the book you showed us, isn't it?'

I nodded.

'I met him once,' he said. 'Greenwell. He was very old by then. It was at someone else's book launch.'

Silence fell. I wasn't interested in someone else's book launch and nor really was he. His face had become grave, the eyes half closed. I said that I supposed he hadn't said anything to Andrew.

'No, and I'm not going to. We're not going to. Think about it, Grace. What would be the point? You might say, who benefits? Not you or me, certainly. Andrew would be devastated, and that's one instance where that overused word is absolutely apt. He would be. And he would hate us both. I know how jealous he is. You don't. You can't. So who benefits?'

'Truth, I suppose,' I said, feeling like a prig. 'What politicians call transparency.'

'Oh, please.'

We sat there, looking at each other, for a while in silence, then starting the argument all over again. I stopped it by reaching or apparently reaching his point of view. 'All right,' I said, 'we'll say nothing. We'll even try to forget it.'

'Thank you, Grace. I don't think you'll have any regrets.'

Before all this started, I would have expected, had it reached this end, to feel enormous guilt, but I didn't. What I felt was relief, as if all along I had wanted to avoid telling Andrew, and perhaps I had. Once James had gone upstairs, had kissed me on the cheek and held me in a sexless hug for a moment before saying I had saved his life for the second time, I felt a burden lifted from my shoulders. I had agreed to do something I had thought was wrong and I would never agree to; whatever he said, I wouldn't do it, and suddenly I was agreeing to it. I felt fine. It was all over, my brother and I would be to each other what we had always been, there would be no recriminations, no pain, no accusations and bitter reproaches. All things would be well, as that weird woman Julian of Norwich said. I sat down at the computer and got back to my thesis.

*

Andrew had a week's holiday owing to him and he and James went to Italy, to Lucca, where neither of them had ever before been. They had never disturbed me and I hope I hadn't disturbed them, but I was able to work better while entirely on my own, and by the time I saw them again I was well into the thesis.

While they were away some kind of notice had come – the sort of thing that's called a 'communication' rather than a 'letter' – telling James that he wouldn't be needed as a witness at Kevin Drake's trial. Apparently, the police had enough witnesses without him. He and my brother came to tell me, inviting me to have dinner with them. While we were in the restaurant, the now happy and enormously relieved James told me that he wanted to apologize to me. While they were away he'd read a piece about a particularly dreadful kind of social engineering in Spain in the 1930s but, almost incredibly, continuing until the 1980s. Under this scheme the Franco regime and the Catholic Church removed babies from unmarried mothers and, telling them their children were dead, placed them with women of higher moral character. At first he could hardly believe it, but he checked it out and found it was well known and not only in Spain, where all over the country there are children's graves containing nothing but stones. He was sorry he had said I exaggerated the suffering of the mothers of illegitimate children.

We were all happy after that. I told them I was still only halfway through the thesis, though Carla had told me not to hang about with it too long. She had once had a graduate student who could never bring himself to relinquish his and finally given up.

Perhaps it was strange that I could now look at James and talk to James without thinking about the 'incident' in the study. It was over, it was past, and just as I had no urge to repeat it, so I was sure he hadn't. I did think of it enough to marvel that I had ever considered telling Andrew. A good principle in my philosophy is to be careful never to confess something to a friend or a lover (or I suppose a husband or a wife) unless you can be entirely sure you're not doing so out of self-indulgence or even, God forbid, pride. Yet nothing like that had prompted my powerful need, immediately after the 'incident', to admit the whole thing to my brother. Luckily, it wasn't an impulse that had lasted long, and now I felt the same as James: keep silent, forget.

Nothing now, I thought, could make me feel that need to confess to Andrew, nothing could impel me to come out with the truth. I was wrong.

8

They called it 'being in a fix' in those days, though Martin Greenwell doesn't. It never crossed my mind. I had taken the occasional
risk before, being a sporadic user of the pill, and never had a scare.
Now it was six weeks since my unexpected encounter with James,
my period had failed to come and the pregnancy test I'd bought had
tested positive. Of course I had to put an end to it, I refused to be in
a fix. 'Abortion' is a nasty word and the euphemism 'termination' is
only slightly better. But I didn't have to think about that yet. So long
as I had it done by, say, the end of August everything would be fine.
I was not one of those girls in fiction whose attitude to their pregnancy must have been a constant dwelling on it, from ghastly
realization through cringing acceptance to death wish.

There was no need for James ever to be told. I had seen him in
Andrew's company and he was much, much better. Andrew said
James was suddenly light-hearted, went out for long walks and
hadn't touched the oxycodone since that 'communication' came.
The book he was halfway through he had abandoned, but he told
Andrew that when the trial was over he might write a novel about
the murder of Bashir.

I worked on the thesis, resisting – I'm not sure how successfully –
an urge to enter into the emotions of some of these girls who
found themselves heading for disgrace or disaster. I did allow
myself to dwell a bit on the almost uncanny power of marriage, a
ceremony, 'a piece of paper' as it's often called, that in two or
three promises and a hymn or two or a couple of names and a
few words could save a life or transform a life or bring with it
unimaginable relief. All gone now, of course, but once a cornerstone
of social life, the magical process that made women pure and
children honourable.

So I was careful to keep things cool – 'businesslike' was the word that came to mind – while all the time this undercurrent of dread and a strange kind of excitement were running along beneath the surface. The weeks passed, summer was coming to an end. One evening my brother and James were going out to celebrate Andrew's birthday and they asked me to go with them. I said I would, then said I wasn't well. I couldn't face being with the two of them, both of them ignorant of what was happening to me, but Andrew much more so than James, Andrew *innocent*.

I didn't go with them. I began again on Greenwell's book with its highly appropriate theme, the subject of the thesis and of my life at present. Next day I booked myself into an abortion clinic, telling myself all the time I gave my details and saw the doctor and fixed on a day that I was so lucky compared with all those poor girls I'd been writing about. I didn't have to have a baby if I didn't want to. It would be *wrong* for me to have a baby that was my brother's lover's child. That, I told myself, was true immorality, betrayal, treachery, positive cruelty. This way, I could have the deed done, it would be quick, no doubt I would be able to walk to the clinic and go home afterwards on the bus.

James need never know, Andrew certainly need never know. In a year's time, in less than a year, it would be as if none of this had ever been. I finished *The Child's Child*, rather pleased with it and gratified in the way we are when we read something that is so close to home as to be taken for a coincidence. My email to Toby Greenwell told him that I thought the book was publishable but I would like to read it again if he didn't mind. By this time I was a little worried that I hadn't given the book the concentration I would have if I hadn't been pregnant. No, I must correct that and say, if I had not been guiltily pregnant. As all those girls were, of course, but in quite a different way and for a different reason. If termination had been possible in their day as it is in mine, so easy, so straightforward, surely by this time without any moral censure, they wouldn't have believed my talk of guilt. They knew what real guilt and shame were; they lived with them every day of their lives.

*

I told myself I hadn't been able to get James alone but that was not true. I could have managed it in a hundred ways, but fear got in the way of every one of them. Now something else had happened. I had started throwing up in the mornings. This sickness had brought it home to me that unless I did something about it in the next few weeks I was going to have a baby in seven months' time. This was reality, which it hadn't been before; this was me carrying another person inside me. The idea of having an abortion and so putting an end to all this now seemed distasteful. It had gradually grown on me, this feeling, getting a bit worse every day. I was fascinated for a while, comparing my sensations to those of all the girls I'd been writing about – well, contrasting really, because I was living in a different world. I couldn't even say I too was a young woman witnessing changes to my body, because those other young women were largely ignorant of what was happening to them. They knew they were in danger of dreadful physical damage and death; opprobrium, if that's the word, loomed over them, disgrace awaited them. None of this applied to me. Like them, I worried, but for very different reasons. I couldn't sleep at night, but that was through worrying about having to tell James and, worse, perhaps Andrew – tell Andrew and James together. If I had a termination – horrible word – I wouldn't have to do any of that. I hadn't told Fay. I sometimes caught her giving me strange looks, suspicious looks, but not without a touch of amusement. She said nothing and neither did I.

The doctor at the clinic asked me if I needed counselling before the abortion. I didn't think so then and I certainly don't now. I know I wanted the baby, beyond a doubt I wanted him or her. It was Andrew and James that troubled me, because I knew only too well that telling them might lead to Andrew's deciding he couldn't continue to share this house with me. It might split them up, for what James and I had done could be seen as a double betrayal. When someone betrays you, you believe that the treachery was deliberate, malicious, vindictive, but it probably wasn't. You believe it was intentional, even vengeful. Very likely the betrayer didn't think of you at all, perhaps forgot for a time that you existed. I had never been the victim of a betrayal, but I had read enough instances of it in literature to think it must be common. Now I knew what it was like from the point of the perpetrator, and I didn't like it.

Every time Andrew and James and I met – and we seemed to do so quite often those days, and amicably – I asked myself something else. Would we ever meet again after I told them? Would they move out of here or would I? Clearly, I had to tell James first and James on his own. That wasn't as simple as it sounds. He and Andrew were always together, except of course while Andrew was out at work and James was upstairs writing.

I remembered how shocked Verity had been when her next-door neighbour had phoned her. How much more disapproving would she have been if she had known me to make a call to someone living in the same house? To someone born in the 1920s, someone who never had a phone in the house until she was ten years old, phoning an occupant of the same house who was sitting no more than a few feet away from you was both extravagant and lazy. Of course I could have gone upstairs, walked down the passage and knocked on the study door, but my reason for phoning was to ask if I might do this. I thought James might not answer but let his caller leave a message, which I wasn't anxious to do. But he answered. He said, yes, of course, and come and have coffee.

I'd rehearsed no preamble and I plunged into the middle of things. 'I'm pregnant. It's yours, so please don't ask.'

He was silenced as he well might have been. 'I thought for a while I'd have an abortion, but now – well, I can't. I want this baby. If I got rid of it I know I'd regret it all my life and I might never have another.'

A flush had crept up over his face and dyed it a dark red. He looked like a young boy caught in some misdemeanour. 'I'm not going to ask you to do that, I wouldn't do that,' he said. Then he said the one word, the one name. 'Andrew.'

'I know. I thought of telling him and you a lie, saying it's someone else's or the result of sperm donation. But there are objections.'

He or she may look like you.' Looking at James's handsome, sensitive face, pale again, I felt for the first time that I hoped it would. 'I even hope she or he will. As for you, tell me if I'm wrong, it may be your only chance of being a father. And I'm Andrew's sister, which makes the baby halfway to being his as well. You see I've thought of all these things.'

'I'll get the coffee,' he said, and when he came back with it, I saw his hands were shaking. The tray was shuddering in his trembling hands. I took it from him, set it down, wished the coffee had a hefty shot of brandy in it, that alcohol I'd make myself give up for the next seven months. 'I don't think Andrew will see it that way,' he said. 'Another possible lie is that it *was* a sperm donation.'

That made me laugh, though I didn't feel much like laughing. 'Wouldn't we have asked his permission first?'

Another silence fell. I drank the coffee, which was very strong, and asked myself if it could be good for the baby. Apart from eschewing alcohol, this was the first time I'd had such a thought, though it wouldn't be the last.

'Do you want me to tell him?'

I said that I couldn't leave it to him but that we should both tell him together, all three of us together. This was a gross mistake on my part, but I didn't see it at the time. James sat in silence and for a while he closed his eyes, then made a gargantuan effort to change the subject, asking me about my thesis, which I told him I'd sent off two weeks before. He was obviously in shock.

'I'm sorry, Grace. I'm trying hard to get off the subject, but I just come back to you and me and Andrew. Would you mind leaving me alone now to think about it?'

So of course I left him alone and went outside and sat in the garden. It was a lovely day, and though I thought I ought to be unhappy and anxious, I wasn't, not a bit. The second flowering of the roses had come and the hollyhocks and Japanese anemones were out. The sun was warm but not hot and I lay back and lifted my face to the clear, still light. For some unknown but surely stupid reason, I felt sure things would be all right. Forget all ideas about an abortion.

How could I have considered it? I was going to have a baby and it was going to make me so happy.

That theory of mine about the baby being halfway to Andrew's as well because I was his sister still seemed sound. Both James and I would be blamed at first, but Andrew would get over that. James would be the dad ('father' is becoming an obsolete word, as 'mother' is) and Andrew would be his or her uncle. Nothing wrong with that. We would be a family. I smiled up at the sun, not seeing what a crass fool I was being or how I would caution or even reprimand any friend who said things like that to me of her own experience.

'No worries' is what people say today and for many it means 'thank you'. I think it started in Australia, though I'm not at all sure about that. When I was a child it used to be 'no problem'. Anyway, having told James and having not been denounced or made to feel wicked (another word I use in its correct sense), I had no worries apart from a little, niggling fear that my thesis might not meet with whole-hearted approval. Well, of course it wouldn't, I would have to defend it, but no real worries.

This afternoon I was going to have a look at the Grand Union Canal and try to match it up with the descriptions in *The Child's Child*. So after lunch I went out and got on the 46 bus, which took me to Maida Vale. As in Martin Greenwell's book, the canal was coated with bright green weed today, a kind of algae, I supposed. Why it was there or where it came from I didn't know, but I'd seen it before and knew it might all be gone by tomorrow. Quite a lot of people were about, so I walked along the canal bank on the south side for a while, but past the second bridge and the pub that used to be called the Paddington Stop I left it and walked up to the path that runs along here past the church dedicated to St Mary Magdalene with the tall spire. All the other buildings here are modern – well, post-Second World War. Nothing of the old Victorian houses remains. There would have been terraces of them, a slum of the kind that clustered round great railway termini and in some places still do. Greenwell's description is probably sound, a grim area of tiny, overcrowded houses, and one would say the bombs did good service but for the loss of human life. St Mary Magdalene was built in the shape of an isosceles triangle, with one end sharply pointed, and was probably made that way to fit in among the streets of houses. It is of red brick, red-tiled with dark stained-glass windows.

I supposed the canal would be straight, but it soon started to curve like a river and had a beauty of its own. I was back on the towpath now, along with the cyclists who used the path and politely thanked me for moving back against the walls of warehouses to let them pass. On the opposite bank were pagoda-like blocks of flats whose common garden, dense with shrubs and trees, stretched down to the water and reminded me of that bit in *Hamlet* about a willow 'that shows his hoar leaves in the glassy stream'. It was all a surprise to me that everything was so rustic and charming. Then came Victorian four-storey houses whose rear walls were actually in the water itself and I wondered if they ever flooded. Then I remembered being told that the water level in the canal barely changes no matter how much rain falls. Those houses must have been there when Greenwell has John Goodwin drown, his death perhaps based on a real drowning he had heard about.

In places the water's surface was covered with weeds. The geese and coots glided through them, apparently oblivious of the green coating. Their bright colour showed up the empty bottles that bobbed up and down and the drifting plastic bags. Then it was all gone; I reached a stretch of clear, weed-free water and on the other side was the back of a black-painted pub called the Grand Union, with a garden full of topiary box trees, spherical and the size of footballs. In the distance were the two gasometers that marked the edge of the great cemetery, as thick with dark evergreens as a forest. I could climb the stairs now on to a blue-painted bridge and catch a bus in the Harrow Road, but I decided instead to walk back the way I had come and I turned sharply, nearly getting knocked down by a cyclist.

I stood still, leaning against the wall for a minute or two after this, the cyclist having brushed against me, actually touching my hand and making my arm swing. I thought of what might have happened and it frightened me. If I'd fallen, for instance, if I'd crashed face-downwards – womb-downwards. I soon recovered, of course, but I didn't stop thinking about the baby, protecting the baby. That was when all doubt went and I knew how much I wanted the baby and how absurd it was for me ever to think I could destroy it.

If Teds Caff had still been here I would have gone in and asked for a cup of tea. But it was long gone and where it had been there ran a brick wall with buddleia branches and long, purple flowers hanging from its top. Ted would have been dead for years and Reenie too, I expect. Here, on a day when no green weed was masking the water, the man who was based on James's great-uncle died, struck on the forehead by a heavy wooden oar. Did that really happen, as it does in the book? Now that I was here, at the scene of the crime, I shuddered at the thought of it, the pain and the fear of death. Although his being pushed in can never have appeared as a joke to John, he may have thought Bertie saw it as a joke until suddenly it changed from a gross comedy sketch to intentional death-dealing, and the death dealt by someone he loved with all his heart. The thought of it upset me, and I realized I was far more easily upset than I used to be if I could be distressed to this extent by an incident in a book. I was pregnant, that was the reason, and I said to myself, It's fiction, it didn't really happen.

The beautiful day was drawing to a close. The sun had clouded over and I realized I was alone down here, a notorious place where not long ago a gang of boys murdered a woman by throwing her into the canal and leaving her to drown. Normally, I wouldn't be in the least afraid. It was daylight, it was still just about summer, I was only a few yards from the Harrow Road, but I was afraid. I thought of the child I was carrying, a child I wanted to be fit and healthy, safely carried to full term, and I walked 'inland' over the green slopes to Westbourne Green.

Was it pregnancy which was making me into a creature not only of fear but also of moods? I woke in the night; it was only one in the morning and I had woken to an appalled sense of what I had done.

Was James even now telling Andrew? I had a feeling, aghast and sick (though my morning sickness was a thing of the past), that James wasn't the kind of person who put off the evil day. He spoke out when he had to and God knew he had to now. I got up and walked down the passage until I was close to the door of their bedroom, expecting to see the glow of light round the door. But all was in darkness, there was no sound, and I decided they must both be in there, sleeping side by side. Or in each other's arms, as novelists say, though actually doing this is uncomfortable. At least I couldn't hear angry voices.

Time was passing and I had told no one but James. But I had told the abortion people that I'd changed my mind and kept my first appointment at the hospital. All appeared to be well, very well, and I felt extremely well. Except that I was tired. The explanation was simple. I couldn't sleep. I woke up worrying about Andrew, and now, of course, the whole thing had assumed huge proportions. I knew that if I didn't tell him soon he would be able to see for himself. My jeans were so tight I'd had to give up wearing them and my skirt waistbands wouldn't do up.

Another dilemma was how to tell Fay. Should I do it before the inevitable showdown with Andrew or wait until after? The difficulty was that I didn't know how bad the confrontation would be or even if it would be bad at all. Fay wasn't the kind of mother to take offence at apparently being excluded from her children's business, but this could be different. Being unmarried is no longer an issue and hasn't been for years, but being unfaithful to one's brother with his lover is and always will be.

It was Saturday, so Fay would be at home. Instead of phoning to say I was coming, I walked across the few streets to where she lives. It was a dull, miserable sort of day, grey, dry and still, and I realized how many English days were like this. I also realized, after I'd rung Fay's doorbell, that it was only seven-fifteen in the morning. Malcolm opened the door in his dressing gown, a mug of tea in his hand. He asked the inevitable question when someone does something out of the ordinary.

'Is everything all right?'

I told him it wasn't, not really, but no one was dead or injured or ill. He said that that was all right then and if it was my mother I wanted to confide in, she was still in bed but awake and would I take her tea up with me? So I found myself carrying two cups of tea up on a tray.

'Look at your face,' she said when she saw me. 'As miserable as sin, as my mother used to say, though I'd have thought sin was more happy and triumphant than miserable. If you've come to tell me you're pregnant, I spotted that weeks ago.'

I hadn't realized how prominent my stomach had become, doubtless because I pulled it in every time I stood in front of the mirror. 'It's not just that,' I said. 'It's James's.'

'Who's James?'

'Andrew's James.'

'Oh, Gracie.'

She only called me Gracie when I'd surprised her or even upset her. So I sat on the bed, took a great swig of my tea and told her all about it, ending with, 'And I'm keeping it.'

'Does Andrew know?'

'He may do by now.'

In these past few days I had become a terrible coward, staying awake half the night in case my brother hated me, running to Mummy with my troubles, looking ahead to a friendless future, my family all turned against me.

'I know it's stupid, but I'm afraid to go back.'

'In case you're counting on my going with you, I'm afraid it's no. I'm not getting involved in this, Grace. Malcolm and I are going out to lunch and before that I've some very complicated case histories to read through. Give me a call when you've had your confrontation – if you do – and then we'll – well, I don't know what we'll do, but no one's going to kill anyone or even smack them.'

'I hope you're right.'

Of course I put it off for a few hours more, thinking that maybe they would go out and I wouldn't be able to do it. I started the walk home, thinking that no pregnant woman in Victorian times could have used the phrase I'd used, 'I'm keeping it.' She had had no choice. I thought about this for a while until I was overcome by an awful feeling of foreboding as I approached our house but before it came into sight. I didn't know what I expected, but maybe – I was now in some realm of fantasy – Andrew and an army of loyal friends standing in the front garden with the gagged-and-bound James, all of them armed and ranked in a row waiting to advance with a war cry as soon as I appeared. When I got there the front garden was empty and all that had changed was that a window in what was their bedroom was half open, the upper sash lowered a few inches.

Trollope says somewhere that any piece of unpleasant news is best imparted by letter. Well, he says something like that. This was all very well in his day, the day of all those poor girls disgraced by having babies without getting married first. Imagine telling your brother by email or text that you're going to have his lover's baby. Or even on the phone. No, it had to be a confrontation and it had to be today. I knew myself so I knew it had to be done on an impulse. I had to be doing something else, maybe starting on a second read of *The Child's Child*, and suddenly in the midst of it, jump up, run across the hall and burst in on them. With my news, my news that it was not too far-fetched to say could ruin my brother's life.

9

I saw from their faces that Andrew knew but had perhaps only just known. I guessed that James had told him a few hours or even minutes before. None of us said anything for quite a long time. Andrew looked at me, then he dropped his head and shut his eyes. I half expected James to stand up and say he'd get a drink of something because neither Andrew nor I was going to do that, but James didn't, he went on sitting there, very still, his face blank. It's odd what we think of at times like this, incongruous, irrelevant things. It occurred to me sort of out of the blue that neither Andrew nor James had ever told me that James was coming to live at Dinmont House. I had worried myself into sleepless nights over it and then somehow I had forgotten about it, worked on the thesis, read *The Child's Child* and the whole thing had gone out of my head. And now James was sitting here with a hangdog look – whatever does that mean? I must look it up – refusing to catch my eye, I too probably with the same cautious and miserable expression, while Andrew presided like the embodiment of despair.

I thought he was never going to speak, and then after a long time he did. 'I don't think I can remain in this house with the two of you. Or perhaps I should say, the three of you. I've been thinking about it and thinking about nothing else since James told me yesterday.' So it had been longer ago than I suspected. Hours and hours he had known and said nothing to me. 'I can imagine that you, Grace, fixed up a pretty little scenario in which your baby has a daddy and an uncle and looks a lot like all of us. It might be a kind of *Design for Living*, a twenty-first-century one Noël Coward didn't write, but in that comedy there's no infant.' It was so near the truth that I felt myself blushing, one of those blushes that deepen and darken until your face is burning. 'I don't suppose it's too late for an abortion,' he said, 'but I wouldn't ask you to have one, I wouldn't dream of it. I wouldn't ask you to have a baby adopted either, of course not. You wouldn't anyway. But I shan't be able to bear to see it or see James with it or see you with James, even if you never so much as touch each other's hand. So I shall go away.' Andrew turned to look at James. 'I'd like you to come with me, just you. We could go and live in your flat.' Like a child Andrew said, 'Would that be all right?'

James just nodded.

'I don't know how I'll feel in a year's time,' Andrew said. 'We never know that, do we?'

There were a thousand things to say but I knew I could say none of them. Not now. Perhaps one day. I got up and walked out of the room, closing the door quietly behind me. That night I dreamt I had a miscarriage, a flood of blood inundating the bed and the carpet. It was one of those dreams you believe to be true and I woke up shivering and crying, certain I'd lost the baby. But it had been, as they say, only a dream, as if a dream were nothing much to get upset about.

Two days later, days I'd spent in isolation and utter idleness, I watched from the study window the departure of Andrew and James. They had wasted no time. Even people who bring no furniture into a house have an awful lot to take out. They accumulate so much, computers and books and devices for reading books, devices for playing music and quantities of other electronic stuff. Andrew and James needed a van to take it all to James's place and Andrew was going to drive it. I saw James come back into the house. He knocked on the study door.

'I can't just go,' he said. 'You've got my phone number, you know where I'll be. I'll want to know how you get on.'

'Once upon a time,' I said with a little laugh, 'you'd have offered to marry me. Funny, isn't it? It's not so long ago but it seems like a thousand years.'

'Goodbye, Grace.' Then, and it was the last thing I'd have expected him to say: 'This will bind us together for ever, won't it?'

'I suppose it will. Goodbye, James.'

He kissed me on the cheek. His lips were cold.

Andrew was already sitting in the driving seat, waiting impatiently, it seemed to me from the window. I realized then – I don't know why then – that although we'd spoken in the past few days, about practical things, about arrangements, he hadn't once called me Sis.

I phoned my mother and said I'd something to tell her. She said she'd come to me on her way home from work. It was going to be a case of what do you want first, the good news or the bad, but I wasn't going to put it to her like that. I was thinking about that, and that doom-laden enquiry that seems to amuse people so much, when I felt a sort of shifting sensation inside my body. For a few seconds I couldn't think what it was and then of course I knew. The baby had moved.

A flutter. A touch, no more than that, as if a small finger had brought a light pressure on to the wall that confined it. I wondered when it would come again, and as if in answer to a speculation I hadn't uttered aloud – but I wouldn't have to, would I? – it, he, she touched me again and I began to cry. The tears were still coming, scrubbed away but still falling, when my mother arrived.

'Oh, dear,' she said, looking at my face, 'this won't do.'

'It's not that I'm desperately unhappy or anything.'

'Emotion makes us cry, not unhappiness.'

I had given up wine 'for the duration' but she hadn't, so I drank elderflower water and she had some Sauvignon and I told her about the baby moving and Andrew's departure.

'He's impulsive,' she said. 'Like you. He rushes into things. He'll come round.'

I asked her what she meant by that, that he'd change his mind or physically come to the house?

'Well, both.'

That was the end of August and in the first week of September they told me my baby was a girl. Whatever the fate of my thesis, it seemed to me appropriate to call my daughter after one of those girls I had been writing about and, not hesitating for long, I named her after Hardy's Tess.

In the second week of that month I read Martin Greenwell's book for the second time.

1929

The Child's Child

I

He knew it was wrong of him, but his life today was so full of wrong actions that it seemed to him one long sin. Some of it he could put right and the letter of resignation he was carrying to the post would begin that process. He dropped the letter into the pillar box and stood for a moment looking at the building opposite, a school like dozens of other schools in the country: brown brick with red-brick facings to the windows and red-brick arches over them, double doors painted black, a little pointed belfry with the school bell inside, and all around the broad, asphalted playground. Turning away, he was beginning the half-mile walk homewards when a voice behind him called out, 'Johnny!'

Only one person ever called him that. John had sometimes wished he had been born a woman, had been one of his three sisters, not the only boy, so that now he could hold out his arms and take the man who had called him into them, could kiss him. And then all that would happen would be young women passers-by giggling and old women clicking their tongues. It was impossible and always would be. They stood in front of each other, afraid to touch.

'I'm awfully pleased to see you,' John said.

'Me too. You got any money so we can go out to supper some-where?'

'Home first, though.'

They walked up the Edgware Road and turned into Orchardson Street. The district was dull but not squalid, the terraced houses grim-looking because of their grey brickwork, the colour of ash. When John let himself and Bertie into Mrs Petworth's house his landlady was in the hall tidying up the tumble of letters and pile of old newspapers on the mahogany table. She said, 'Good evening, Mr Goodwin,' smiled, and nodded to Bertie. A widow, desperate to be thought respectable, she was strict with her lodgers when it came to young ladies in their rooms. Such visitors must be out by nine o'clock. Innocent but cautious, she believed that sexual intercourse took place only after ten, but she was taking no chances. She infinitely preferred young men who had no young ladies – that should come later, when they were fiancées – but chose for their companions members of the same sex. That was suitable and proper.

To show her approval of Bertie as John's visitor, she remarked to him as he set foot on the first stair that it had been a fine day and would seem that spring had come at last. Bertie agreed, and he and John climbed to the second floor. John was always in two minds about locking the door. If Mrs Petworth tried his door – a most unlikely eventuality – she would think it strange, almost sinister, that he had seen fit to lock it. Why would he? What was he doing in there? Drinking? Playing cards? On the other hand, he dared not leave it unlocked. The truth, in her eyes, would be so much worse than the whisky or the cards. She would send the girl who helped in the kitchen for a policeman. His life and Bertie's life would be over.

Knowing nothing of what went on in John's head, Bertie was stripping off his clothes without the least inhibition. John did so too, but even though Bertie had been his lover for a year now he still felt shame showing his naked body. That was the way he had been brought up, never to show nakedness, never even to speak of it.

They made love. At the moment of climax Bertie always cried out, making a sound John believed anyone passing the door or standing outside must be able to identify for what it was. He himself only sighed with pleasure, his hand clamped over Bertie's mouth to hush the noise.

In the café where they had a beefsteak and mashed potatoes, washed down with a pint of beer each, John told Bertie what was in the letter and what he planned to do. Bertie showed very little emotion. He nodded, he went on eating.

'You mean you'll get a job teaching in a school down there?'

'Somewhere in Devon, yes. I've applied to Devon County Council and they're interviewing me next week.'

'But what are you doing it for, Johnny?'

'I don't want to say anything to hurt you. I don't want to upset you.'

'You won't,' said Bertie. 'I'm hard. You'd best be hard in our game.'

'I know, but I can't be.' John laid his knife and fork across his half-empty plate. He could eat no more. 'I said I don't want to hurt you and I don't, but I believe that what we do, what all men do who do it together, I believe that's a sin. It's a crime, of course, but it's a sin too and that's worse. We sin, you and I, but it's an even worse sin when we go to those places where there are all men like us, all Uranians behaving like us.'

In an incredulous voice Bertie said, 'You'll go to hell, will you, when you die? Come off it. We don't do no harm, we don't hurt no one.' Bertie was a clerk in an office but not earning much, the lowest rank, the one who made the tea and fetched the post. 'We do all right together, don't we?'

'I'm not saying we don't enjoy it. That's why we do it. Maybe we hurt ourselves, damage our characters, I don't know.'

'That's too deep for me,' Bertie said. 'Can I come and see you when you're living in Devon in a cottage?'

'You know what would happen then, don't you?'

'That's why I'd come.'

'You see, Bertie, I intend for it never to happen again.'

Bertie shook his head, half smiling. 'I can't believe that.'

'What we did just now, that was the last time for me.' John looked about the café to check that all the customers were occupied with their own business and then he took Bertie's hand under the table. 'It was lovely. It was a great joy to me. But it must never happen again, never in all my life. I've got to be – well, like a monk. Women aren't anything to me, just as they're not for you. So the only choice I have is to go with men or be celibate. That's the word, celibate. And I will be. I'll teach in a school out in the country and I'll live there and there won't be any people like us. There won't be any temptation.'

Bertie was silent, staring at him. At last he said, 'What about me? What am I going to do?'

'I don't know. You'll find someone. The time may come some day when men like us aren't hunted down and persecuted, when we're allowed to – to love each other in private, but it's a long way off. I'll write to you, Bertie, I won't deny myself that. Will you write to me?'

Bertie said nothing but he nodded. On and off as if he would never stop.

2

The Great Western train was half empty, not unusual at this hour on a weekday. John noticed the name on the side of the engine, the *George V*. It was heading for Penzance, but he would leave it at Exeter St David's, where his interview was to take place, and when that was over take another train to Bristol. The expense, even travelling third class, was more than he could really afford. It would have been much cheaper to have bought a return ticket and gone back to Orchardson Street – just a short walk from Paddington station – but he hadn't been home since Christmas and he was longing to see his mother and his sisters, Sybil, Ethel and Maud. His father too, but his fondness for his father was tempered with fear. He was always afraid that his father would find out.

He got into the train with his *Daily Telegraph*, his packet of sandwiches prepared by Mrs Petworth and the Player's he had bought at the tobacconist's on the station. He was early, so easily found a seat in a smoking compartment. The difficulty would have been to find one where smoking was forbidden. He rationed his cigarettes to ten a day for economy's sake and he had already had two. An old man sat in the best window seat, the one facing the engine. He still wore his overcoat but had put his homburg in the luggage rack. John put his attaché case up there at the other end, sat down and lit a cigarette. He had been travelling three or four times a year on this line for four years, but he still felt a thrill when the guard blew the whistle and they were off. A great plume of steam swept past the window and drifted up into the air as they headed for Reading and Taunton and the long, dark Whiteball tunnel into Devon.

When he was alone, in bed at night, or as now, travelling some long distance, he let his thoughts take a journey of their own and remember how he and Bertie had met. At the same time he wished that it had been somewhere else, some green country place perhaps or a foreign city of beautiful buildings and antique treasures, where of course he had never been, instead of a pub in Paddington. He saw it as a sordid place, crowded with dirty, hoarse-voiced labouring men and presided over by a fat landlord and a sluttish barmaid. His own idealistic dream of such an encounter – for it had been love at first sight for him – would have had them meet each other alone and with eyes for no one but one another. But it had been the Prince Alfred, half a mile from where Bertie lived in Bourne Terrace, round the back of Paddington station and a little further than that from Orchardson Street, and it had been a cold, wet evening. Bertie's beauty, his grace, his height and his wonderful blue eyes had lit the place for him, and his smile, with his golden head held a little on one side, promised a lovely, happy future.

What they did that evening and subsequent evenings, even though often in squalid places, brought that happiness for a while, but gradually guilt had closed in. It was wrong. He couldn't get away from that. He tried hard to persuade himself that though lust could be wrong, love never could. His sister Ethel was allowed to love Herbert Burrows, her fiancé, allowed to linger on the doorstep with him exchanging kisses before he went home. John's kisses shared with Bertie had to be taken and given in the deepest secrecy because society and he too knew that while Ethel's were right and good, his were wrong and bad. All that lovemaking was wrong and must be abandoned for good.

The train emerged from the tunnel into Devon.

The three men who were the panel had liked him, he could tell that. They only said they would let him know, but he could tell he had pleased them, due perhaps to his having his degree from the University College of the South West of England just up the street. The others would have only teacher-training qualifications or no more than Higher School Certificate. They would be surprised too that he was giving up a teaching post in London, and the extra money called the London weighting, to come to work in a small Devon country town. Perhaps they would be suspicious, but he was sure they wouldn't guess the truth. They had asked him about his wife and he had had to say he wasn't married. Then one old busybody suggested that perhaps he had a fiancée, and John, feeling guilty and ashamed, lied and said that there was someone. They were saving up to get married. He was afraid one of the panel might say that in that case he was surprised John was giving up a better-paid job, but none of them did. Fiancées, nearly as much as wives, met with approval.

He had a long wait for his next train, the one that would take him to Bristol, and he was hungry in spite of the sandwiches. In a café he had a cup of tea and a poached egg on toast and sat thinking about the lie he had told. He told lies all the time, he was more or less resigned to that, and most of them were concerned with when he was going to find a girl or when he was going to get married. Because the only social life he had was with Bertie and the men Bertie knew, he came into little contact with middle-aged women who might try to foist their spinster daughters on him. He teetered too on the border of being a gentleman. A doctor was one but not a schoolteacher, though he might be if he was head of a school. This meant he would never be invited to tennis parties or tea dances, he would be asked to tea only with women teachers, and he would be expected one day to marry one of them. He had lied to them as well, talking in a vague way of a girl in Bristol living in the same street as his parents.

Half an hour before his train was due he made his way to the station at St David's and sat on a seat on the platform. A good many more lies lay ahead of him. His parents would want to know why, if he must leave London, he couldn't take a job in Bristol; his sisters would ask about the girls he knew. They would all enquire as to what he did at the weekends. His parents were Methodists, as he and his sisters were or had been. His mother would want to know if he went regularly to church, and to this question too he would lie as he would to all the others. He had never set foot in the little Methodist chapel round the corner from Orchardson Street.

The train came and he got into an empty carriage, wondering why he had longed to see them all, to come home. Not just now but for always, he would have no real relationship with any of them because what love for them he had, what companionship, would be distorted and made pointless by lying. He realized then, sitting in the train, that even when he became celibate, he would still be constrained to lie. The older he grew and the longer he remained single and unattached, the more his mother and the three girls would question him about women friends (or the absence of them) and the more hold out to him the pleasures of marriage, ending, probably every time they spoke of it, in asking him if he didn't want children.

3

Maud wanted children one day, two at least, when she was married. At fifteen, attending a school where the pupils stayed till they were eighteen, she thought she was probably the only girl in the County High School who had had relations with a man. Those were the words she used to herself, 'relations with a man', because she knew no other except 'the act', but she hadn't connected it with what her mother called 'offspring'. In a daring, almost incredulous way, she was proud of what she had done. It made her grown up, a woman, even though it was the deepest secret, and though she had surrounded what they did and its circumstances with romance, she had decided that once – well, twice – was enough. The preliminaries to it, cuddles and kisses, caresses like those in the silent films she saw, she much preferred. The culmination that he had insisted on and she hadn't resisted for long had hurt, and she had bled nearly as much as when she had her monthlies. The second time there had been no pain but nothing much else either, a disappointment, though she hadn't told him that.

Now two things were due in her life, the visitor that was her brother, John, and the visitor, as her mother called it, that she and her friends called the curse. John was coming on Friday evening, the curse should have come ten days ago, on the tenth of April. If she had been irregular like her friend Rosemary Clifford, who sometimes went five or even six weeks between visitors, she wouldn't have given it another thought. She tried to remember if anything like this had happened before in the three years since the first visitor, but all she could recall was that once it had come two days late.

Ronnie was Rosemary's brother. She hadn't got to know him through Rosemary but because she was in her school choir and Ronnie was in the boys' school choir. The choirs met when they were giving concerts together in St Mary's church hall and after the performances or the rehearsals Ronnie walked her home. Her parents didn't like her singing in a Church of England hall, but she calmed them down by reminding them that it wasn't the church itself. Now she wished she had listened to them. They didn't object to Ronnie. They thought he was a nice boy. As far as Maud was concerned, he wasn't nice, he was gruff and he grinned too much, but he was by far the best-looking boy in the choir. Besides, as far as Maud's parents knew, Rosemary was with them. The Goodwins lived on the outskirts of Bristol and Ronnie walked Maud home across the fields. On one of those walks home they went inside a barn doorway and he kissed her, but it was too cold to hang about. Two weeks later, when it happened, it was a lovely evening, exceptionally warm for early spring, and a slightly cooler evening the second time.

Until she tried it, Maud had only a vague idea of what relations with a man consisted of, but she knew all about pregnancy, which she called 'expecting', and quite a lot about childbirth. Her mother had had a fifth child three years before, but it had died when it was a day old. On the morning of the Friday John was coming, she woke up early in the room she shared with Ethel, and the first thing she thought of was not John's arrival in the evening but that eleven days had passed since the curse was due to have come. It wouldn't be a curse to her. She got up and went to the bathroom they all shared, praying for a trace of blood on the lavatory paper. But someone else was in there and had turned the key in the lock. She wasn't desperate to go, only desperate for that blood. Now she was reaching a stage when she could no longer tell herself the delay was due to the cold she had had the week before last or that she had miscounted. It must be that she was going to have a baby. A little sound like a whimper escaped her and a quiet sob followed it. The bathroom door opened and Sybil came out.

'Was that you making that noise?'

'What noise?'

'Like you were crying. You weren't, were you?'

'You imagined it,' said Maud in a lofty tone.

Her sister went off to her bedroom, tall, slender Sybil, a dressing gown over her peach-coloured slip, her hair at this hour falling down her back like a brown silk cloak. Maud used to speculate if Sybil, eleven years her senior at twenty-six, had ever done the act with a man and was sure she hadn't. Maud went into the bathroom, sat down on the lavatory seat and pushed her forefinger into what another girl at school, not Rosemary, had told her had the Latin name 'vagina'. The finger came away damp but bloodless.

She must be careful not to make a sound. She wanted to scream or howl like an animal in pain but she couldn't. And she couldn't have a baby. That would be appalling, outrageous, impossible to contemplate. A girl down the road had had an illegitimate child; 'born out of wedlock' was how Maud's mother put it. Everybody in the neighbourhood knew, and if any friend called who didn't know, this girl was pointed out and her story told. The Goodwins' charwoman had a niece who was expecting without being married, but she never had the baby. She drowned herself in the Bristol Channel. Maud thought of drowning herself or putting her head in the gas oven, but not yet, not yet. It could still be all right, God would make it all right. Why did she go to chapel every Sunday morning, why had she gone to Sunday school every Sunday afternoon and sung hymns in the choir and prayed and prayed if God wouldn't show mercy unto her? He couldn't punish her like this for something she had done in those sunset fields, in the long grass among the coltsfoot and the celandine and hadn't even enjoyed – could He?

The Goodwins were far from rich but they were 'comfortable'. John Goodwin had inherited a bookbinding business from his father and it had always done fairly, if not spectacularly, well. He had married a woman he met at chapel, the only child of Jonathan Halliwell, who kept a draper's shop in the High Street. On his daughter's marriage he gave her and her husband a thousand pounds, a huge sum. John and Mary Goodwin used it to buy a house up the street from the chapel, because both of them were deeply devout. Jonathan died shortly after this purchase had been made, leaving his widow rich. She furnished the young couple's new home for them with some valuable and beautiful pieces and several paintings, including a Burne-Jones and a Holman Hunt, though these were not much valued at the time.

Was it a happy marriage? They never asked themselves or each other that question. They were together, they were used to each other, they had four children, none of whom had given them much trouble. John had a BSc in biology and a teaching job, Sybil was a typist, Ethel worked for her uncle, who now managed the draper's, and Maud was still at school. It looked as if she might be doing well enough at her schoolwork to go to a university, unheard of among the Goodwin females and her mother's family, the Halliwells, but the University of Reading's school of art was a possibility and she might get a scholarship.

Goodwins and Halliwells seldom if ever thought about anything deeply. Young John was the exception. Life had made him think. In politics his parents were Conservatives, and if Mary was triumphant or joyous at having just got the vote for herself and her two older daughters the previous year, along with all the other women of Britain over twenty-one, she gave no sign that she was even aware of it. Their religion was laid down for them, no thinking necessary there. The same went for their moral values. They had absolute faith in their children's holding the same views as they did. With their parents' example before them, why should they stray?

If not exactly worried about it, Mary was uneasy about Sybil's failure to find a young man since a previous boy had jilted her, but Mary dealt with her mild anxiety by thinking as little about it as possible. Ethel was engaged to a man seven years older than herself who worked for His Majesty's Customs and Excise, a highly suitable connection. Ethel and Herbert Burrows had met through a cousin of Mary's whose husband's nephew he was. If, as Mary put it, it was 'high time' Ethel at twenty-two and especially Sybil at twenty-six were married, in his father's estimation, John at twenty-five was 'far too young'.

That Friday evening, when John told his parents about the interview and the panel's enquiry into his matrimonial prospects, his mother said, 'Well, they've got a point there, John.' He sighed to himself, thinking, It's begun.

They had just had high tea, for although the Goodwins had graduated to a live-in servant, always known as 'the maid', they had never progressed as far as eating dinner at seven-thirty. The maid, Clara Gadd, served cold ham, tongue, a salad of lettuce and tomatoes, beetroot in malt vinegar, and bread and butter, followed by tinned peaches and tinned milk. Mary had her snobbish side and would have liked to call the maid by her surname, simply Gadd, but she didn't quite dare. When it seemed that John was about to talk of salaries and accommodation, Mary shook her head at him and put a finger to her lips. If Mary had known any French, Maud said to him later, she would have said, '*Pas devant les domestiques.*'

Herbert Burrows called in the evening. He and John had met just once before. John thought he was a bit of a stuffed shirt but could see that his parents would approve of him. It was Friday, not Sunday, when Maud knew anything of the sort she proposed would be out of the question, but when she suggested putting a record on the gramophone and Ethel and Herbert and she and John dancing to it, their parents too if they liked, she was surprised when her father shook his head and, using a favourite Goodwin phrase, said it 'wouldn't be suitable'. Herbert, too, supported him and said, 'Not a good idea,' in ingratiating tones. Maud had only suggested it for something energetic to do, something to take her mind off what was always on it, however much she tried not to think. Her grandmother Halliwell, a fit and vigorous old woman, who had also come round for the evening, said young people ought to have a good time while they were young, but her opinion was ignored in spite of her wealth.

The parents were the first to go to bed, departing soon after Herbert left. Ethel hadn't come back into the living room after saying goodbye to him with kisses on the doorstep, and sharp at ten Sybil too went to bed. Grandma, as even her daughter and son-in-law called her, left soon after in her motor car, driven by her 'man', the husband of her housekeeper. John and Maud were left. More than ten years were between them, but they had always been the closest of the siblings since Maud was a toddler and John the big brother who carried her or pushed her pram.

'I'm sorry they wouldn't let us dance,' he said. 'I'd like to dance with you, Maud, but perhaps it can never be in this house.'

She was desperate for someone to tell. It was too early to know, she knew that, but just to have someone to talk to about her fears would help her, someone to share her terror. Soon it would be time to go to bed and in the night-time the worst of it would return to her, feeling the swelling of her body, the fear of someone noticing. Before that happened she might be sick in the mornings. When she thought like that, lying in the dark, panic rose into her mouth and she had to stop herself from screaming. She could remember her mother when she was carrying the little girl they called Beryl, though she had lived only a day. If she had a baby and it lived only a day that would be wonderful, a relief and a release. Better still, if it came away first from her in a miscarriage, for then there would be no disgrace and no shame. She could bear the pain and maybe blood and pain, anything to be back where and who she was before this horror came upon her.

'You're very quiet tonight, Maud.'

'I wasn't quiet when I asked if we could have a dance.'

'That's true. Afterwards when you hardly said any more I thought you might be sulking, but you don't sulk, do you? You're usually a cheerful soul.'

'John. John, do you believe in God?'

He raised his eyebrows. 'That's quite a question in this house.'

'I know, but do you?'

'I don't know, Maud. I used to think I did. I think the trouble is, if it's a trouble, that I know too much science now to believe in a creator. There's no need for a creator, it could all have happened without God.'

She said as if she were near to tears, her voice hoarse, 'I don't know about any of that. It's just that I'm afraid it's all lies. God *isn't* love, He *doesn't* answer prayers, He *isn't* merciful.'

'Oh, Maud. What's wrong? Come here.' John took her hands. In that household they didn't hug or kiss. 'There's something very wrong. Won't you tell me about it? You can tell me.'

She was sobbing by then. 'No, I can't. I can't tell anyone.'

He handed her the clean, white handkerchief Mrs Petworth had washed and ironed for him. Maud scrubbed at her eyes, but he took the handkerchief back and dried her tears tenderly. Even with her face crumpled and red from crying, she was the prettiest of his sisters, her eyes large and a clear greenish blue, her skin pale yet flushed and quite unblemished. Of the family, through some throwback, she alone had long, elegant hands with tapering fingers. While he held her, gently patting her back, he thought she must have been rejected by a boy, some fool without taste or discernment. Or a bunch of schoolgirls, bitter with jealousy, had insulted and abused her.

'Don't tell me I'll feel better in the morning,' she said.

'I wasn't going to. You'll feel better one day, though. We all do that.' And we feel worse again, he said to himself, it's the way life is.

She was sitting up straight now, her swollen eyes meeting his directly. 'When will you come back here?'

'If I get the job, and I think I will, I'll leave at the end of the term, that's late July. I'll have to come back here to live until I can start at my new school in September and find a place nearby.'

Suddenly her face took on a look of deep seriousness. 'If things aren't better by then, if this thing that's worrying me hasn't gone away, I'll tell you.'

She got up quickly after that and ran away up the stairs to bed.

4

He started to do what he had never before done. He began writing to Maud. Letters to his mother he had always written, but never to any of his sisters till now. In the first letter he told Maud that he had got the job. She need not tell their parents because he was writing to them too. He was still at Mrs Petworth's but would leave in the last week of July. How was she? He had been worried about her. She had seemed so sad and anxious. Would she write back, please? He needed to know how she was and if she was better. She didn't reply. The true cause of her trouble, that she was *in* trouble, as people said, never occurred to him. Such things never happened in families like his. He wrote again in the middle of May, telling her that he would be teaching at the grammar school in a town in Devon called Ashburton, south of Dartmoor. The countryside was so beautiful he longed for her to see it.

The next time he wrote she meant to answer his letter. She knew what he said already because her parents had told all three girls. He would like to come home on Saturday 27 July, be in Bristol for Ethel's wedding, go back to London to pack up and fetch his things, then return to Bristol until 2 September. By then he hoped he would have found himself a cottage to rent in one of the villages near Ashburton. His father and mother were immensely proud of him. At only twenty-five he had succeeded spectacularly, his was an intellectual triumph. They boasted about him in a modest kind of way to the chapel congregation.

'Fancy asking if he could come home,' Mary said to her husband. 'As if we wouldn't be happy to have him, our only son!'

Maud wrote him a non-committal letter. It took her a long time. At first she meant to tell him what had happened to her, because to write it seemed easier than to confess it to him face-to-face, but after trying she found she couldn't put the words on paper. So she wrote that she had been ill with a stomach complaint – which, she thought bitterly, was literally true – but was better now. It would be good having him here for the wedding in the middle of August. She didn't much want to be a bridesmaid, she told him, but couldn't say no. Her letter occupied only half a sheet of paper.

She said nothing about her thoughts of drowning herself. One evening, when it was dark, she could jump into the Bristol Channel like the charwoman's niece. She couldn't swim, none of them could, so she wouldn't be tempted to save herself. She would sink and die, first seeing her whole life pass before her closed eyes, as they said it did. The baby would die with her, and for the first time she felt a pang at that, at her unborn child dying, instead of looking forward to its possible death with joy. One evening at twilight, before it got dark that summer night, she stood looking down at the water and was too afraid to jump. She found that she was more afraid of death than of pregnancy and disgrace.

The stomach complaint she wrote about to John had been morning sickness. The first few times it occurred she tried to conceal it from everyone, but with only one bathroom to be shared by five people, all of whom had to get up at much the same time, this was impossible. When she threw up on the bedroom floor and refused to say anything Ethel told their mother that Maud had food poisoning. The prospect of going to Dr Collins, who, Maud was sure, would know on sight what was wrong with her, was terrifying. The doctor had a surgery in his own large and rather gloomy house in the next street. Maud and her mother sat in the waiting room, which was full of mahogany chests of drawers and tables and chairs with shabby green velvet seats. One of the two pictures, one on the wall opposite the window and the other on the wall opposite the door, was of a drooping maiden with a wreath on her long hair. She looked as ill as Maud had felt the week before but felt no longer. The second was of a single cow standing in long grass against a background of blue hills.

Three weeks of vomiting had made her thin, for which she was glad. In her box-pleated school tunic no one would have dreamt she was expecting. Dr Collins came into the waiting room, said good-morning and ushered them into his surgery. He took her temperature, looked down her throat and asked her about her bowel movements. Then he gave her mother a prescription which she was to take to his dispensary, where it would be made up. Years later she often wondered about Dr Collins. Had he known? Had he guessed but said nothing? She had no reason for thinking this way except for one small thing. As they were leaving the surgery, her mother going first, she had looked up at him to say thank you as her mother said she should. The words were never said, for Dr Collins caught her eye and, giving a slight shake of his head, smiled at her a slight, indeed tiny, half-smile.

The medicine was a clear liquid with a white sediment. Because, as Mary Goodwin said, Maud was 'a big girl now, nearly grown up', she was left to give herself her twice-daily doses. If Dr Collins had guessed the true nature of her 'illness', as she sometimes thought he had and sometimes was sure he hadn't, he wouldn't have given her anything that would harm her baby. But surely he hadn't or he would have said something. To her mother if not to her. A strange thing was happening to Maud. Much as she dreaded her condition being detected, much as the idea of giving birth to an illegitimate child horrified her, she didn't want to take anything that would hurt the baby. Though she thought of a woman someone at school had told her about who had drunk Jeyes Fluid, and sometimes of doing the same thing herself, that would be the end of both of them, not of her alone or her baby alone. As to the medicine, she sometimes saw a man in the street who had a humped back and a woman half of whose face was blotched with a birthmark, and although she had never thought about it before, she now wondered if these disfigurements had been caused by their mothers taking medicine that poisoned their babies before they were born.

July came in, it was four months since what had happened in those fields, and she noticed she had begun to lose her waist. Her skirt refused to do up. Her mother was already making Ethel's wedding dress, and she and Sybil would make the dresses for the bridesmaids. Maud was in a sweat of fear. If her mother measured her for the dress, what she saw when Maud was in her slip would only add to the vague suspicions she already had. She had asked Maud why the towels she used at the time of her monthlies hadn't been put to soak in the covered bucket of cold water that stood inside the cupboard under the scullery sink. Mrs Goodwin knew to the day when her girls menstruated and expected to see the blood-stained squares of towelling floating in the reddening water.

'I washed my own,' Maud said.

'There was no need for you to do that. The maid always boils them to be sure they're really clean.'

'I got them clean enough.'

'Well, I'd rather you didn't do it again.'

Ronnie she had never seen since that second time. She saw his sister, Rosemary, almost every day, and Rosemary had told her that he had been working for his university entrance. The idea of telling Ronnie was horrible, but perhaps the time would come when she must. Or someone in her family must, and the only possible one was John. She longed for John's homecoming at the end of the month. She would tell him and consult him. He knew what to do about so many things.

The Goodwin household was in a fever of activity about the forth-coming wedding. Maud told her mother there was no need to measure her as she was the same size as she had been for the last dress Mary Goodwin had made her: she still had a thirty-six-inch bust, a twenty-four-inch waist and thirty-eight-inch hips. That was what she said, but it wasn't true. Her bust – none of the family, indeed no woman they knew, spoke about 'breasts' – had increased by two inches and her waist by three. Her stomach had been flat, but now it had grown into a little dome. A week before John was due to come home, Maud told Ethel she couldn't be her bridesmaid.

'What do you mean? Why not?'

'Don't ask me. I just can't.' Maud could think of no excuse. Why couldn't she? The true reason was impossible to say. 'You'll have Sybil and you've got Wendy.' Wendy was a cousin, their father's sister's daughter. 'I don't see why you want three. Everyone only has two.'

'What's Mother going to say?'

'I don't see it matters what she says. It's your wedding.'

Ethel, of course, told her mother.

'I don't understand you,' Mary Goodwin said to Maud. 'I don't know what's come over you. Your father says it's a dreadful unkindness to poor Ethel. He's very disappointed in you.'

What would he say then when he knew she was expecting an illegitimate child?

She always walked to school, and now when she was out in the street she seemed to see pregnant women everywhere. Of course they did their best to conceal it, wearing loose smocks over their dresses, wearing baggy skirts and double-breasted jackets far too big for them. But Maud could tell. Her condition had made her ultra-sensitive. It was high summer so no one wore gloves. She also looked at these women's left hands. They all wore wedding rings. Was she going to have to wear one, maybe a curtain ring?

She was in minor disgrace at home. Her father didn't ask her why she wouldn't be a bridesmaid, he told her to forget 'all this nonsense' and accept that it was her duty to perform this service for her sister that most girls enjoyed. Mary Goodwin took her cue from her husband and Sybil joined in. What was wrong with her? She had never been a stubborn girl. Why was she taking this ridiculous attitude? Rosemary told Maud she was getting fat – well, not exactly fat, but a good bit bigger than she used to be. 'Plump' was the word Sybil used, studying her critically but too innocent to come to the true conclusion.

Maud had decided that she would tell John. She was teaching herself to walk slightly bent over, pulling her increasing stomach as nearly as she could towards her spine. On the eve of Ethel's wedding she told her mother she was feeling ill, she thought she was sickening for something. It wasn't entirely a lie. The sickness of the early weeks was long past, but her nervousness and fear had affected her stomach so that she suffered continual sharp pains and diarrhoea. A cousin of theirs – a married woman, of course – had had a miscarriage at three months. Maud didn't know what her symptoms had been, no one would tell her, that wouldn't be right, but she guessed there would be pains and perhaps bleeding. To her misery, she never bled, but the pains might mean she was losing the baby.

Her mother in pink with a cloche hat and Sybil and their cousin Wendy in their blue, frilly bridesmaid's dresses went off to the church in one hired car, her father and Ethel in another, Ethel in calf-length cream lace and a veil tied round her forehead just above her eyebrows with white ribbon sewn with roses. John refused transport and walked to the church. It wasn't far. Maud, uncaring about her disgrace, oblivious to everything except her looming fate, sat at home on the lavatory in pain, hoping and praying for the blood to come. It never did, and when the others came back, minus Ethel, she had to go downstairs. One good thing, one tiny ray in all this gloom, was that she would now have her bedroom to herself.

She had meant to tell John but she didn't. Suppose it made him despise her as a loose woman? He was going the next day and she hardly spoke to him. Wondering what was wrong, he went back to London to pack up and move out.

5

Leaving the great barracks of a school in the hinterland of the Marylebone Road was no hardship to John. His pupils had not been the half-starved, wretched little creatures of London's East End, but they were deprived indeed and he seldom came across one who showed the least interest in what he tried to teach them. The staff were mostly women, all but two of them unmarried, and the single ones desperate to be married. For most of his four years there one after the other of them had made clumsy flirtatious advances to him, one of them either leaving when he did or lying in wait for him in the playground to ask if she could walk a little way with him. He was never rude, so he couldn't bring himself to say no. Then she would suggest a cup of tea in the nearest café. He could refuse that, though, on the grounds that he had to be home in five minutes. Only one of them ever touched him. That was no more than an attempt to put her arm into his, but his reaction, instinctive though it was, the homosexual's reflex, so distressed her that she ran away from him with a whimper.

Now he had left for good. He had already paid his last rent to Mrs Petworth, his two suitcases were packed with everything he possessed in this world apart from the books he had left in Bristol. Clearing out his life to start a new one, the room bare but for his bedclothes and an empty teacup, he sat down to write to Maud. It puzzled him that she had only once replied to his letters. He tried to think – 'puzzled his brains', as Bertie had once put it – what could be wrong with her and could only come up with the idea he had had before, that some boy had made her unhappy. He wrote that he was looking forward to being at home again in a few days' time, to seeing them all but especially her. He would see *her* and find out, he wrote, but wrote gently, what was wrong with her. It upset him very much that she had hardly spoken to him on his last day at home. His letter was interrupted by a tap at his door. It could only be Mrs Petworth. It was Bertie.

John was so aghast to see him and so overjoyed that he almost fell. He took an unsteady step backwards.

Bertie came in, turned the key in the lock and took John in his arms. 'I couldn't keep away, not when I knew you was going the day after tomorrow.'

'You shouldn't have come. You know what I said, that I wouldn't do it any more.'

'I never believed you.'

John looked at him in despair. 'I love you. I don't know what to do.'

'I do.'

Bertie stayed the night, John's last night at Mrs Petworth's. If she had known she would have objected only because if John wanted a friend there overnight he should have paid the extra rent. Two young men lying close beside each other in a single bed caused her no qualms on grounds of morality. John slept for a while, then lay wakeful, reproaching himself for his weakness of character, for the speed with which he had given in to Bertie's persuasions. John had resolved that the sin of having relations with a man was in his past and he must atone for it by the manner of his future life. That life must be celibate and his friendship with Bertie, if it was to continue with so many miles between them, must be chaste. Bertie turned over in the narrow bed and laid his arm over John's waist. With a sigh that was halfway to a whimper, John got up and spent the rest of the hot, stuffy night in the armchair.

Whatever happened to her in the whole course of her life, Maud thought, she would always remember this day, the *date* of this day, 16 August 1929, three days after John came home to stay. She was fifteen years old, due to be sixteen on 30 December. On Friday 16 August at half-past eight in the morning her mother walked into the bedroom that was now Maud's alone and saw her standing in front of the cheval glass in only her petticoat.

'Oh, Maud,' she cried out. 'Oh, Maud, oh, Maud, oh, good heavens.'

Maud said nothing.

'Maud, do you know you are expecting a child?'

'Of course I do. I'm not an idiot.'

Maud stepped into a skirt, the waistband of which she could no longer fasten, and pulled over her head a loose blouse Mary Goodwin had never before seen. Maud turned on her mother a face of the deepest woe, of utter tragedy. 'Aren't you sorry for me, Mother? Don't you pity me?'

'Pity you? I don't know. I'm in a state of absolute shock. I must think. What is your father going to say?'

Maud opened her mouth to scream, but laughter came out, hiccuping peals of it. Her mother smacked Maud's face, not hard, a token smack, because that was what you did to hysterical girls. It made Maud cry. She sank down weeping on the bed, scrubbing at her face with a corner of the sheet. Mary Goodwin stood there, shaking her head, just shaking it back and forth like an automaton.

'Don't you care for me at all? What will become of me? Don't you care?'

'You have shocked me beyond belief, Maud. Care for you? You have ruined all possible caring for you. You have done a wicked thing.' Mary Goodwin began to pace the room, stopping to stare blankly out of the window, turning to come back and turn again. 'You had better stay in this room. I'll bring you something to eat later. I thank God Ethel is away from here, I thank God she's married. As for poor Sybil – it's better if she doesn't see you, if you keep away from her.' Mary paused, struck by a sudden thought, a possibility. 'Tell me the truth, did he force you?'

Maud knew the word if her mother didn't. 'You mean, did he rape me?'

Mary Goodwin went white.

'No, he didn't. It was just as much me.'

Her mother might have shown some satisfaction at that, some

sort of relief, but perhaps she felt neither satisfaction nor relief. Perhaps rape would have been preferable.

'When is it due?'

'I don't know. December, I think.'

'I shall speak with your father immediately, before he leaves for the office. I don't suppose he will go now. No doubt he will want to talk to you and tell you what we have decided.'

Maud sat up. 'What do you mean, *you've* decided?' She shouted it. She had never before been rude to her mother. 'What do you mean?'

'You'll be told when I've talked to your father.' Mary moved towards the door. 'Of course you can't stay here. He will agree with me there. He'll say we can't keep you here.'

Maud was paralysed by her mother's words, transfixed by a mixture of panic, ignorance and fear. The closed door trapped her like a wild animal shut in a cage. She had never known anyone in her position before, never read a book or a story in which an unmarried girl found herself pregnant, never been told of such a girl as a warning, though now she remembered Sybil pointing out to her a poor, badly dressed woman in the street. She pointed her out and said she had a little boy at home she told people was her brother, her mother's youngest child, but he wasn't, he was hers, 'born out of wedlock'. What had her mother meant by 'you can't stay here'? Where could she go? For the first time in her life she felt utterly alone. Would they put her out on to the street and lock and bolt the doors against her? That thought made her brace herself, tell herself not to be stupid. They couldn't do that, they wouldn't. They were her *parents*.

Then she thought about John. He was at home, in his bedroom, perhaps still in bed. Would they stop him seeing her? Would they make her go away so that he couldn't see her? Why hadn't she told him already? Had she been too afraid? Hysterics came back, making her scream and sob and beat at the wall with her fists. The door flew open and her father came in. It was the first time he had ever come into her bedroom without knocking and she knew without knowing how she knew that she had forfeited all his respect. She sank down on the bed crying.

'Sit up,' he said, 'and be quiet. Making a noise won't help.' She lifted her head, her face red and distorted, wet with tears. 'A fine sight you are. I don't want to talk to you about how you got in this condition. The man can't marry you, you're too young to marry, and by the time you're old enough it will be too late for legitimacy.'

The possibility of marriage hadn't crossed her mind. Only one thing her father was saying struck her and that was his failure to mention the child she carried. He was purposely avoiding that, as if the child were some sort of unmentionable disease, and in so doing he did her some good. He made her angry.

'You can't stay here. It wouldn't be fair on your sister to risk her being contaminated by you. There is a home I know of where women such as you can be sent to live and work. In fact, it is a charity of mine. I contribute, along with several other members of the chapel, to its upkeep. It goes against the grain with me that a daughter of mine should be sent there, it's a shameful thing, but we have no choice.'

Maud shouted, 'I could stay here. This is my home. Why shouldn't I stay here?'

'In *my* house where your innocent sister lives? Stay here where everybody we know would see your disgrace? I think not. You will have to go to Wesley House and think yourself very lucky you've not been turned out on to the street.'

By some instinct or prevision, making a leap of years into the future, Maud knew that whatever he might desire or her mother wish for, this was the last time she would ever speak to her father. If she had to be sent to this home so be it, but she was speaking to him now for the last time. Adrenalin poured into her blood.

'What did you mean by "too late for legitimacy"?'

He looked at her as if she had done something dirty, soiled herself or stripped off her clothes. 'Thanks to this new law which came in in April, sixteen has become the age for legal marriage. You will not be sixteen until 30 December. Your mother tells me you expect to be confined in December. Therefore legitimacy is impossible.'

'I shall tell Grandma. Grandma will help me.'

'You will not tell your grandmother. In any case, she is away on her holiday in Switzerland.'

'John will help me.'

'John won't be allowed to see you. In any case, he has gone out. He has errands in town and will be out all day. By the time he comes back you will be settled at Wesley House, and for the future an adoption will be arranged.'

The last time she would speak to her father for ever . . . Then let it be good, she thought, learning defiance, learning strength. 'My baby will be mine and stay mine and live with me. He will never see you or speak to you as long as I live. When you're on your deathbed,' she shouted, 'I won't see you. I won't go to your funeral. I will never speak to you again. I hate you.' And she burst into hysterical sobs.

6

He had things to buy. At his new school he would be teaching maths as well as general science, so he bought a book to help him brush up on his trigonometry and another which would refresh his chemistry knowledge and included the periodic table. He had meant to go to a tailor in London for the suit he needed but the prices were beyond his means, so he settled for the tailor his father had always used. There he was measured for a suit in the cheapest material they had, a dark grey broadcloth. All this took him less time than he expected, and the bus from the city centre brought him home before lunch.

His parents and his sisters expected him rather later, and he thought it might be displeasing to his mother if he used his key, presuming on his status as an adult and the son of the house. He rang the bell. An almost unheard-of thing happened. His father answered the door. Instead of being at the 'works', as his mother always called the office, John Goodwin was at home.

'Dad, is everything all right? Has something happened to Mother?'

'No, well, no need to trouble you with it immediately. Your mother is quite well. Come in. Didn't we give you a key?'

The house was more than usually silent. In the living room, the largest and pleasantest of all the rooms, Mary Goodwin and Sybil sat in armchairs opposite each other on either side of the fireplace. It had turned cold for August, but of course there was no fire and the fire screen, a framed embroidery of improbably coloured tropical birds, hid the grate. Neither woman got up, but while Sybil continued to look at her hands, folded in her lap, his mother turned a doleful face to him.

Someone must be dead. He went up to his mother, laid his hand on her shoulder and said, 'Where's Maud? What's happened to Maud?'

'Aren't you going to give me a kiss, John?'

Dutifully he bent down.

'Your father will tell you,' Mary said, and, making a grotesque dumb show in Sybil's direction, indicated that no more was to be said about Maud in Sybil's presence.

John tried and failed to say a cheerful 'Hello, Syb.' The words came out like a phrase in a foreign language, inadequately learned. He turned round to face his father, who was standing helplessly behind him. For the first time in his life John felt stronger than his parents, able to handle something better than they could, although he had as yet no idea what it was.

The two men went into the dining room, where the table was laid for the midday meal which would normally be served at this time. Neither of them made any move to sit down.

'Please, Father, tell me what's happened to Maud.'

'She is in her room.' John Goodwin gave a heavy sigh. 'We thought it best for her to remain there.'

'All right. She's ill, is she? What's wrong with her?' John had spoken in the abrupt, sharp tone which in normal circumstances would have called forth a stern rebuke. 'Please tell me what's wrong.'

Because his father turned his face away before he spoke, John failed to hear quite what he said, or rather the term he used was so old-fashioned John thought he must have misheard.

'She's with what?'

'Your sister is with child, is what I said. Don't make me repeat it.'

John pulled out a chair from the table and sat down. 'You mean she's going to have a baby?'

'Don't.'

'I'd have thought she was a child herself, but perhaps I don't know much about these things. I must go up and see her. Poor Maud.'

'You should say, "My poor parents, *her* poor parents." I don't wish you to see her, John. Not yet, if ever.'

Sitting there, staring down at the white tablecloth, embroidered by his mother with a design of yellow daffodils and green leaves, John was thinking of his own situation. If this was how they reacted to a daughter of theirs becoming pregnant without being married, how would they receive being told of the appalling, outrageous, almost unthinkable conduct of their son as a pervert, guilty of the crime people – if they ever dared speak of it – called homosexualism?

Taking John's silence for acceptance of a ban on seeing his sister, his father began outlining the arrangements which were being made for her reception into the Wesley Institute for Unmarried Mothers. Another three weeks must elapse before she could occupy one of the dormitories there, each shared by six young women. The child would be taken from her immediately after it was born and offered for adoption. If Maud remained here in this house and in her room during that time, leaving for the home with either himself or her mother and in a car –

Here John interrupted him. 'Do you know anyone with a car?'

'Of course. Grandma has a car, but I don't wish Grandma to know about this. The shock of it could kill her. I shall arrange to hire one.'

'Does Sybil know any of this?'

'Your mother told Ethel as a married woman and asked her to tell Sybil. That has been done and now she is at home again with us.'

John got up. 'I am going up to Maud now, Father.'

'No, John, no. I forbid it.'

'I am going to Maud now.'

At first John thought of simply taking her away with him, removing her from their parents and taking rooms for them in a boarding house until, if all went well, he had found a place to live near the Ashburton school. Within twenty-four hours he understood that his parents were bewildered. They had no idea how to handle the situation. His father might have made an arrangement with the Wesley Institute, they might have shut Maud away, leaving her food to be taken to her by 'the maid', but they were plainly terrified of the disgrace that would accrue to them if Maud's condition became known. Both of them relied on John far more than usual.

It was as if they had lost a daughter and gained a son, and John's telling them that the Ashburton job was his to start at the beginning of the autumn term called forth extravagant congratulations. He realized that he could be in control if he wished to be. His stated determination to go straight up to Maud after his father had told him not to, his immediate mounting of the stairs, showed his father better than any arguing could have that their twenty-five-year-old son had made himself master.

His father's pomposity almost disappeared that evening, as did his mother's evasion of the facts. Once Sybil had gone out, allowed to visit her friend in the next street only after repeatedly promising 'not to mention Maud's name', only then did they start to let down the barriers and to confide as much as they were capable of. Mary Goodwin began by reverting to what she had said to Sybil. John must never speak of Maud to anyone. If anyone asked after her he must say she had been taken ill and was to go away to stay with a cousin in Hereford. He never knew why Hereford, why the name of the town came into his mother's head. They had no relatives living there. His father spoke of their great shock, that they still hardly believed such a thing of a child of theirs. John saw that what both of them really felt was desperation at the possible loss of their respectable status.

His thoughts went back to his meeting with Maud in her bedroom. She had been lying on her bed, got up and threw herself into his arms. The siblings had never been encouraged to kiss or even touch each other, and he couldn't remember the two of them ever before in such a close embrace.

'You don't think I've committed a crime, do you, John? You don't think I'm foul and dirty and disgraced, do you?'

'Is that what they said to you?'

She nodded and tears began to flow down her face.

'You mustn't cry,' he said, 'because if you do I will and men don't cry, do they?' He laughed when he said it. He sometimes cried and had taught himself not to be ashamed of it.

Still weeping, she said, 'What did *my father* mean about a new law? He said there was a new law that meant women couldn't get married till they were sixteen. What does it mean?'

John thought, then said, 'Oh, yes, I see. Up till this year, if you can believe it, the age for women getting married, if you could call them women, was twelve, and for men it was fourteen. This new law changed that to sixteen for both.'

She said nothing, only gave a little sob.

'Listen to me, Maud. I will look after you. I won't let them ill-treat you. I won't leave you alone either. I'll be up here with you as much as I can.' He was thinking fast and thinking about things which he had never had occasion even to imagine before. 'Maud,' he began, choosing his words with the greatest care, 'Maud, your sweetheart who is the father of your baby, does he know? I hope you don't mind my asking.'

'No, I don't mind. Not when it's you. He's my friend Rosemary's brother. His name's Ronnie Clifford.' She wanted to say Ronnie wasn't her sweetheart any more, if he had ever been, but that would only lead to too many awkward questions. 'Father told me I couldn't marry him even if he wanted to because I'm not old enough. The baby will be born before I'm old enough.'

'I'll tell him, though, shall I? He ought to know. Maud, remember, I'll look after you.'

Now, talking to his parents, he felt surging through him that strength he hadn't known when almost boasting of it to Maud. How he was going to look after her he didn't yet know, but he could tell from the expression on his parents' faces and the tone of their voices that they recognized it too. They recognized it and were glad of it. If they could be relieved of responsibility for their daughter, put their burden on John's shoulders, their former dull contentment that they called happiness might return.

'There's no need,' he said, 'for Maud to go into this home you've arranged for her. It's not as if she has no family. That must be cancelled. I can do that.'

His father had coloured. He wetted his lips, then said, 'I haven't in actual fact done anything about the Wesley Institute. I told her I had, but it was really that I intended to do so.'

You lied to torment her. John didn't say this aloud, but perhaps he looked it. 'She told me she prefers staying in her room. She doesn't want to come down here. Sybil can see her there.'

'It's not right for Sybil to see her,' his mother began. 'Sybil is an ummarried girl.'

'So is Maud,' John said.

Not until the following evening did John finally make up his mind. He had been thinking of it all night and all that day, turning the plan he had come up with over and over in his head. At first it had frightened him, it was so *big*. It was so daring. He doubted he could handle it. Then he presented it to himself as the only possible thing to be done, the only thing that could be acceptable to Maud and satisfy his parents as far as it was known to them. If anyone was to be sacrificed it was he, and he would be. If it worked, and it must work, he would live a life of deception for years and it would be a life of celibacy and chastity, however it might look to the outside world. Maud could hardly object to it, for it would save her reputation and give her dignity. Only he would be sacrificed, but he argued with himself that keeping the vow he had made in Bertie's presence would in any case commit him to a single and sexless life. It would help him. One way of looking at it was to teach himself it was as much for his benefit as hers.

This plan he was formulating would protect him, he must try to look at it like that. For no women would pursue him or try to ingratiate themselves with him, no men would suspect him of being an invert (as some people called it). At his new school the headmaster and his fellow teachers would wordlessly welcome John into the league of married men.

None of this was communicated to the family. Gaining some of his bullying cockiness, his father said, 'Since you've interfered with my arrangements and stopped her –' he never used Maud's name – 'being suitably catered for until her confinement –'

'There was no arrangement,' John said. He was losing the excessive respect he had once had for his parents and with it a lot of his affection.

'No, well, since you put an end to that, have you thought where she is to go? She can't stay here.'

The door opened and Sybil walked in. 'I've been upstairs with Maud.'

'You were told on no account to go in there and talk to her.'

'I'm a grown woman, Father. Maud says she doesn't want to stay in this house.'

Mary Goodwin started crying.

Her husband sent her a glance of contempt. 'It doesn't matter what she wants. She has forfeited all rights to choice.'

John ignored him. 'I shall find somewhere for her and me. She will live with me.'

'Oh, John,' his mother wailed, showing more emotion than he ever remembered, 'oh, John, don't make me lose you too.'

Ronnie Clifford made no answer to the letter John sent, telling him that Maud was expecting his child and asking if they could meet. It was a gentle, polite letter, containing of course no threats and no demands for money, but it came as no surprise to John that it wasn't answered, and he wondered what use a reply would have been. He had obtained the address from Maud, the post was reliable and he had no doubt his letter had reached its destination. The boy was very likely afraid and believed that if he let this news pass un-acknowledged, it would go away. Even if he could be made to marry Maud, it could not be until after the child was born, and anyway, Maud had told John she didn't want to marry Ronnie.

Would she want to marry, or appear to marry, *him*?

7

Ten days had passed and he had told Maud nothing of his plan. He took the train to Exeter St David's and thence to Newton Abbot. A Western National bus took him to the village of Dartcombe, where, having answered an advertisement in one of the papers he'd bought when last in Exeter, he was due to look at a cottage that was to let in a few weeks' time. The bus took him along narrow lanes between banks lush with flowers, the primroses and violets long over by this time, but buttercups and heartsease, campion and meadowsweet, and, on the edge of a little stream, yellow musk in full bloom. Green hills rose behind them, some dark with woodland, others divided into little patchwork fields where red-and-white cows were pastured. The villages of granite cottages, churches with tall spires and one or two 'gentlemen's' houses differed from one another only in the arrangement of these dwellings, in the beauty of the little gardens, the predominance of thatched roofs and the size and antiquity of their church. Dartcombe was one of the prettier places, made so by the height of the wooded hills which enclosed it on three sides and the ancient oaks on the village green.

No. 2 Bury Row, the street so called, John supposed, because of its proximity to the little churchyard that was adjacent to the church of All Saints, wasn't one of the prettier houses, being the second in a row of terraced cottages not much more than twenty years old. Its owner lived at No. 1, and while wondering if this would be a disadvantage, he knocked on the door, met Mrs Tremlett and was shown over the four rooms and kitchen of the cottage she referred to as 'next door'.

He felt a mild embarrassment, a kind of guilt, at the lies he had to tell, even though they were told in a good cause. He had been telling himself for a long time now that the end can never justify the means and now he was discovering that adhering to this principle was not as simple as it sounded. Mrs Tremlett was assuming that the larger of the two bedrooms would be shared by 'Mr and Mrs Goodwin', and he let her assume it. The other bedroom, she suggested, would become the 'nursery' used by the child John had told her his 'wife' was expecting at about Christmas time. There was no bathroom, but in the scullery beyond the kitchen a strange innovation had to be explained to him. Under a wooden cover was a hip bath shaped like an armchair and fed by a cold tap. You heated water on the range which, added to the cold contents of the bath, made sitting in it tolerable.

Better than nothing, John thought. The house had a garden full now of flowers, asters and dahlias and early Michaelmas daisies. He decided that he might enjoy gardening after he came home from school, though he had never tried doing any before. An outdoor lavatory, clean and freshly whitewashed, adjoined a small tool shed. John said he would take the cottage and paid the first month's rent, though Mrs Tremlett requested payment by the week. Would it be all right for him to stay the night, this coming night? As far as she was concerned, Mrs Tremlett said rather suspiciously, but where was his wife?

John was able – almost – to tell the truth: 'With her parents in Bristol. I'll be going back there tomorrow morning.'

He had intended to get himself a bed, if he could, in the inn called the Red Cow or else get the bus back to Exeter. This would be better. Would they feed him at the Red Cow?

Mrs Tremlett assured him they would. Her brother, Mr Lillicrap, was the landlord. Meanwhile, her momentary suspicions gone, she would make him a cup of tea and let him have a packet of tea and a jug of milk for the morning.

The afternoon clouds departed, leaving a clear sky. It had been mild; now it became quite hot. John went for a walk, exploring the village, noting a shop and making his way into the church. Like all country churches, even on the hottest day, inside the silent nave it was cool and still. Along the pews, in front of every place, was a hassock embroidered in bright wools with the symbols of Christianity, a white fish on a blue ground, a yellow lamb on green, and many crosses of all colours. Two large vases of flowers, hollyhocks and day lilies, stood in front of the altar. John wondered if Maud would come here on Sunday mornings or if she, like him, had abandoned her faith. He remembered what she had said about not wanting to believe in God any longer and doubted if she would adhere to Methodism after her treatment by their parents.

If he had been a character in a book, he thought, sitting here in a country church on a summer afternoon, the incumbent of this parish would have come in, a vicar or rector, walked up to him and asked if he needed help, and perhaps he would have poured out his heart to this kindly clergyman. But he wasn't in that fictional church, he was here in All Saints, Dartcombe, and in future if he needed to confide or confess it would have to be to Maud. He went back to No. 2 Bury Row, observing its neatness, the rather shabby but well-kept furnishings, the staircase covered, he supposed, in that fabric called drugget. He would give Maud the bigger bedroom with the double bed and the view of the village street and this church. His would be the smaller room at the back, where he could look out on the garden and the wooded hills beyond.

Sensing that it would be a wise move to order the local drink in the Red Cow instead of his usual pale ale, he asked for a half-pint of cider. It seemed a good choice, and Mr Lillicrap extended a large, calloused hand across the bar when he introduced himself. The other men looked at John and looked away, but one or two of them nodded. John thought that perhaps he should have gone into the saloon bar and that sitting in there at a table would have been more acceptable to these men, who were obviously farm labourers. None of them would have been in any doubt that he was a professional man. Nor would he be able to bring Maud in here. He doubted that any Dartcombe woman had ever set foot in the Red Cow, or any other public house. Mrs Lillicrap would be the only female to be seen here. A large woman, whose Devon English was almost unintelligible, she served him soup followed by ham and eggs in the small parlour, where he understood that the family usually ate.

Something about his parents' home made writing to Bertie impossible within its walls. Guilt and shame were only two among the many emotions even thinking of it made him feel. So he had brought paper, an envelope and a stamp with him. His fountain pen was always clipped over his breast pocket. He had written once before since he'd come home but had done so, feeling absurd and stared at, sitting on a bench in the park, the paper resting on a book on his knees. Now he was alone with no one to see and as he sat down at Mrs Tremlett's ring-marked but well-polished dining table, he felt a fullness of the heart that is one of the feelings lovers have, of a joyful breathlessness, the whole body charged with longing.

The long letter was the most passionate he had ever written. He told Bertie how terribly he missed him, how in saying he could give him up and never be with him again, he had written the worst of lies. Without as much inhibition as he had once had, he wrote of the things they had done together, sinful in most men's eyes no doubt, thought of by John as wrong when he spoke of them to Bertie, but now clearly appearing as entirely right because they loved each other. The letter covered several pages and when he reread it he expected to be ashamed of some of the things he had put down in ink on paper, but he felt no more shame than he would in reading a love poem of John Donne's or a scene from Shakespeare.

Upstairs, he was surprised to find the single bed in the back bedroom without sheets or pillowslips. There was linen inside a cupboard, but he was too tired to make up the bed and, stripping off his suit and shirt, he got under the eiderdown and on to the blanket-covered mattress without any other covering. It was only eight o'clock. He fell asleep at once and slept until he was awakened by the loudest and most tuneful choir of birds he had ever heard.

John had accomplished a lot, but he still had more decisions to make and these perhaps were the hardest. How much to tell Maud?

Something would have to be said to his parents and then there were his sisters, but Maud's opposition was what he had to expect and what he might have to overcome. When he returned home he found her still up in her room, but now it was a voluntary incarceration. She had stuck to her resolution to never again speak to their father, she was cool to their mother, though she seldom saw her, and Sybil was spending most of her time before and after work up there with her sister. Ethel, the married woman, had chosen to join her parents in a disapproval of Maud that amounted to horror, made all the worse by Maud's refusal to admit her shame.

Maud was drinking the tea Clara Gadd had just brought her. John studied her appearance searchingly and she, mistaking his motive, supposed he was noticing that her pregnancy was becoming apparent.

'It shows, doesn't it? If I went outside in the street people would see.'

'I wasn't looking at you for that. I was hoping you'd pass for eighteen or nineteen. I think you would. We could pass you off for eighteen.'

'What do you mean by "pass me off"?'

He told her. He told her about the cottage and Mrs Tremlett and the pretty village and how everyone would be told she was John's wife, expecting their child.

She blushed deeply. 'Oh, John, I can't.'

'Yes, you can. It will be easy once you get used to it.'

'Won't they find out?'

'How? We'd be Mr and Mrs Goodwin, John Goodwin and Maud Goodwin, which is what we are now. I'll get you a wedding ring. I've already told the woman next door that you're my wife – she's our landlady. You'll like it there, Maud. The birds sing so loudly in the morning, you won't believe it. I shall get myself a bicycle so I can ride to school and you'll buy our food in the village shop. People will notice your figure and they won't be disgusted or angry, it will be just what they expect in a young married woman. They'll congratulate you.'

She listened in silence. To her it was as if he were telling her a fairy story, something that couldn't be true, couldn't happen. 'They won't let us. Mother and Father won't let us.'

'They will.' He didn't say what was in his mind, that they would be glad to get her off their hands. In spite of the depths her relations with her parents had reached, she would still be hurt if she felt that they didn't want her. 'They will let us.' He had already hinted to them, and more than hinted, that he had found a place in Devon for Maud where she would be looked after and mentioned Mrs Tremlett's name as a reliable woman to care for her, and at last he had told Maud that he and she would be living under the same roof. 'You mustn't worry,' he said. 'There's nothing for you to worry about except keeping fit and well for the sake of the baby.'

Her mind was travelling ahead. 'After the baby is born what shall I do? Where shall I go?'

'Stay with me, of course. As far as other people are concerned, it will be our child, we shall be its mother and father. We shall live together and everyone will think we're married.'

'John, would you leave me alone now? It's a lot to take in at once. I'd like to be alone for a while just to think about what you've said.'

Next day, she approached the question he knew must be asked and which he dreaded.

'There's a teacher at my school who used to say to us that we'd got all our lives before us. It was because of women over twenty-one getting the vote last year. You can do great things now, she said, all your lives are before you. Well, I was thinking, all your life is before you, John. Mine may be over, we can't tell what will happen when my baby is born, but you, John – you'll want to get married, really married, you'll want children of your own.'

'I shall never marry.'

'But you don't know that. You'll meet someone and fall in love and want to marry her. Why not? She won't want me in the house with my baby.'

'I shall never marry,' he said again.

Now was the time to tell her. He sat there in silence, thinking of the words he would use. Whatever he said must sound hideously coarse to her, perverted, gross, scarcely believable. You know what happened between you and Ronnie, he would have to say, well, it's like that in a sort of way, only we're both men. He would explain that they loved each other, try to tell her that sexual intercourse could be beautiful between men just as it could between a man and a woman. Maybe talk about the Greeks – those *damned* Greeks, he swore to himself. The opprobrium most people, in which nearly all people, held men like himself reared itself up in his consciousness like a monster, a hairy Caliban, crocodile-headed, an embodiment of all that was evil in mankind. It might be that she too, from what she had picked up at school or heard whispered in scorn by Ronnie Clifford, had given a place in her mind to that monster. He couldn't tell her. And strong as he was teaching himself to be, he leaned on the coward's resource. One day he would tell her, but not yet. One day he would tell her and tell her too that he had given it all up, it was all over for him.

She said goodbye to her mother and gave her a cold kiss on the cheek, but Maud stuck to her resolve not to speak to her father and she walked past him without a word, preceding John down the steps. John had arranged for his clothes and books to be sent on ahead for Mrs Tremlett to take in. Maud's clothes, or those she could still get into, he carried in the two suitcases in which he had brought his own. She said she was a good seamstress, had come top in the needlework class at school, and told him she would make all her own clothes in future and the baby's. John promised that once they were settled in he would go into Exeter and buy her a sewing machine.

Sybil asked her to write and Maud promised she would. In this way any news she had to tell would be passed on to those parents with whom she had no desire to communicate. John could write to them if he chose, she said to him when they were in the train. On the third finger of her left hand she wore the wedding ring

John had bought for her. If her parents had noticed it they had said nothing, probably thinking that in her condition, now obvious, it was the only course for her to take. The train steamed along through fields that were the rich, damp green the cattle loved and occasionally yellow with ripened corn. Looking out of the window but seeing little of all this, Maud was conscious of being happy for the first time since that day her mother had walked into her bedroom while she was dressing. She was happy and dreaming now of a home that would be a real grown-up house, hers and John's and where, in the wintertime, her baby would be born.

8

The climate of opinion and behaviour Maud had grown up in had led her to expect the life ahead of her to centre on wifely devotion, accomplished domesticity and motherhood. Recently, because of her success at school, her parents had talked about the possibility of her going to university, the college at Exeter perhaps, but she had known that though this might lead to her becoming a teacher, such a job would last only until she married and then those woman's duties would overcome other aspirations. Now they had come upon her in a rush. She would not be a wife to John but would find herself with something like a wife's function; the cottage would demand tidying and cleaning and linen-washing, and in only a few months motherhood would arrive.

She thought of this as they travelled in the bus from Exeter to Dartcombe. The countryside around Bristol was lovely enough but not so lush as this, not so richly green, so that you wondered how the bus could manage to tunnel through the narrow lanes with their steep banks and tree branches which almost met overhead. The earth was dark red, the fields small and square, enclosed by hedges and alternating with dark woodland. If she had not been told by her English teacher that while you may compare art to nature when writing, you must never compare nature to art, she would have been reminded of the patchwork quilt her mother had made and which covered her bed at home. She would never see it again and that thought brought a small, almost silent, whimper. But John heard it and took her hand.

Seeing this and the tender look he gave her, an old woman sitting in a nearby seat caught Maud's eye and gave her an approving smile. Her pregnancy, beyond concealment, was very apparent now, as was the gold ring on the third finger of her left hand.

'Are you feeling all right?' John asked her. 'This bus is rather bumpy.'

'I'm very well. It's nice here, it's lovely.'

She could tell that pleased him, and she was aware of how fond she was of him. Still, it was a shock to her when, after a short walk from the bus stop to the cottage in Bury Row, John introduced her to Mrs Tremlett.

'This is my wife, Maud.'

It had to be so, of course, but was it wrong to tell such a huge lie? It had to be told. You might say that the whole purpose of their coming here together and living together in this place, confronting this grim-faced but kindly woman, was founded on that lie. The alternative was the hideous truth, for that was how it now appeared to Maud.

Mrs Tremlett was too polite to say what she was evidently thinking, that this young wife was very young indeed. She herself had been married at sixteen, and Mr Goodwin's wife was not much more than that. Like her own, the wedding was one that had had to be because of a coming child. But she said nothing, only ushered them in to where the table was set with tea things, and although it was warm and still summer, a fire was laid in the grate.

'Your bed's made up,' Mrs Tremlett said, 'so you'll have nothing to do. Mrs Goodwin can have a good rest after her journey.'

The bed was the first sign of what they would have to contend with in the future.

'We shall get used to subterfuge,' said John. They were upstairs in the bedroom and Mrs Tremlett had gone. 'I shall make up the bed in the other room for myself and somehow that will have to be concealed from our kindly neighbour if she's going to do our cleaning.'

'I can do the cleaning, John. We don't need her.'

'We shall, you know. When the baby comes. We'll let her come once a week for now to keep her hand in.'

'We have to pretend we're sharing this bed?'

'Of course we do. Think about it, Maud. What's *she* going to

112

think if this young couple, newly married, sleep in separate beds?'

'Not that newly married, I hope, John.' Maud put her hands to her swollen stomach, laughed and burst into tears.

'Come on now, it's all right. Everything's going to be fine, Mrs Goodwin. I'm going to do the bed now and then we'll have our tea.' He found sheets initialled MT – for Margaret Tremlett, he supposed – in a drawer in the bedroom tallboy and set about making up the bed. The last time he had done this it had been for himself and Bertie, and knowing that they would never again share a bed he felt a pain that was physical.

Thursday was to be Mrs Tremlett's day. She came early but John had already gone, because it was his first day at his new school, and Maud was up washing clothes in the scullery sink. The kitchen range she knew how to operate, but the copper in the scullery puzzled her. How did you get hot water into it and, come to that, out of it when the washing was done?

Mrs Tremlett opened the door in the bottom of the copper, inside which a fire was laid. 'You leave that to me, my dear,' said Mrs Tremlett. 'You mustn't use that dolly in your condition. Thicky little old sheets can come next door with me and I'll see to them.'

She always spoke in a gentle, friendly way, but it only made Maud wonder what treatment would have been meted out to her if her landlady had known the truth, that she was fifteen and unmarried, could never be married. She wasn't sure what a dolly was but guessed it might be the wooden pole with a kind of wooden plate on the end of it that stood in the corner. How was she to wash John's sheets? Perhaps by hand, using a bar of yellow soap and rubbing the linen against that wooden board with the bars across it. She would ask him when he came home. The sun was shining and she went out into it, standing in the front garden, holding up her face to the warmth.

They had been there a week and she had learned all about the village shop, where you could buy tea and sugar and meat and fruit in tins, as well as candles and string and oil for the lamps. Eggs and potatoes came from the farm on the hill, and a horse and cart laden with churns brought the milk which the dairyman poured into her own blue china jug. For a butcher and a baker you had to take the bus into Ashburton or Newton Abbot, and she had done that once, at the former not knowing what cuts of meat to buy and very aware in this warm weather that whatever she bought must be cooked at once or it would go off. John said it would be best if he bought their meat after school and brought it home with him, two lamb chops, for instance, or mince to make rissoles or a cottage pie.

How thoroughly she had been looked after and tended to at home! While it went on, she had never thought about it. It just happened and she took it for granted. Mother and 'the maid' did it all, with the charwoman whose niece had drowned herself coming in once a week to 'do the rough'. Somehow Maud doubted if that life would ever be her own again. She had put an end to it by one of the two 'acts' people called love she had performed with Ronnie Clifford in the meadow on the way home from choir practice. If she thought of Ronnie now, it was with bitterness.

The postman was coming up the village street, carrying his sack, which must be heavy even though it held mostly paper. All those letters coming to friends and relations from friends and relations. I wish I had a friend, she thought, my relations have been no good to me. Well, John has, but John is now my pretend husband. And Rosemary is lost to me because of Ronnie. The postman was opening their gate and coming up the path. He said good morning and Maud said good morning, and he handed her a letter, but of course it wasn't for her. It was addressed to 'J. Goodwin Esq.' Maud took it into the house and sat down in the sitting room. 'Esq.', she knew, was short for 'Esquire', a polite way of addressing a man, better than 'Mr' and perhaps the next best thing to 'Sir' or 'Lord'. Some people said they could tell from the handwriting if the writer was a man or a woman, her father said he could, but Maud was sure she would be unable to do that. This writing sloped backwards, which she had been taught was bad and should be stopped when the writer was a child, just as left-handedness should be stopped and changed to right-handedness, as had happened in Ethel's case. The man or woman who had written this envelope had put a little circle over the 'i' in 'Devonshire' instead of a dot, and that was a solecism her English teacher had called 'illiterate'.

The letter might be from a friend, someone John had met at college perhaps, or it could be from a girl. Maud hoped in a way it was from a girl. Maybe a girl was more likely to put a little ring over an 'i'. He had said he would never marry, but young as she was, she knew people said things like that and changed their minds when they met the right one. Her thoughts flew ahead to after the baby was born and John's girl came here to visit them. Before they married, she and John would have to move so that the neighbours didn't find out, John and the girl would have a wedding, and they would all live together in the new place. Maud would say she was a widow, and they would all get on well, the new Mrs Goodwin loving the baby as much as if he or she were her own. Maud put the letter, which had given rise to such daydreaming, on the sitting-room mantelpiece.

After Mrs Tremlett had gone, carrying with her a big basket full of linen to be washed, Maud sat down on the floor with the sewing materials John had bought for her: pins and needles, reels of black and white cotton (the coloured ones would come later), a pair of scissors, a paper pattern for a baby's nightgown and a length of white lawn. She knew she was not so good a seamstress as she had led John to believe she was. The sewing machine was yet to come and she would have to learn how to use it. Meanwhile she tried pinning the pattern to the fabric, cutting it out and tacking the pieces together. She was still at work when John came home, carrying a paper bag, itself wrapped in brown paper in case the blood from scrag end of beef came through.

'The butcher's shop was full of women,' he said. 'I was the only man, and I think I was the only man to be in there all day. The butcher was too polite to laugh. When he'd served me he said, "It's not often we see gentlemen in here, sir. They do the eating of it and the ladies do the buying."'

John had never before seen Bertie's handwriting but guessed the letter was from him. Who else would be writing to him? His mother or father perhaps. He had written to them, telling them he was settled in Bury Row with Maud nearby in the care of Mrs Tremlett. 'Nearby' was the word he used, not wanting to commit himself to writing 'next door'. It was unlikely they would even think of writing to Maud. He wrote about the beauty of the village and the countryside, the ancient church and the churchyard, where a famous poet of the last century was buried, the bicycle he had bought and the ease of the journey to school. No answer had as yet come. The letter that had come he opened carefully, his heart beating faster.

His own letter to Bertie, written on that night he had spent alone in the cottage, had been full of passion as well as tender love, but Bertie's reply was devoid of that. It was short and the personal part contained descriptions of acts they had certainly performed together, as well as words Bertie had often used while they made love, but still John was profoundly shocked by them. This aspect of their love he felt was sinful, led to policemen and police courts, to violence in the streets, to prison and a whole spectrum of ugliness and shame. These were the words that went with 'sodomy' and 'buggery' and which led to stringent laws being made to plant in the minds of young men a horror they dared not overcome. Yet they excited him, they seemed inextricably associated with Bertie, his beauty and his voice and his powerful attractions. Should he try to write to some extent in this vein when he answered? If it would make Bertie care for him more, need him and love him – yes, he thought he would.

But when he had read the letter again and again, knowing it and the terrible, beautiful words by heart, he decided to wait until Maud had left the kitchen to lay the table and then he would open the door of the range and put Bertie's letter on the burning coals inside.

Doing this would hurt terribly, but he dared not leave such a document – he thought of this sheet of paper as a document because of the words it contained – in the house for Maud or even Mrs Tremlett to find.

While keeping his eyes on the little passage and the kitchen door beyond, he put the letter in his trouser pocket, where its presence reminded him of what he had to do. One day, he thought, not now, not yet. If Maud asked him about the letter, for instance, she might ask whom it was from, expecting him to say from a woman. Even though he had told her he would never marry, he knew that such a denial would carry no weight with her, would carry no weight with any woman. She would like him to have a girl, and if he did it would naturally lead to marriage. When he imagined her response to his telling her the truth, he felt sick with self-disgust. You could never say this to a girl. Girls didn't know that such tastes, such behaviour, such desires, existed, or if they had heard it hinted at with sniggers or downturned mouths and mock shudders, their reaction was to recoil. 'Queers', men like him, wore women's brassieres, with padding to resemble breasts, and put red ink on their underpants to look like the blood that came from women once a month, but just the same they hated women. Bertie had told him all these things. John knew only that he was different, yet he could never say so.

Sometimes he encountered old men who lived alone but were not widowers. One such was living in their street in Bristol, and probably one in this village. John knew they were like him, unable ever to tell anyone the reason for their solitary lives, condemned to answer their families' repeated suggestions that it was time they married with the response that was not a reason, that they were 'confirmed bachelors'. It was rather better when two single men shared a house, for so repressive was the taboo on homosexualism – he hated the word, but what else could you call it? – that few if any people guessed why they were together.

Maud's emergence from the kitchen with a tablecloth over her arm and a handful of cutlery interrupted this unhappy reverie.

Through the open doorway he watched her lay each place with a knife, a fork and a spoon, and when she went to fetch water glasses from the sideboard, he slipped into the kitchen and pushed Bertie's letter into the range.

9

Time passed and John never said a word. Autumn came, bringing wet weather with it. Maud was learning that Devon is so green because it rains a lot. Her belly swelled more and more and the baby moved. Contrary to John's expectations, Mary Goodwin wrote to Maud, and Mrs Tremlett had to bring the letter in, believing that Maud's mother had mistaken the number in Bury Row.

'You can read it,' Maud said to John, her eyes filling with tears. 'Not that it's worth reading. It's unkind and mean. She says that she hopes I'm learning my lesson now, but that there's not much chance of that, the way I'm living in comfort with a kind lady and my brother next door. She knows it's next door now, John.'

'I'll have to tell her another lie. I'll write and tell her to send your letters care of me, give her some excuse, but I dare say she won't write again.'

'We'll have to let them know when the baby comes.'

There was no doctor in the village. Dr Masonford from Ashton, five miles away, paid his visits to patients in a pony and trap, just as his predecessor had done half a century before. Mrs Lillicrap from the Red Cow told John when he asked her that if all went well it shouldn't be necessary to call the doctor. With her experience in midwifery, she would come herself to deliver the baby. John remembered the monthly nurse who had been in the house in Bristol when his mother gave birth to Maud. Ethel had had to move in with Sybil to provide her with a bedroom and remembering this made John see insuperable difficulties. Any nurse he engaged would require a bedroom and this would mean giving up his room to sleep with Maud. The nurse and Mrs Tremlett and Mrs Lillicrap would see nothing unusual in this. Indeed, they would assume that this was what was happening all along. The idea of a monthly nurse must be given up, and he and the two women would take on the care of Maud and the baby. He saw that he had begun to weave a tangled web when, by the means of an invented marriage, he first practised to deceive.

Letters were regularly exchanged now between John and Bertie. John, at least on paper, was losing his inhibitions. He saw the absurdity of quoting from the Song of Solomon in his outpourings but couldn't resist addressing Bertie as 'thou whom my soul loveth', telling him he had dove's eyes and a mouth like 'lilies, dropping sweet-smelling myrrh'. Knowing that a generally held view was that the Song referred not to love between two human beings but that which existed between Christ and His Church – while thinking this attitude ridiculous, John still feared he might be writing blasphemy. Bertie never commented on these extravagances when he replied. Perhaps they made him feel awkward, or else he didn't understand them. John thought the latter more likely, as he had never known Bertie to be embarrassed.

All Bertie's letters John burned. It became a ritual, waiting for Maud to leave the kitchen, then moving quickly out there to open the door of the range and push the single sheet of paper inside. Bertie wrote in pencil on cheap lined paper. No doubt he didn't possess a pen. John tried not to feel shame on Bertie's behalf for the bad spelling, the little circles instead of dots over the letter 'i', the lack of punctuation, but it did nothing to lessen his love. In a way he was relieved to burn the latest letter, because then he could no longer see the illiteracies while holding in his memory the passionate expressions.

Bertie wanted to come and visit him in Dartcombe. Having made a kind of vow never to make love with him again, John had broken this undertaking almost as soon as the opportunity came. Bertie made it plain that he wouldn't take any further protestations of celibacy seriously, though he put it in far cruder terms. John longed to see him and asked himself constantly if there was any way this could come about. If at last he could bring himself to confess the truth to Maud, would that make a visit from Bertie more or less possible? The trouble – or the joy and glory – was that if Bertie came to No. 2 Bury Row they would make love and how could that even be imagined with Maud in the house? Whatever happened, he must bring himself to tell Maud before she had the baby.

She was big now, 'as big as a house', according to Mrs Lillicrap. She commented approvingly when Maud said the baby was moving so vigorously that he or she had pushed a plate off her lap and sent it flying.

'It's a boy,' said Mrs Lillicrap, the expert. 'You're carrying him low and that's always a sign. Strong too. Girls don't kick and shove like that.'

Maud thought it would be nice to have a girl because you could give her a pretty name. This was a proper way for a young wife to feel, Mrs Lillicrap said approvingly, but unfortunately it was a boy.

'Best to be a man in this world. You want to think of it like that. And Mr Goodwin will be pleased. A man wants his first one to be a boy.'

'He won't mind what it is,' Maud said, and how could he when it wasn't his?

She still estimated she had two weeks to go, but Mrs Tremlett, who had had eight of her own against Mrs Lillicrap's three, said it would come sooner than that.

All the leaves had fallen by now and so had a great deal of rain. But the past two days had looked like summer, apart from the bare trees, the sky bright blue although the sun was never far from the horizon and set early. Maud no longer went out as she had become embarrassed by her bulky shape, and when she sat at the sewing machine, she hardly knew where to put her great belly, so she gave that up too. A small wardrobe of garments suitable for either sex had been created not very skilfully and now, sitting in an armchair with her feet up on a stool, she was finishing off the white shawl she was knitting.

At this stage of her pregnancy John chose to tell her he had been and would always be, whether he practised his 'vice' or not, a homosexual. He wasn't being callous or insensitive, he told himself, it would mean little to her, she would not even be much interested, it was too alien to her even to concern her, but he had so driven himself, his mind racked by keeping this vital fact of his existence from her, that he felt he could not remain silent for another day.

When he first began, talking in a veiled way and with many euphemisms for relations between a man and a woman, she blushed a fiery red. She laid aside the needles and the white wool and, hanging her head, looked down into what remained to her of a lap.

'It can be like that,' he said, 'when it's not a man and a woman but two men together. Do you understand what I mean?'

She said nothing but shook her head vehemently.

'It is like that for me, Maud. That's why I can never get married.'

Suddenly she burst out, 'But it *can't* be. It's not possible. Men and women aren't made the same.'

He shook his head. 'That's not the important part, that's nothing.' Wasn't it? Was it really nothing? 'It's love that's important, isn't it? Love like you had with – with Ronnie.'

A look came on to her face that he had never before seen there. It was compounded of anger and contempt. 'You call that love? That wasn't love. It was two animals in a field.'

It was his turn to blush. After that he didn't know what to say. The silence was awful. If only she would ask questions, but she sat as if petrified in her chair, her belly filling all the space between arms and cushions while her arms and legs looked thinner than ever, her slender neck longer. She was all the child she carried, it had taken her over, and it was motionless now, waiting to be born and set her free. Inconsequentially, he thought he now knew for the first time what that phrase in the Bible about a woman being delivered really meant.

He made himself go on. 'I made up my mind when I came here with you that I would never be like that with a man again. That has to be over for me – well, for ever.'

She seized upon that one word 'again'. 'You mean you did that while you were in London? What you said a man could do with a man? You did that?'

Instead of replying, he said, 'I promise I never will again.'

'I don't understand what it was you did.' Turning her face away, she said, 'I don't want to. I don't want you to tell me any more.'

It had been dark for hours but was still only eight in the evening. The silence that had fallen was like a physical barrier between them, a wall. John thought he had never in all his life felt so lonely, not when he first went to live in London, not when he told Bertie they must never make love again. This kind of loneliness makes you feel you would never again speak to a living soul, never feel a human touch. Maud picked up her knitting to put it away, the way women do, rolling up the finished work, placing the two needles side by side and pushing them through the ball, before tucking the little parcel it made into her red-and-blue crocheted knitting bag. She got heavily to her feet, one hand in the small of her back.

'I think I'll go up now.'

'Maud, wait a little while, please.'

'No, I'll go up now.'

As the people who lived in these cottages and these villages had done since time immemorial, she put a light to her bed candle and lumbered upstairs with it. There was no gas in Dartcombe, and while Dartcombe Hall and the rectory and one or two other houses had electricity, most residents used oil lamps downstairs and candles on an upper floor. Maud, who had learned these things quickly, carried her candle in its blue enamel holder in her right hand, shielding the flame with her left. This meant she couldn't hold on to the banister.

'Let me help you,' John said.

'I shall be all right on my own.' Her voice was cold and tremulous.

He understood that she didn't want him to touch her. His touch would be a contamination. He sat down there, deep in thought, for half an hour, then another half-hour. What was he to do? The fire died to a red glow, then to grey ash with a spark at the heart of it. He fed it with small pieces of coal just in time, having no wish to go to bed himself, the strange idea coming to him that he would be even more alone up there, even lonelier. The way Maud had reacted was not at all as he had expected, though he hardly knew what he had expected. Perhaps he had thought that she would say it was all right, things weren't the way they used to be, the world was changing. 'You fool,' he said to himself. 'She's a child, she's *fifteen*. You have shocked her to the core . . .'

As if summoned by his words, which he had spoken aloud, she appeared at the top of the stairs, this time clinging to the banister. Her candle she must have left in her room. In a ballooning white nightgown she had a ghostly look, half lit by the light from the single oil lamp on the table in front of him.

'John, it's started. The baby's started.'

He sprang to his feet. 'Oh, Maud, it's all right. I'm here.'

'I've had an awful pain and I'm having another one now.' She would have doubled up her body if she could have. 'How long does it go on?'

He forgot about loneliness, forgot despair. 'I don't know. How would I know? I'll go and fetch Mrs Lillicrap.' The absurdity of this woman's name struck him now and not for the first time. 'I'll fetch her. You must go back to bed.'

'All right. I'm sorry I was so horrid to you, John.' She stumbled back into her bedroom. 'I wish you hadn't told me, though. I really do wish that.'

10

A set piece carried in John's mind was of a man pacing up and down a passage while on the other side of a door hung with a white sheet a woman was screaming. His mother's labour was nothing like that, even if he had been in the house to hear it. Perhaps he hadn't been in the house but he and Sybil were sent away to an aunt or grandmother, he couldn't remember. Pacing wasn't possible outside Maud's bedroom door, the space was so small he would very likely have fallen downstairs. Nor was a sheet hung over the door and she wasn't screaming, but a soft moaning reached him from behind the door. Still fully dressed, he sat downstairs where he couldn't hear those sounds, drinking tea.

It had been half-past nine when Maud had told him her pains had started and it was now two in the morning. Mrs Lillicrap, a mountain of a woman but light on her feet, had set water to boil on the kitchen range and lit a fire in the bedroom grate. She had emerged several times from attending to Maud to tell him all was well, been up and down stairs, gone back into the room, emerged again and said there was nothing to worry about. Keeping his own fire going – he seemed always to be carrying scuttles of coal these days – he thought of what he had told Maud and how she had said to him that she was sorry for being horrid to him. 'Horrid', that schoolgirl's word. Would they raise the subject again, he or she? In his experience of his family, when something unpleasant had been spoken of or even discussed, it would be put away and, if not forgotten, never mentioned again. So it had been when a young man of Sybil's had got engaged to someone else, and a similar silence had prevailed when a second cousin of his father's had been divorced. John's confession might meet with the same fate. Would it be so bad if it did?

A different sort of sound upstairs brought him back to reality and to his feet. Not a scream but a long howl such as a cat or a dog might make. Silence followed, then a steady whimpering, and he returned to his seat. Another half-hour of self-questioning and self-reproach passed before the bedroom door opened and Mrs Lillicrap came out.

'You have a lovely little daughter, Mr Goodwin. Would you like to come up and see your wife?'

Suddenly exhausted, though he had done nothing, he climbed the steep little staircase and went into Maud's room.

She was sitting up in bed, resting against pillows and holding the baby in her arms. 'Oh, John, look what I've done. Look at my little girl. I'm going to call her Hope.'

'Maybe her daddy would like a say in that,' said Mrs Lillicrap, laughing.

'It's Maud's choice.'

In that woman's presence there was nothing to be done but kiss Maud, lay a gentle finger on Hope's cheek and utter the biggest lie of all, that this was the happiest day of his life.

II

In the second week of December, when Hope was a fortnight old, Maud sat downstairs in the armchair where she had sat when John told her of the life he had led, holding the child to her right breast. Because John was in the room, she had covered herself in a voluminous white shawl so that modesty might not be offended. The confession he had made to her had never been mentioned by either of them again, though he was constantly aware that he had made it and of her reaction to it.

'You told me,' said Maud, 'that up till less than a year before Hope was born girls could get married at twelve and boys at fourteen? Is that really true?'

He said it was. He took an interest in acts of Parliament and the law.

'Then they made it so that everyone had to be sixteen. Why did they have to do that?'

'I expect it was something to do with women getting the vote the year before.'

She said nothing for a while but stared beyond the lamplight into the dark corners of the room. 'People used to believe that you could stop a baby being born by tying knots in things. I read that somewhere. If you had a bed with curtains you tied knots in them and you tied knots in your stockings.'

'It's just a superstition. It wouldn't work.'

'No, I don't suppose it would. But I was thinking, suppose it did, I could have tied knots in things and made Hope not be born till New Year's Day and Ronnie and I could have got married the day before and she'd have been a legitimate child.'

If that swine had been willing, John thought, you could have, if he could have been found and run to earth, but in the long run whose happiness would that have led to? He remembered what she had said about two animals in a field and thought how that had shocked him as much as his telling her about him and Bertie had shocked her. He watched the small upheavals inside the woolly folds of the shawl as Maud gently shifted the child to the other side and he asked her if she'd like a cup of tea before he left on his bicycle for the last day of term. She nodded, smiled at him, a rueful smile as she reflected what a difference to her life that change in the law had made. John would bring his Christmas present to her back from Ashburton that afternoon, the promised dress-length for her to make herself a frock. On his way out he picked up from the doormat a letter that had come from Bertie.

He would treasure it, read it several times before it met its inevitable fate, the fire or the kitchen range. Keeping such letters was more than he dared do, even though they were innocuous these days compared to his to Bertie, dull letters of the 'hope you are keeping well' and 'mild for December' kind. This one, which he read in the shed where he kept his bicycle, was typical, but it was all he had. It ended, though, on a different note, Bertie asking when they could meet. He had a week's holiday due to him. When could he come down to Devon and to Bury Row? Bertie said nothing about the baby, Hope, though John had mentioned her birth the last time he wrote.

He put the letter into his pocket, reasoning that even if it was stolen or happened to fall out, not a word in it indicated that he and Bertie were anything but the friends any couple of young men might be. But his mind was full of the empty phrases Bertie had written, repeating over and over sentences such as 'life goes on much as usual' as if they were verses composed by Keats or extracts from one of Shakespeare's sonnets. His own letters often had quotations from these sonnets. Although no teacher had ever told him that Shakespeare might have been homosexual, he read inversion in certain lines. Writing to Bertie back in November, John had told him that his was a face 'by Nature's own hand painted' and called him 'the master-mistress of my passion'. In that instance Bertie did refer to the content of John's letter, saying that he hoped John wasn't calling him a woman.

Cycling along the narrow, deep lanes, the hedges white with hoar frost, a precursor of the snow soon to come, John planned in his mind the letter he would write in response to Bertie's. That Bertie should want to come here to see him, to be with him, was a delight and John had not dared suggest it. Now he longed for it but asked himself how it could be possible. He had begun to regret having told Maud of his sexual nature. If he had said nothing, instead of gritting his teeth and bringing himself to the agonizing point of telling her, Bertie could have come to Bury Row and they could have shared the bed in John's room without attracting comment. Men often did that. But now she would remember what John had told her and be horrified. She might say Bertie couldn't come, and John, though he paid the rent and bought the food and was in her eyes and everyone else's the master of the house, knew that he could never bring himself to defy her. He might be 'queer', as even homosexuals themselves called it, but he was always aware of the opprobrium in which ordinary, 'normal' people held men like him and Bertie. Maud was one of those ordinary, normal people. He remembered too the promise he had made her, saying that what he had done when he lived in London would never happen again. Months before that, he had made a vow to *himself* that it would never happen again, he would be chaste in thought, word and deed. In thought that promise had already many times been broken.

Apart from John, Sybil was the only member of her family that Maud felt at all close to, so she had written to Sybil to announce the birth of Hope, enclosing a letter in the only Christmas card she sent. She asked her sister to tell their parents, then scratched out 'parents' and substituted 'mother'. Having sworn never to speak to her father again, she hadn't relented but clung to this vow. She wished him no harm, plotted no revenge, even if such a thing had been possible, but knew that she would never rid her mind of the words he had spoken, that she could 'contaminate' her sister, that she was to be sent away to a home 'to work', among many other dreadful things. Sybil hadn't replied. Perhaps she had been told not to.

Maud bathed her baby in the scullery sink. It made a perfectly adequate bath. When Hope was dried and creamed and powdered in the way Mrs Lillicrap had taught Maud, she laid her on one of the towelling squares John had bought in the shop in Ashburton (surely receiving many strange looks), folded it round her tiny but solid stomach and buttocks, and fastened it with a big safety pin. Hope cried little, perhaps because she was mostly in her mother's arms or close beside her, but now she began to whimper for milk. When Maud had put the baby to her breast, she thought of writing again to Sybil. This time she would ask her to tell Rosemary Clifford about Hope. She couldn't bring herself to do it, but surely Sybil would. Sybil could tell Rosemary and tell her too that this baby was Ronnie's as well as Maud's. Having driven him out of her mind for months, now Hope was born she admitted him again. If he wanted to see his child he could come to Bury Row. He could come, but she knew he wouldn't. He might even say that Hope wasn't his, but Maud rather doubted this. You had only to look at Hope to see his face, the face that had so attracted her in the first place, the dark blue eyes, the classically straight nose, the fair hair.

Maud was longing to take Hope out in the second-hand pram passed on to her by Mrs Tremlett, but Mrs Lillicrap said not yet. Give it another week. And only then if the weather was right. It was far from right at the moment, the white frost lying every morning on walls and hedges and five-barred gates and roof tiles. The leaves on the ilex in the churchyard, usually nearly black, were edged in fluffy whiteness. Mrs Lillicrap said Hope must go to All Saints to be churched the first time she went out and Maud thought she would abandon Methodism and go at least once to the Church of England. All the Methodists had done for her was be unkind and punishing, so she might as well try another kind of God she no longer believed in.

She finished the feeding, realizing that Hope would need changing again. She didn't mind. Washing for her little daughter was a pleasure. Lifting her up in her arms, looking into Ronnie's eyes, she talked to her as she often did, telling her the things she could tell to no one else.

'My darling, I love you so much, more than I've ever loved anyone. You are my treasure and my precious. I am so glad to have you. I'm happier than I've ever been. When I think how I hoped you weren't inside me and I longed for you not to be, I think I must have been mad. Oh, my darling little Hope, I do love you so much.'

A long dribble of curds and spit trailed out of Hope's mouth. Maud laughed. Everything her baby did, even regurgitating her feed, Maud thought amazingly clever.

Understanding how a woman feels with her first baby, that her whole life is bound up with that baby and all her thought processes are concerned with it, completely eluded John. It eludes most men. If he thought of it at all, he supposed that Maud felt about Hope much as he did: she was getting used to having a baby in the house, the 'maternal instinct' made her look after Hope and care for her, but as with him the crying rather exasperated her and like him she was glad when Hope was put to bed upstairs. He had no idea of her total involvement with Hope and her passionate love for her. Therefore he thought that when he broached the subject – if he did – of Bertie coming to Bury Row, even just paying a daytime visit, his sister would immediately recall every detail of his confession and would behave as she had the night before Hope was born and run away from him, disgusted by his revelations.

But still he made plans for how Bertie could be accommodated. If he asked Mrs Tremlett or Mrs Tremlett's daughters Gladys or Bertha or the Lillicraps or all of them whether they could put Bertie up for a few nights in one of their homes, wouldn't they wonder that his friend couldn't stay in John's own house, where they knew he had a spare room? Perhaps they need not be brought into it. He could make himself a makeshift bed on the living-room sofa and give Bertie his room upstairs. It was a possibility. After all, he had sworn to both Maud and himself that he would never again make love with a man, and he hadn't, except in his thoughts. He could spend time with Bertie but never touch him. This way, if they slept far apart, they would never be alone together and that was for the best.

That night, sleeping in the room he would give up to Bertie, he dreamt of him in this bed. He had shown him to the room and was lying on his not-very-comfortable couch downstairs, but he got up and climbed the stairs as quietly as he could, listening to the baby crying in Maud's room but not allowed to cry for more than a moment before, he guessed, Maud began to suckle her. He got into bed beside Bertie and the touch of his naked body was so over-whelming that something happened which he had never before experienced in Bury Row. He ejaculated so explosively that he awoke with a groan. Slime that Bertie called 'spunk' was all over the sheet, mercifully only the bottom one. He pulled it off the bed and rolled it up, not daring to leave it for Maud or Mrs Tremlett to find.

That sheet became a curse to John. Curiously, it seemed to take on a life of its own, eventually haunting Maud as well as himself, though he was to know nothing about that. It was like the white sheet a ghost wears, a figment of his dreams, never again to be looked at but never to be destroyed either. The household at No. 2 Bury Row was not so well off that he could afford to sacrifice a nearly new item of bedlinen that was not, in any case, their own, but had the initials MT embroidered on it. Maud might not know what that stiff stain was, but Mrs Tremlett, the married woman, certainly would. She too would ask herself and maybe ask Maud why 'Mr Goodwin' was sleeping in the spare room instead of with his wife. In answer to that, John imagined a whole drama in which 'Mrs Goodwin' refused her husband marital relations for six weeks after the baby was born, so he was obliged to sleep in the spare room, where, unable wholly to restrain his lust, he indulged in soli-tary self-abuse. Or perhaps she would simply say that her husband needed his sleep away from a crying baby. This second explanation left out any accounting for the stain. Afford to or not, he would have to destroy it.

It worried him disproportionately. He dared not leave the rolled-up sheet to be discovered, so he hid it in a paper bag stuffed into the basket on his bicycle handlebars. After school he went into the Ashburton draper's and bought the cheapest single sheet they had. The cold weather continued for another week and then it began to grow mild. After several nights without frost, John announced on the Saturday morning that he intended to do some gardening. He had no tools but borrowed a spade and fork from Mr Lillicrap at the Red Cow and started work on the soft, wet earth. When he had dug a sizeable pit, he buried the sheet in its paper bag and covered it with a layer of soil about six inches deep. The new one went into the drawer to await the time when it would replace the one that was at present on his bed. One of his fellow teachers at school had been reading a detective story and every day in the common room regaled the rest of the staff with bloodcurdling details that included the secret burial of the murderer's wife's corpse in the garden. Maybe his neighbours, watching from their bedroom windows, would credit him with similar concealment of a crime.

12

After the burial was over he went on digging, rather enjoying this activity while his mind was occupied with thoughts of Bertie and how to have him to stay without distressing Maud.

'Can I ask you something?' John had come in from the garden and washed his hands at the scullery sink.

Maud was sewing. Concentrating on keeping the thin tissue-paper pattern and the material perfectly flat, she simply nodded.

'I'd like to ask a friend of mine to stay for New Year's Eve and maybe a few nights after. Would you mind?'

She didn't look up. 'A friend that's a man?'

He realized that he was responding with the same sort of embarrassment that a 'normal' man would feel if he had been asked if his friend was a woman. 'Yes. He's a man.'

She lifted her eyes, still holding a pin between the forefinger and thumb of her right hand. Was she going to make the connection with what he had confessed to her? Apparently not. 'Where will he sleep, John?'

'In my room, I thought. And I could sleep down here on the sofa.'

She nodded. 'Will I like him?'

'I think so.' John didn't really know. 'His name's Bertie. Bertie Webber.'

'So I'll call him Mr Webber.'

'Maybe to start with.'

Perhaps she had forgotten what he had told her. He had read somewhere about amnesia and how people forgot what had happened just before an accident. It might be true that women forgot what they had been told just before labour pains started. There was no one he could ask.

He had written to his mother, an apologetic letter telling her he would not be returning home for Christmas. Her reply, which arrived on Christmas Eve, was an enclosure inside a card with a picture on it of a robin perched on a fir tree, signed 'from Mother and Father', though John had not mentioned his father in his letter, just as his mother didn't mention Maud in her cold letter. John was beginning to feel about their father much as Maud did, not wanting any contact with him. A card also came from Ethel and Herbert, and, to be treasured, one from Bertie wishing John 'the seasons' greetings' and accepting the invitation to come to Bury Row on 31 December. Managing to ignore the position of that apostrophe, John slept with Bertie's card under his pillow.

It was the day after Maud's sixteenth birthday and Bertie was coming. Some aspects of his visit John had not foreseen. He had looked forward to Bertie's coming in a breathless fever of anticipation, all of which he had had to conceal over Christmas as best he could from Maud. Fortunately, she was too occupied with making Christmas perfect for Hope, who was too young to notice, to pay his feelings much attention. She had decorated the living room with paper chains for Hope and acquired a tiny Christmas tree from Gladys Tranter's husband. John's longing for Bertie went little further than how ecstatically it would be gratified when John watched his train come in and his lover step out of it on to the platform. He would be happy then as he hadn't been since the last time he and Bertie met in London. How Bertie would feel about the weather, colder and wetter than London, how he would see the village and, come to that, Maud and the baby, John hadn't considered. If John had thought about Bertie's reaction at all, he supposed that his lover would feel as he did, that meeting again was enough and every difficulty, if difficulties there were, was lost in the rapture of once more being together.

The morning of Bertie's arrival was cold and John was afraid that if it snowed the bus to Newton Abbot might not run. Anxiously he watched the sky for that ominous yellowish greyness in the clouds that would foretell a heavy snowfall. But none came, the clouds parted a little, and John set off absurdly early, soon after their mid-day dinner, to meet a train that wasn't due till four.

A terrible dread assailed him that when the train came Bertie wouldn't be on it, he had had some sort of accident or his mother – the only relative he seemed to have – had been taken ill. Even if Bertie had 'wired' him, John had left so early he wouldn't have been at Bury Row to receive his telegram. Again he was worrying needlessly. Bertie stepped off the train just as John had anticipated, was all smiles and stuck out his hand for John to shake it. The touch of his fingers was such bliss that John wanted never to let go.

The bus was half empty and they sat in the front, side by side. Bertie took a blanket out of his big canvas bag to cover their knees. His hands were soon busy under the thick folds, but John had to stop him, fearing an incident like that with the bedsheet. Bertie stopped but laughed so much that passengers stared. John tried to distract him by pointing out the beauties of the countryside, a pretty church, the woodland and green meadows and, as they approached Dartcombe, crossing the river bridge, the ancient manor house where the Imber family lived.

A visitor was only of interest to Maud as a possible new admirer of Hope and so far every caller at the cottage, members of Mrs Tremlett's family, the Lillicrap daughters, neighbours in Bury Row and the Reverend Mr Morgan and his wife, had satisfied her expectations. Hope was a lovely baby, they all said so, and many, especially the women, wanted to hold her, lost in admiration that Hope never objected to being passed from hand to hand. Bertie, however, though charming to Maud, remarking on her beauty, which he said he hadn't expected, took no notice of the baby. Though held up in Maud's arms, Hope might not have been there as far as he was concerned, and John noticed the little frown that appeared on Maud's forehead and the stiffening of her shoulders as she stepped back.

But she had made the spare bedroom as nice for Bertie as their limited resources allowed, their new towels folded on a chair, coat hangers in the cupboard free of John's clothes, which she had transferred to her own wardrobe, the bedcovers turned back and pale yellow winter jasmine in a jug on the windowsill. John showed him up there; the door was closed behind them and at last they were in each other's arms. Again John had to restrain Bertie, repeating in a whisper what he had told him on the walk from the bus stop. It must be enough for them to be here together, sitting side by side, holding hands perhaps when Maud wasn't there, exchanging a kiss when she was out with the baby – something which was only just beginning to happen and then not every day.

Bertie said, 'We'll see about that,' and laughed that incredulous laugh that had made people stare on the bus. 'Who's to stop us?'

'My sister, that's who.'

'Your wife, don't you mean?' And Bertie laughed again, treating the whole thing as a joke.

That, it appeared, was how he saw John and Maud's subterfuge, a joke that no one could take seriously for long. That first evening John had to keep reminding Bertie that it wasn't a joke, that in the presence of Mrs Tremlett (who had brought in her scales to weigh Hope) and the people at the Red Cow it was important to remember that the Goodwins were husband and wife and to speak accordingly. That only made Bertie laugh again, though he promised he would try.

But New Year's Eve went reasonably well. In the evening Bertie and John walked up to the Red Cow and brought back a jug of cider and another of beer. Maud refused to drink anything but tea and water because she feared the alcohol would get into her milk. John could tell she was offended when Bertie filled a glass with cider for her and urged her to try it. Far from staying up to see in the New Year, Maud went to bed at half-past eight, making no excuses for such an early departure but taking her candle and saying only a curt goodnight.

'Alone at last,' said Bertie, moving from his chair to sit beside John on the sofa and throwing an arm round his neck.

John removed the arm. 'No, we mustn't.'

'Why not? She won't come down again, will she?'

'I don't know. I don't think so, but it's an awful risk. Suppose she saw us even just kissing?'

Bertie moved up to the end of the sofa and said quite seriously and rather crossly, 'Suppose she did? She's not going to run and tell the village copper, is she? Look here, Johnny, who pays the rent and buys the grub? You do, unless I'm much mistaken. She knows which side her bread is buttered. She's not going to turn you out, is she? You never heard of killing the goose that lays the golden eggs?'

It was true but horrible to hear in plain words, and words which showed him Bertie as John had never known him. The trouble was that none of that made John love Bertie less. 'Maud's not much more than a child,' John said. 'I can't expose her to that.'

'A child who got herself in the family way when she was still at school.'

Upstairs the baby began to cry. Maud may have fallen asleep, for it was a full two minutes before she was able to quieten her. Bertie cast up his eyes and slowly shook his head. John had picked up a book and begun to read it, afraid that if he told Bertie something of Maud's 'fall' he would sneer and then they would quarrel. But when Hope was quiet again, half the beer and cider had been drunk and their silence somehow become more companionable. Bertie returned to his former place next to John and again put an arm round his neck.

As usual at this time of a winter's evening, it was quite dark in the cottage, the only light coming from the oil lamp that was barely bright enough for John to read by. He laid aside his book and said, as he had the night before, 'I'll just go up and light your oil stove so that it'll be warm for you.'

'Don't come down again.'

'What do you mean?' John didn't understand.

'I mean, I'll join you.'

They didn't see the New Year in. When All Saints' Church clock struck midnight and the bells began, they were asleep in each other's arms.

13

That was the first instance of John breaking his promise to himself, the New Year's resolution he couldn't keep. It was followed by several such. He had got up after the change-ringing awakened him, whispered to the still-half-asleep Bertie that even if they kept him awake the bells were lovely to listen to.

'What's that?'

'The bells are lovely.'

'Can't hear what you say for the noise of those bleeding bells,' Bertie laughed.

John worried that Maud might have heard them in the next room, but if she had she gave no sign of it, though it was plain, at least to him, that she disliked Bertie and he her. In spite of this Bertie was not at all anxious to go home on 4 January and said he would like to stay a few more days. John's school term began on the 7th and Bertie had told him he was due back at work then too.

'That's what I *said*.' They were out for a walk in the village. 'As a matter of fact, I won't be going back. I've got the sack.' Bertie laughed to take the sting out of what had been even more than usually ominous words since the General Strike of a few years before. 'You needn't look like that. I'll find work when I want to. I've gone back to live with my mother.'

John had taken it for granted that Bertie had a return ticket, but apparently not.

'So you can see I'm free as air.'

'I'll buy you a ticket to London. Of course I will.'

'I don't believe you're that keen to get rid of me.'

Bertie knew John wasn't, but perhaps he didn't know how great a strain having him to stay had put on John's income. Bertie had contributed nothing to the household expenses and now John saw that Bertie couldn't have afforded to. He had saved nothing from his wages, which for a short while had been more than John's salary. John was beginning to see that his passion for Bertie was no help to his understanding of his lover, any more than Bertie's for him gave him insight into John's character and ways of thinking. Now, though, John could see that Bertie was indifferent to what went on in another's mind. He simply believed that everyone was like himself or, if not like him, naive, credulous and ignorant of the real world. But every night they made ardent love, Bertie having a signal he gave John before he climbed the stairs to the overheated bedroom where he kept the oil stove lit day and night. Even in front of Maud, when he made for the stairs he would turn, face John and raise his eyebrows while giving a small smile. In the months and years to come, John would see that smile and those raised eyebrows in his dreams.

The day before Bertie was due to leave – he had finally agreed he must return to London on the appointed day – he asked John how long he intended to live with Maud. They were walking down to the Red Cow, the usual destination of their walks, for Bertie had no interest in landscape, beautiful old houses or the river.

'I hadn't thought about it,' John said, surprised. 'For always, I suppose.'

'And call yourself her hubby? Bit of a joke, isn't it?'

'Not to me.'

'You could take another cottage down here and have me to live with you instead of her. How about that? I could get work. Old Lillicrap says he wants a barman now his missus is in the family way again.'

'I can't afford two homes, Bertie. Besides, how could I leave Maud? She's only sixteen.'

'She's got all her pals. That Tremlett woman and that big, fat Gladys and the other woman, what's she called? They're dropping in every day. She's never alone. And how about that Ronnie who got her up the duff? Can't you get that sod to marry her? Or find some country yokel who'd do it for a hundred quid?'

Bertie's words upset John so much that he couldn't speak. But in spite of the ugliness of the way Bertie put things, John could see the attractiveness of the idea. If only Maud could marry! If he could live with Bertie! That night on the sofa, after he had left Bertie's bed in the hot, airless room, he indulged in waking dreams of sleeping with him all night long, of no longer being troubled by Hope's crying, of keeping some fraction of his salary for himself. The plan to take care of Maud and at the same time become chaste and continent was proving far more difficult than he had supposed when he'd made those promises to himself and her. And not just difficult, impossible. But before he slept he had put all this away from him. In the morning Bertie was to leave for London.

John bought a single ticket for Paddington and gave Bertie enough money to pay for food on the train. They had exchanged a passionate kiss in the cottage in Bury Row before they left, but John would have liked another, that farewell embrace, forbidden to them but which any 'normal' lovers could have. The train came in and Bertie boarded it with a laconic 'So long.' Watching heads emerge from windows and hands raised in a wave, John hoped for a last glimpse of his lover and a wave for him. But none came and the train moved off. John kept it in sight until it dwindled into nothingness in the far distance, the only sign of it that remained the great plume of white smoke rising into the low, dark clouds.

He turned away, aware that he was returning to worries and shortness of money. He and Maud were usually comfortable, but his income couldn't stand a profligate guest. Bertie had kept his bedroom heated day and night, when they shopped he had spent John's money on expensive cuts of meat and a seemingly endless supply of cigarettes. The cottage stank of paraffin and tobacco. Every day jugs of beer and cider had been brought in and more drunk in the Red Cow. The first thing John was conscious of when he walked in after seeing Bertie off was the stale odour of those cigarettes and that oil stove.

'I know,' were Maud's first words to John. 'And it's too cold to keep the windows open.'

'I'm afraid you and Bertie didn't get on.'

'No, we didn't. What's the use of pretending?' She was silent for several minutes, sitting at her sewing machine and spreading out a hem under the needle. When she had worked the treadle for a while, stitching the seam, she took back her hands and laid them in her lap. 'I didn't say anything, I felt I couldn't, but I know what you and Bertie were doing in the spare room. It was him you did it with before, wasn't it? I know it was. You said you never would again, John. You promised.'

He flushed a deep, dark red. 'I know.'

'Do you know how I felt? It was the way he looked at me and the way he spoke and never took a scrap of notice of my baby.' John was horrified to see the tears fall from her eyes and roll down her cheeks. 'I felt he wanted to get rid of me, he wanted me to go so he could be alone with you. He did.'

'Don't cry. Please don't. That will never happen. Never. I know I broke my promise before, but I won't again. I promise we'll always be together. Look at me, Maud. I promise.'

He had promised before and she no longer trusted him. From that day she began to change, to grow colder, more shut in and suspicious. Perhaps she was only becoming like their mother. But that was yet to come and now she managed a smile. From the Moses basket came a sudden, loud yell. Hope had woken up and wanted her food. That evening John wrote to Bertie, sitting up in bed in the now cold spare room, a long, passionate letter, recalling details of their lovemaking, regretting that Maud had changed the bedsheets and therefore deprived John of the scent of his lover through the night.

14

John wrote to Bertie far more often than Bertie wrote to him, but John knew this was because writing never came easily to Bertie. Sometimes his letters were plainly a third or fourth effort, copied from corrected earlier versions. Far from troubling him, John was touched. These revised letters showed how much Bertie cared for John's opinion and wanted to impress him – surely a sign of love.

Little correspondence came to No. 2 Bury Row and rarely for Maud. Her Bristol friends ignored her, as did her parents and sister Ethel. There was nothing from her grandmother, and Maud supposed that she didn't know where her granddaughter was, had perhaps been told that she had gone away to school. Only Sybil occasionally wrote, simple unimaginative letters asking after Maud's health and Hope's and dwelling exhaustively on the weather. Any friends Maud now had lived in Dartcombe and had no need to write to her, but in spite of this lack of attention from the outside world, she always picked up the letters from the door-mat. She seemed, in John's view, to have an uncanny instinct for sensing exactly when the postman was coming, or else her hearing was better than his. She would bring a letter from Bertie to the breakfast table and lay it beside his plate, saying when John appeared, always unwilling to use Bertie's name, 'Another letter from your friend.'

They were infrequent enough, John thought, but still they came too often for Maud. One morning, about a year after Bertie had been to stay, with Hope on her lap, she picked up the envelope he had set aside, delaying reading its precious contents until he was alone, and said she hoped he wouldn't be inviting his 'friend' to stay with them again.

'Certainly not,' said John with unusual sharpness. 'I know and he knows he wouldn't be welcome.'

'You broke your promise. You promised you wouldn't do those disgusting things but you did do them and I can't forget it.'

'Evidently. You won't let me forget it either.'

How she had grown up since the birth of Hope, quite suddenly becoming a woman, and the kind of woman common in their family: narrow, censorious, quick to pass judgement. The sweet innocent was gone, the young girl who respected and admired him as if he really were her husband. 'Disgusting' wasn't a word she would have used a year ago. She sounded like Ethel. He remembered how wistfully she had spoken that day before Christmas when she had talked about the Age of Marriages Act and about a superstition that was a means of delaying a birth. He was disappointed in her rather than angry. Although he had never put this feeling into words before, not even in his thoughts, he had supposed that because she herself had transgressed and been punished for it, she would more readily understand transgression in others, would have become tolerant and forgiving. He expected too, if unwillingly, that she would feel some gratitude towards him for providing her with a home and financial support and a shield of respectability.

Knowing that going along this path would lead him to feelings he didn't want to have – resentment, indignation and, worse, a sense of being unjustly treated – he took his letter and went upstairs to read it. There was more this time than usual. Bertie had at last succeeded in finding a job, serving behind the counter in an ironmonger's shop in the Edgware Road. The pay was poor and it was as well he was living at his mother's because he couldn't afford rent. He said he wanted him and John to meet and soon. They mustn't go on like this, just communicating on paper. If his tone wasn't exactly cold, the terms he used made it look as if he and John were business acquaintances who needed to meet to discuss some kind of proposal. John's house wouldn't do because Bertie knew he wasn't accepted by John's sister. Perhaps they could have a 'rendezvoo' in a hotel somewhere, but it was important not to delay too long.

John wondered why Bertie wrote in this fashion when he himself poured into his letters so much adoration and passion and promises of enduring love. The answer must lie in the awkwardness Bertie felt about writing, his inability to select suitable words and phrases. John knew he would think about this question of their meeting all day, while he was supposed to be teaching boys Boyle's Law, while he was marking essays, trying to find a way round this seemingly insoluble problem. Staying a weekend in a hotel was impossible. He couldn't afford it, and Bertie certainly couldn't. With Bertie's poverty in mind, he wrote him a loving note and, not for the first time, put it in an envelope with two pound notes he took from the tin he kept in a drawer. Maybe it was less than two weeks' wages to Bertie, but it would help. John took the letter with him when he left for school and Maud, who was standing in the tiny hallway, stared at it and no doubt read the address.

Life was quiet and dull at No. 2 Bury Row. Events which enlivened it were, for John, Bertie's occasional letters, and for Maud, Hope's cutting another tooth or, now that she was approaching two, uttering her first words. Maud had hoped the first word of all would be 'Mama', but in fact it was 'Dada'. Where she learned to call John that Maud never knew, only guessing that she had heard Gladys Tranter's little girl call her father Dada, or perhaps some other one among her friends had encouraged Hope to give John that name. It was the only possibility open to them, but neither of them liked it, John because he saw it as teaching the child to lie, Maud because, secretly, she believed that at some time in the future she was going to have to tell Hope the truth of her parentage. And what would happen if there was ultimately a reconciliation between herself and her mother and Ethel? For her father, Maud still kept unchanged hatred and resentment. Or if Sybil, who wrote to her quite often now, wanted to visit? She never spoke of these things to John, sure he would neither understand nor care.

Rosemary Clifford, not Sybil, was the first to come. The doorbell rang at No. 2 Bury Row one afternoon soon after Maud and Hope had finished their midday dinner and Maud had laid the baby down for her nap. She expected to find Daphne Crocker, her new neighbour at No. 4, on the doorstep. Instead, it was Rosemary, but a Rosemary transformed into a smart young lady, her hair marcelled, lipstick on her mouth, wearing a linen skirt and a black-and-white jumper, her feet in black patent shoes with double straps across the instep.

Nothing was said for a moment.

At last Rosemary said, 'Can I come in?'

'It's not very tidy.' Maud thought immediately that this was a stupid thing to say, but she made it worse with 'It's a bit of a mess really.'

Rosemary laughed. 'I knew you lived here. I mean, in Dartcombe. Sybil told me. But not exactly where. My Auntie Joan lives in Dartwell Magna, and I'm staying with her so I begged a lift from Mrs Imber – my mother knows her – and asked at the Red Cow, and they sent me here.' Rosemary laughed again, apparently from sheer happiness, and sat down in the middle of the sofa. 'Where's the infant, then?'

'She's asleep. She has an afternoon sleep.'

'And you live here with John?'

'Yes.'

'What's she called?'

At this moment a wail came from upstairs. Maud sprang up. 'I'll fetch her.'

She could have carried Hope down at once, but she wanted her to be seen at her best, so she hurriedly dressed her in the latest frock she had made, pink and blue flowers on white winceyette, elaborately if a bit unevenly smocked. Hope had white socks on and pink shoes with straps.

'Hold Mummy's hand and we'll walk down.'

They got to the fourth step from the foot and Hope put up her arms and said, 'Mummy carry.' She was shy of the strange lady.

'Her name is Hope,' said Maud.

'That's a good choice. I expect you needed all the hope you could get.'

The little girl looked as if she might cry, but she didn't. Perhaps she was fascinated by Rosemary's scarlet mouth and matching fingernails, or perhaps by the way the strange lady was staring into her eyes and smiling.

'I thought as much,' Rosemary said. 'I wondered as soon as Sybil told me and now I know. She's exactly like Ronnie.'

Maud blushed a fiery red. 'Yes. She's his. There was never anybody else.'

She would have liked to tell Rosemary everything, the way her parents had wanted to put her into that Methodist home, the things her father had said to her, how he had threatened her with the adoption of her baby. Above all, she would have liked to talk about her feelings, her misery, her dread, the temptation of suicide, the loneliness until John came to her rescue. But she couldn't. It was impossible. In some play somewhere, when she was in school, she had read the expression 'I cannot heave my heart into my mouth', and that was exactly how she felt. Not just to Rosemary but to everyone who hoped that she would confide in them, even John, particularly John. Talking about her feelings, even weeping while she spoke of them, had once been possible, but no longer, and John and Bertie together had, so to speak, by what they had done, shut her emotions up inside her just as if they had taken hold of a full bottle of water and pushed a cork tightly into it.

To Maud's amazement, Hope had climbed on to Rosemary's lap and was sitting there playing with the contents of her black suede handbag. Clever Rosemary had understood that if there is anything a two-year-old likes to play with it is the powder compact, the comb, the lace handkerchief, the purse, the lipstick and the cigarette packet she finds in a lady's bag. Rosemary had her cigarettes in a case with her name cut into its silver surface and now, having first offered it to Maud and been refused, she took one out and lit it.

Hope said, 'Hope have cigarette.'

Rosemary laughed. Had she always laughed so much? 'Not till you're grown up.' She put Hope on the floor with the bag and its contents, excepting the compact and the lipstick. 'You don't want sticky red stuff all over your furniture. I'm going to tell Ronnie. Is that all right?'

'He won't believe you.'

'Yes, he will. He's come down from Oxford and he works in a bank. I don't mean behind a wire cage like those people who hand out money when you give them a cheque, I mean something called a merchant bank. Would you like to see him?'

Maud said, 'I don't think so.'

'Oh, why not? He'll be thrilled when he knows this little sweetheart is his.'

'I doubt that.' Maud's friend was so sophisticated and so clever, yet Maud thought she knew more about men than Rosemary did. Maud had been through more, she had lived.

'We could all have tea. You could bring her and we could have tea in that nice hotel in – what's it called? – Newton Abbot.'

This time Maud laughed, a harsh, metallic sound. 'I think I will have that cigarette,' she said, though it would be only the third one she had ever had in her life.

'That nice hotel' in Newton Abbot was the one Bertie had seen after arriving at the railway station. That was what John thought of when Maud told him as much as she wanted him to know of Rosemary's visit. He and Bertie had seen each other a few times over the past two and a half years, meeting in London in the school holidays for just an afternoon, once in a boarding house in Reading because it was on the Great Western main line. Bertie had remembered the nice Newton Abbot hotel, but it was well beyond their means. In the boarding house Bertie had told John without shame, or even supposing that John would be hurt, that he sometimes went on Hampstead Heath, picking up young men, or found a guardsman in one of the London parks who would 'do it for cash' though he wasn't 'queer' himself. These confidences had brought John savage pain and jealousy, but when he protested to Bertie, all his lover said was, 'I dare say I'd give it up if you and me shared a place down where you live.'

John was ashamed of his reaction to Maud's news; his heart leapt when he'd heard that Rosemary intended to tell her brother that Maud had had his child. Ronnie had failed to answer John's letter telling him of Maud's pregnancy, but he was older now, they all were. Maybe he had changed. This might lead to Ronnie offering to marry John's sister, taking her away and thus leaving John free to live with Bertie. It was a giant leap to make – but was it? It rather depended on what kind of a man Ronnie Clifford was, and John hadn't high hopes of him after having had no answer to his letter. If it were me, John thought, I would be so excited at the thought of being a father I would rush off at once to see my sweetheart and my daughter and after that . . . But he couldn't imagine doing what was necessary to father a child, couldn't imagine wanting to do it. He had never made love to a woman and knew he never would.

Regularly he burned the letters he received from Bertie. He was afraid Maud might find them if he kept them to read and reread. Because he pressed Bertie for a photograph, he finally sent one, a picture of himself with his mother in a tiny garden with a wire fence round it. Bertie's mother wore a crossover flowered overall and bedroom slippers and looked as old as the hills – well, more like seventy than fifty-five. This John refused to burn but he cut Bertie's mother off it. He looked at it every night, wishing it were of Bertie on his own. By day he hid it, firstly in one of the drawers in his bedroom, then, realizing that Maud or Mrs Tremlett opened this drawer to put his clean shirts inside, in one of the pockets of his overcoat. But truly, nowhere was safe from these women. He often lay awake at night, asking himself but never getting an answer, why the world was so horrified by Uranians and so furious with them, when in fact they harmed no one by what they did.

Another disturbing thing was happening to him. He had begun to think that he had been wrong, or, rather, unwise to set up this little household with Maud and Hope. When he first thought of it, the arrangement had seemed so good to him, the answer to every dilemma: his homosexuality, the trap Maud had got herself into, where they were to live and how they were to live, the illegitimacy of Hope. Moving in here and pretending to be husband and wife had indeed solved these difficulties, but it depended on his celibacy; that which he had believed would be easy enough to stick to had turned out to be nearly impossible. He was now brooding daily on how he could escape from this situation of his own making, asking himself if he could afford to keep up two homes, one for Maud and the child and another for himself and Bertie. It pained John that every time Bertie wrote these days, he asked for money. John was afraid of losing Bertie if he refused and now found himself regularly making a contribution to Bertie's expenses, which amounted to doubling his wages.

Whether Rosemary had ever told her brother about his child Maud didn't know. Time went on, Hope was three years old, and no letter came either from Ronnie or from his sister to say she had told him. This caused Maud no distress, only resentment. All her feelings were for Hope, whose father seemed to have no longing to see her, sweet and beautiful as she was. When the doorbell rang Maud half expected to see Ronnie there, as if making surprise calls on people you hadn't seen for years might be a family trait.

It was years too since she had seen Sybil, though they wrote to each other. Then her sister invited herself to visit and stay the night if Maud was happy with that. Maud wasn't happy, but, as she put it to herself, she could put up with it. She cleaned the house from top to bottom, baked a Madeira cake for tea, changed the sheets on her own bed for Sybil to sleep in – Maud would sleep on the sofa – and dressed Hope in the new dress she had made for her, white lawn, trimmed in pink and with pink smocking.

Nothing about Sybil's appearance was eye-catching. She had always been rather dowdy and now, at thirty, she looked what people would call a typical spinster. Her shoes were flat-heeled lace-ups, her costume dark grey broadcloth, just like a man's but for the skirt substituted for trousers. Sybil had never cut her long, dark auburn hair and now she wore it in an unflattering bun at her nape. But her pleasure at seeing Maud and her reaction to Hope with her fair curls and dark blue eyes were all Maud could have longed for.

Sybil had brought Hope a present, a fluffy terrier on wheels, that the little girl received rapturously and, remembering her mother's teaching, said thank-you for.

'She's lovely,' Sybil said. 'Not much like any of us, but that doesn't matter. She looks a happy child.'

'I think she is. I hope so. I wish she had more children her own age to play with, but Mrs Tranter and her husband have moved to Dartwell and their little girl too, of course.'

'Maud, I have to ask you, I hope you won't mind, but the people here, do they know about Hope?'

Maud knew very well what Sybil meant, but still Maud meant to ask her to spell it out. 'What do you mean, about her?'

'You know.' Sybil looked uncomfortable. 'That she's not – well, born in wedlock.'

Maud spoke stiffly, 'John and I call ourselves Mr and Mrs Goodwin. Everyone believes Hope is his child.'

'Oh, Maud.' Sybil placed her slice of Madeira cake back on her plate, looking as if the news she had received had spoilt her appetite. 'Oh dear, Maud, was that wise? Didn't you think about the consequences?'

'What consequences?'

'Well, what if John wants to get married? What if you do?'

'I won't and he won't. Hope thinks John's her father and there's no reason why she won't go on doing so. Now let's change the subject. How's Mother? How's Ethel?'

Sybil, who plainly didn't want to change the subject, told her that Ethel was 'expecting' her first child in January, and took no notice of Maud's flashing eyes and pursed mouth. 'No one told her she was a disgrace to the family, did they?'

'Oh, Maud,' was all Sybil could say to that. She expected a happier response when she told her sister their mother was well, missed Maud a lot and would like to see her. 'She says bygones will be bygones if you'll only come and maybe stop with us for a couple of nights.'

'I could, but I don't want to see our father.' I make him sound like

God, Maud thought, but didn't know how else to put it, and he had behaved like God to her, a jealous god, punishing disproportionately. Reaping where he had not sown, she remembered from her churchgoing days, and gathering where he had not stored. 'Mother could come here,' she said, 'if she misses me so much.'

Never the soul of tact, Sybil said, 'She wouldn't do that. You see, if you came to us, she says please could you not bring the child. She doesn't want to see her.'

Maud's reaction was far from anything Sybil expected. She thought her sister might protest that she had no one with whom to leave Hope or that she had never been separated from her and wasn't about to start now. But Maud screamed. She screamed and burst into violent tears, seizing hold of the little girl, who had been playing with her toy dog, and clutching her so tightly that Hope also began to cry and howl. The two of them rocked back and forth, sobbing and grabbing at each other's clothes and hair. Sybil turned white. All she could say was, 'Oh, Maud, Maud, don't. Please stop. What have I said that's so terrible? Please stop.'

Into the midst of this John walked. 'What on earth is wrong?' He looked from one sister to the other. 'What have you said to her?'

'Nothing, nothing. I only said that if she'll come and see Mother, not to bring Hope.'

Maud's tears had subsided. Hope was still whimpering and hiccuping. John laughed. 'I can see that would start the fireworks.' He said to Maud, 'You don't have to go anywhere if you don't want to. You're making a fuss about nothing. Have another cup of tea, that'll do you good.'

Sitting up straight, directing a look of enraged distaste at Sybil, her face bright red and wet, Maud said, 'I will never go near that house again. I'll never go to Bristol again. You can tell her I don't want to see her as long as I live or she does, and as for Father, he's dead to me already.'

Sybil stayed the night in Maud's bed and Maud slept downstairs, Hope in her cot pulled close to the sofa. In the morning, before he cycled off to school, John showed Sybil the vegetables he and Maud were growing behind the house in a patch Maud called the kitchen garden.

'It helps us make ends meet.'

'But you have a good salary, don't you, John?'

'There are three of us to live on it. Down here I don't get the London weighting.'

Sybil left on the bus for Ashburton, rather peeved because Maud wouldn't come too to see her off.

'You could leave Hope with Mrs Whatshername.'

'Tremlett. Her name is Mrs Tremlett. I don't know why everyone is always trying to get me to leave my little girl with other people.'

So they parted on waspish terms.

Maud, whom John had once described as a cheerful girl who never sulked, was sullen and morose that evening. When John asked her what was wrong all she said was, 'I wonder what Sybil would say if she knew about you and your *friend*.'

15

When John had said that he had three people to support on his income he wasn't telling the whole truth. For the past few months he had been supporting Bertie as well. The days when Bertie received money from John only when he asked for it were gone, the days when John put a pound note or two into an envelope and sent them with a covering note were in the past. Now, each week, he sent his lover a postal order for nearly twice the sum that Bertie earned serving behind the counter in the ironmonger's shop. John couldn't afford it, and every time he sealed up the envelope and dropped it into the pillar box he thought that he was buying Bertie's love.

In the past he had sometimes planned to save enough, even if it took him weeks, to take a room for one night in that hotel Bertie coveted. John didn't get far. Hope needed new shoes, she had a rash or a cough and the doctor had to be sent for, the roof of No. 2 Bury Row sprang a leak and Mrs Tremlett refused to pay for mending it, so John had to. John said nothing, just accepted, but Maud reproached their landlady, calling her a skinflint, which led to her asking for an extra five shillings for their cleaning. 'If that's what I am,' she said to Maud but with a grin, 'I'll need my pay going up.' Learning to be 'a real dressmaker', as she put it, Maud needed more and more fabric to work on and more paper patterns to buy. The hotel plan came to nothing and now never would. All John's spare cash went to Bertie.

A letter came from him unexpectedly. He never thanked John for the postal orders and John attributed that to his lover's embarrassment at being given money. A letter these days was rare, and Maud, picking it up from the doormat, brought it to him held out between thumb and forefinger at arm's length as one might carry a bag of rotting food. John, eating his breakfast, was growing tired of pandering to her whims. More and more he was resenting the way she took everything as if it were her right and gave nothing in return beyond doing the housekeeping, which was more for herself and Hope than for him. He opened the letter in front of her. It told him that Bertie's mother, who was only in her fifties, had died of a growth in her throat. His sister's husband had paid for the funeral.

The tone of his letter wasn't sorrowful but almost exhilarated. His mother's house was a poor little place in Paddington, not far from the station, but it had been hers and now it was his. John expected an invitation to follow, but there was nothing. Still, he refused to be downhearted, knowing how hard Bertie found writing anything and how composing a letter tired him out. John got up from the table and told Maud Bertie's news, not so much to annoy her as to make her realize and accept that Bertie was his friend and his doings of the greatest interest to him.

'I don't want to hear,' Maud said.

'What has Bertie done to make you dislike him so?'

'It's what you and he have done together. I'll never forget the noise you made in the next room to mine and me with my innocent little child.'

He said nothing. Later that day, when school was over, he sent Bertie his usual postal order and put a note in with it asking if he could come and stay a night the following weekend. Knowing how writing was so difficult for Bertie, he added that there was no need to answer if it was all right for John to come on Saturday the 16th. Only if it wasn't convenient was Bertie to 'drop me a line'.

Most days Maud sat down at her sewing machine once Hope was bathed and dressed and playing with her toys, to teach herself procedures more difficult than turning up hems and sewing on buttons. Perhaps she could find an evening class in Ashburton, where a teacher taught tailoring, and leave Hope just for a couple of hours with John. While she was thinking along these lines, resenting John yet feeling guilty about him, the doorbell rang. She wasn't expecting anyone. She got up and looked out of the window, from where you could sometimes see who it was on the doorstep. But what immediately caught her eye was an enormous and extremely elegant black car parked outside the house, a Rolls-Royce. It was the only make of car she recognized, everyone knew it at once from its gable-shaped front, a gleaming silver. Of the woman on the doorstep she glimpsed a tailored suit and fox fur, unsuitable for a country village, and a bright splash of yellow hair.

Maud went to the door.

The woman said, 'Alicia Imber, and you must be Mrs Goodwin. How do you do?'

Maud knew you were not expected to reply to this enquiry but say, 'How do you do?' in return. She was so taken aback by the sight of her caller that she could only say, 'Come in,' but resisted the temptation to ask her to excuse the mess, of which there was none. Hope, who had been playing with her wooden farmyard, transferring painted-metal Jersey cows from the farmyard to the meadow, left the herd to wait behind the gate while she stared at the newcomer, who said a smiling hello to her.

'I see you've been sewing. Heaven knows how you find the time. I know I never should.'

Mrs Imber was tall and thin. Maud judged her age at forty, which was the callous overestimate of youth's instant dislike, as Alicia Imber was only thirty-four. The fox fur's sharp nose and furry forehead nestled against her rouged cheek. Maud asked her to sit down, but instead of doing so, she hovered over the sewing machine, picking up and scrutinizing the half-finished winter coat Maud was making for Hope.

'Very nice,' she said, smiling. She laid the coat down. 'It was about your sewing that I came. Mrs Clifford – I think you know her niece – told me the smocking you do is very good and I was wondering if you could make a dress for my little girl. Would you like to show me a sample?'

Mrs Clifford was Rosemary and Ronnie's aunt. What business

had she to put this patronizing woman on to her? Maud was thinking as she went upstairs. She brought down what she considered Hope's prettiest dress, green with white and red flowers, the smocking red. Mrs Imber scrutinized it as if she were a judge in a needlework School Certificate examination, but she smiled. 'Well, yes, very nice.' She laid the dress down on the arm of a chair.

'Can I wear it tomorrow, Mummy?' Hope said, darting a suspicious glance at Alicia Imber as if she thought the woman intended to steal it.

'If you like,' Maud said, then asked her guest, 'How old is your daughter?'

Like most mothers of a family when asked about one of her children, Mrs Imber took the question to apply to all of them. 'My boys are eight and nine and they are called Christian and Julian, and my little girl, Charmian, is six. As you can imagine, I miss my sons dreadfully and so does their sister, with no one to play with, but they are away at their private schools and what must be must be.'

'If you could bring Charmian here I could take her measurements and tell you how much material to buy.'

'Yes, well, we'll see. Charmian isn't very strong and I was hoping you would come to me at Dartcombe Hall.'

Maud summoned up all the nerve she had. 'It would be best if you came here.'

'Oh dear. You do like to make the rules, don't you? I'll come next Tuesday, shall I?' Maud knew that 'shall I?' was a mere figure of speech, meaning nothing. 'Goodbye, my dear,' Mrs Imber said to Hope. 'I don't know your name.'

That evening Maud relayed the conversation to John, but with exaggerations as people with paranoid tendencies do, and adding a phrase she had read somewhere, the first of many such inventions.

'You don't have to have that woman here,' he said, 'or make a dress for her child. We can manage without that.'

'What does *noblesse oblige* mean, John?'

'Why do you ask?'

'It's what she said to me when she was leaving,' Maud lied.

'It means an aristocrat owes it to himself, or maybe God, I don't know, to bend to the needs of lower-class people.'

'Thank you.'

John wished he had lied. Any translation, such as the almost incomprehensible 'nobility obliges', would have done. It soon appeared that Maud's work wasn't good enough. John, when buying her the sewing machine, had hoped she would use it and earn something to augment their income, but he knew now that this wasn't going to happen.

He found it easy enough to be untruthful when he told Maud he was going to London and would stay the night, with whom and why. One of the teachers at school had invited him to come with her to visit her parents in a place called Twickenham. This was half true, for Elspeth Dean had invited his 'wife' as well, but of course he had politely refused. The great thing was to get Maud to believe him, and it appeared that this time she did.

Bertie hadn't replied. John had said not to do so if coming on Saturday was all right, so evidently it was. Everything seemed to be going smoothly if you didn't count Maud's pressing enquiries as stumbling blocks. Who is she? Why have you never mentioned her before? Do you like her? And worst of all, 'Do you love her?' It wasn't the first time he had left Maud alone. On two occasions, taking a room in a boarding house, he had stayed a night away. It had always amused him (and been hilarious to Bertie) that the landladies wanted to see the ring on the third finger of the woman's left hand when it was a couple hoping to stay, nearly asking for their marriage certificate and making them sign the visitors' book, watching to see if the woman forgot and signed Jean Brown instead of Jean Smith. No landlady had suspected anything untoward of John and Bertie: they were obviously pals who would quite naturally be happy to share a bed, not just a bedroom. But no such minor incidents this time. They would share their bed in Bertie's late mother's house.

It was the first time John had visited the house. He knew more or less where it was and set off from Paddington station through a maze of dirty, little streets in the direction of the Grand Union Canal and the one beautiful building to be seen, the tall and narrow Gothic church of St Mary Magdalene, with its tapering spire, that stood almost on its bank. On this cold, dry, grey autumn day, a sharp wind whipped round street corners. A galvanized-iron dustbin stood on the rectangle of concrete that served as Bertie's front garden and beside it, leaning against the house wall, was a motorbike with badly worn tyres. There was no doorbell. The flap on the letter box had welded itself to its rusty surround, so there appeared to be no way of announcing his arrival. About to bang on the door with his fist, John tried the blackened brass handle first. The door opened and he stepped inside.

The house smelt unpleasant, a combination of paraffin, fried fish and urine. The door to the front room had fallen off its hinges and been left leaning against the wall. Every surface in the room and the passage had been painted dark brown, but so long ago that much of it had bubbled up and was peeling away to show the tinned-salmon colour underneath. It was cold. John called out Bertie's name. Nothing happened and he called again.

A door slammed upstairs and Bertie appeared at the top of the stairs. He was naked but for a pair of cotton trousers and the braces which held them up. 'Oh, it's you,' he said. 'Bit early, aren't you?'

'I think I said the afternoon.'

John took in the situation even before Bertie's companion had emerged from the bedroom. Once, not long ago, John wouldn't have understood, but in the intervening year or two he had lost his innocence. He had discovered Bertie *in flagrante delicto*, a term John had come across somewhere but never expected to experience himself. Yet he knew Bertie now. He knew how he lived and what he did. It was still a terrible shock.

The man who was now behind Bertie seemed to have hurriedly put on a shirt and trousers and, a good six inches taller, could clearly be seen struggling to tie his tie. Bertie came a few steps down. He said, incredibly, 'I don't suppose you've had your dinner. You get along to Delamere Road, there's a café there. I'll join you in ten minutes.'

If only he had had the sense, John thought as he walked away from the house, to have told Bertie to write if his visit *was* convenient, not if it wasn't. But would Bertie have written at all? He didn't care, he had no feeling for John's feelings, he had made it plain that he thought men such as them could have as many partners as they liked (partners in crime) and no one was to mind, no one was to be jealous. John was experiencing the sorrow of the man who knows that he passionately loves someone who is unworthy of his love. Even thinking that way made him ashamed of his arrogance in considering himself better than Bertie. He found the café and walked past it – he felt food would have choked him – down to the bank of the Grand Union Canal. He had heard people refer to it as a river, not knowing the difference between this still, stagnant water and a flowing stream. This water was a greenish brown and quite opaque. A narrowboat went by, low enough to pass under the first bridge and the second and through the tunnel at Maida Hill, not far from where he had first lived in London. In the wake of the boat came a pair of Canada geese and a bobbing coot, the white flash on its head bright on this dull day. John had never before thought of putting an end to things, but now it occurred to him that to fill his pockets with stones and slip into that cold, brown water would bring him a peaceful death. He turned away and walked to the station.

A train for Penzance had just gone. He was cold but a fire was in the waiting room and no one sitting on the horsehair settee that was near to it. Strangely, the warmth made him feel better. It wasn't simply a physical improvement but a mental cheering up. Perhaps he had been too hasty, perhaps he should have stayed, got Bertie to send the tall man away, talked to his lover, explaining how unhappy Bertie's infidelities – that was how John saw them – made him feel. In spite of the hunger which was now returning, he fell asleep with his head resting against the slippery black fabric. At some point he was aware of a porter coming in with a coal scuttle to tend to the fire, the man calling him sir and asking if he was all right. John thought he might be turned out on to the platform, but this didn't happen. He was aware of other people coming and going, but they took no notice of him and he went back to sleep.

This time it was only a doze, broken by waking dreams, as he began once more to think what he should do. He was ignorant, apart from what he had read in English literature, of how hard it is to give up someone with whom you have an intense sexual bond. His eyes still closed, he tried to imagine life without Bertie, the emptiness, the longing that would need to find expression in a howl of grief. He knew now, he knew what the books had never told him.

Outside, it was dark. He sat there, half lay there, wondering how hard it would be to walk to the end of the platform and, when the great train came in from the West Country, still going fast, to slip off on to the rails and lie down quietly to let it pass over him. He heard the porter come back but, instead of kneeling in front of the fireplace, he sat down beside him on the settee. John opened his eyes and saw it was Bertie.

'So this is where you've got to. Fine dance you've led me and I'm bleeding frozen.'

John wanted to do what he thought he would never do again and certainly dared not do here, throw his arms round him and kiss him the way a man and a woman were allowed to kiss. All he could do was murmur that he loved him.

'Then you'd best come back to my place like you said you would. Never mind Davy, he's just rubbish. He don't count. Come on now. Pull yourself together and we'll go get ourselves a slap-up meal first.'

So John went with him, hating himself but powerless to refuse.

16

Mrs Imber came back in the Rolls-Royce, bringing Charmian with her to be measured for her frock, and consented to be given a cup of tea. The two little girls, much the same age, got on well, rather better, Maud thought, than Hope did with Maureen Crocker, and Maud hoped a closer acquaintance might be possible. But when she suggested that Charmian might come again to play with Hope's wooden farmyard and the metal animals or in the little wooden house John had built for her in the garden, Mrs Imber looked almost shocked.

'I don't think so,' she said. 'Perhaps you didn't know, but Charmian often isn't quite well.'

'That woman is the worst kind of snob,' Maud said to John. 'There's nothing wrong with the child. It's just that we're not good enough for them. Gladys told me the Imbers are basically brewers. All their money comes from beer. Two generations back they were farm labourers.'

John was content for Hope to have her village friends. She would soon be going to school and make more. Since she had become three, he was more and more conscious that while she called him Daddy, he wasn't her father, was indeed her uncle, and 'living a lie', as he put it to himself, was increasingly upsetting to him. Since the episode of Bertie's flagrant and apparently guiltless unfaithfulness, their encounters had always taken place in the little slum house in Paddington. No one ever cleaned it. Plainly it was not only filthy but disintegrating, and although in receipt of money from his lover whenever John could afford it, Bertie spent nothing on his home. He seemed not to notice the smell or the slowly failing plumbing. What primitive electrical wiring there was had ceased to function, a failure Bertie attributed to the cables being chewed through by mice. But John had seen a rat when arriving there one evening, the half-tame animal sitting beside the dustbin and staring insolently at him. Bertie laughed when John told him.

Bertie had never again visited Bury Row. The only visitor from John's world was Elspeth Dean, the music teacher and one of only two women on his boys' school staff, and she came not at his invitation but at Maud's. The illusion that John and Maud were a married couple had to be sustained and not just in the village, but whereas John knew that this must be permanent, Maud hoped that if, for instance, they moved somewhere new, they might revert to being brother and sister. She thought that if Elspeth became her friend and John saw her in their domestic setting, he might grow fond enough of her to see her as a possible wife. As for herself, ever since Rosemary's visit – never repeated – she had wondered about Ronnie and for months half expected him to write or even visit. Though the months had stretched to years and he had never come, she still thought it a chance that they would meet and the love they had never had for each other would blossom like a long-neglected plant which, when fed and watered, might come into bloom.

John too hoped for changes, but of a different kind. To him, Elspeth, though pleasant and pretty and possessed of a lovely singing voice, was rather a nuisance in the house in the evenings, someone he had no wish to converse with, someone who seemed to be growing fonder of him when he knew and expected Maud to know that he was irrevocably 'one of those', or 'queer', as he and Bertie put it. The changes he wanted and saw as happening in the future were much the same as Maud's, that they might move away and become brother and sister again, that someone would come along and marry Maud, so that she was supported otherwise than by him, thus leaving him free to take a house somewhere to share with Bertie.

At least now Bertie seemed to look upon their relationship as permanent, John coming up to Paddington once every two or three weeks and sending him a couple of pound notes in an envelope between visits. They no longer discussed it, but John was sure that

Bertie's occasional adventures with Davy and his kind still took place and always would. He decided that he could bear it so long as he was told nothing about it and was never again to be shocked by the sight he had had on his first visit to Bertie's house.

At home in Bury Row, Hope started school in the autumn after she was five, the little Church of England school attached to All Saints that was also attended by Georgie Tranter and Maureen Crocker. Maud took Hope, holding her hand, and fetched her home in the afternoon. She and her daughter had been so close and so much together that Hope cried disproportionately when Maud left her in the playground, but by the next day she was better and ran towards the school door to find her new friends.

Mrs Imber had been less than delighted with the smocking on Charmian's frock; the stitches were not quite even and the hem was not as neatly done as she'd expected. She paid Maud but told her she wanted no more work from her; Maud, easily disheartened, abandoned her ambition to become a professional dressmaker and made clothes for herself and Hope alone. She missed Hope more than she had thought she would, having even looked forward to her starting school as a time when she would have 'more time to myself'. With no resources but her child, no hobbies but one she felt she did less than well, not much of a reader, she saw life stretching bleakly before her. She was like a traveller setting forth along a path he believes will lead to the city but who rounds a bend to see a limitless desert stretching before him. To compensate, she went frequently into Ashburton to the shops and sometimes to Newton Abbot, from where she took the train to Plymouth, spending more money than the family could afford on high-quality food and buying ready-made dresses, hats and shoes. Meanwhile, Hope went down with chicken-pox, which made Maud worry her face would be scarred, and then with measles. These, the inevitable result of starting school, had little ill-effect on her.

John had given up expecting letters from Bertie unless he had something exceptional to tell him. Apart from a telegram there was no other means of communication. Although several people in Dartcombe had the telephone – the Imbers, someone had told him, made long-distance calls on theirs – John had no ambitions in that direction. He couldn't afford it. He confessed to himself that he had hoped Maud might make a success of her dressmaking, become a good businesswoman and augment their income. But, no, he told himself, he should have known better. He was appalled by her extravagance and the frivolous items she bought. Money was always short. He had occasionally gone to Bristol to see his parents, but now these visits had to be cancelled. He was even sending less to Bertie, something which so distressed him as to keep him awake at night. Soon, with no enclosure to put in the envelopes, he wrote less and less often. Even when he had no replies to his letters, he would have gone on writing over the years because this, though one-sided, was the only contact he had with Bertie. But it occurred to him that Bertie might find his letters annoying, and he pictured Bertie's exasperation, but abandoning the correspondence, such as it was, was almost unbearable, as if life itself were over. Six months, a year, then two years, had passed since John had last spent a night in Bertie's house, more than a year since he had heard from Bertie. John's nights were haunted by the dreams of the jealous lover; scenes of Bertie frolicking with hand-some young men drifted past John's sleeping eyes, so that he often woke with a groan of misery and shame. His love remained un-diminished. He thought that the worst had happened to him and he had sunk into the depths of misery.

His heart leapt – he actually felt it take a jump of joy – when one morning, just as he was leaving for school, Maud brought him a letter she had picked up from the doormat. Bertie's backward-sloping handwriting was now known to her almost as well as it was to John, but the difference in the emotions they felt when reading the address was evident in the pursing of her lips, the wrinkling of her nose and the way she held the envelope almost at arm's length.

'Give it to me, please,' John said. 'If you don't care to touch it why not leave it where it was and let me pick it up?'

She made him no answer. In future, he thought, if this letter made things better between Bertie and himself he would invite his lover here and she must put up with it. Self-pity and resentment engulfed him. He had given up all chance of his own happiness for her, lied for her, earned for her and her child, given up a lot of comforts – such as a good bed in a good bedroom – to which he was entitled, and his reward was to be denied the company of the only person in the world who meant anything to him. He still hadn't opened the letter and now a dread took hold of him, a fear that Bertie was telling him what he already knew but had never put clearly into words, that all was over between them. Inside that envelope must be bad news, the confirmation of the fears John dared not face, for Bertie never wrote a simple love letter and certainly would not be telling him he was sorry not to have written before but that everything was all right and he longed to see him. That wasn't Bertie's style. The cowardly side of John suggested he might leave the letter unopened, hide it in his bedroom. The braver John gritted his teeth, stuck his thumbnail under the flap and ripped open the envelope.

It was quite short. He read it once, then again, scarcely able to believe the words on the paper.

17

John went to work, cycling through the teeming rain. He had the fifth form for his first class that day and was teaching them geology, volcanoes and igneous rocks. John never had difficulties with keeping discipline, largely because his pupils liked and respected him, though he was aware that some of them were noticing that his mind was not on the lesson. Still, he could be confident that they would never treat him as this same group of adolescents had treated poor Mr Carrington, all twenty-seven of them climbing out of the window and sitting on the flat roof of the science lab before the teacher came into the classroom. After John had let them finish the hour by reading contemporary accounts of the Lisbon earthquake of 1755 and was gathering up his books, a boy called Walter King came up to him and asked if he wasn't feeling well. This was so kind and so obviously sincerely meant that John felt tears come into his eyes as he thanked Walter for his thoughtfulness but said he was quite well, just a little tired.

The day seemed long, but it was not one he wanted terminated by going home. He felt like that passage in the New Testament about the foxes having their holes and the birds of the air their nests but the Son of Man with nowhere to lay his head. He was very conscious of Bertie's letter in his pocket, as if this single sheet of lined paper and flimsy envelope were made of lead and weighing him down. When school was over he encountered Elspeth Dean in the staff cloakroom, not someone he specially wanted to avoid but, along with the rest of the world at present, someone he was indifferent to. She was putting on her coat as he was putting on his. She came up to him and said how much she had enjoyed a recent visit to see his wife and would he ask Maud if he and she would come to tea with her in Ashburton. John said he was sure this could be arranged, trying to keep the impatience out of his voice. Elspeth was a perfectly pleasant woman and he liked her, but at that moment he wanted no one, only to be alone. Once he was on his bicycle he made his way not to the road for Dartcombe but to Ashburton's little park, where, forbidden by a by-law to cycle, he pushed his bike along a path that branched off the main ride, found himself a seat and sat down to read Bertie's letter for the third time.

Dear John

    It is a long time since I have herd from you. I don't know what I have done rong. As you must know its hard making ends meet. This place is cold and offen I do not have enuf to eat. When you sent me a £ note if not very offen things was better. I had best come to the point quick. I kept all the letters you sent me and if the polis was to see them you know what will happen. You are rich with a gentmans work. You can send me £2 per week and not miss same. Just do it and we can be frends agen.

Hoping to stay youre frend,

B.

Blackmail, it was called, and Bertie was doing it. This was his usual way of ending a letter, with the initial B. instead of his name. Steeped in bitterness, John asked himself if Bertie had done this with his eye always on the main chance of extorting money with menaces some day to come. That, too, was why he had rarely described reflecting on the pleasures of their lovemaking, while John, the loving innocent, had poured out his heart on paper as, when they met, he had poured out his body.

All these things were suddenly clear to him. He had never before thought about them, while always knowing that his love for Bertie was greater than Bertie's love for him. Things would be less bad, he thought, if with Bertie's words and his threats John's love for him had been extinguished. But this hadn't happened. Just as Bertie's illiteracy had never made John despise him, so this criminal betrayal had no effect on his passion and his longing. He still knew that if the man who had been his lover were suddenly to appear in the darkening park and come walking towards him along this path, smiling, merry, with his head a little on one side as he often held it, John would spring up, his heart brimming with joy, and take Bertie in his arms. Always looking about him at first, of course, to be sure they were not being observed.

The time hadn't yet come for him to decide what to do. It was too soon. First he had to take in exactly what the menace of the letter was. Bertie, whom he felt closer to than to anyone else he had ever known, had threatened, in what he now saw as plain words, to show John's letters to the police, knowing that every line made clear that John had repeatedly committed a serious and universally loathed criminal offence. Buggery, sodomy, he wasn't sure of the wording of the law, knowing only that it carried a long prison sentence for the convicted man. Spelt out as his 'crime' would be, his parents would know, his sisters would know, he would lose his job and probably his home. Yet strangely enough, or perhaps not strangely at all considering his love for Bertie, all these consequences shrank to mild hardships when compared to his lover's betrayal, when set beside what Bertie, the object of John's absolute devotion, had already done to him with apparent ease, almost with indifference.

Rereading the letter wasn't necessary. He knew the hateful words by heart. He folded it again, replaced it in its envelope and walked back out of the park to begin the ride home. It was night now and he disliked cycling in the dark with only the feeble lamp on his handlebars to light his way and alert any other traffic that he was there. But there was little of that. On his outward and homeward journeys he might meet or pass maybe one car. More frequent were the horse-drawn farm carts, but it was too late for them. He was alone in the dark, silent lanes, the birds long gone to roost, the cattle gone from the fields for the night. John thought, if only one big car – maybe that Imber car – would come too fast round that bend in the road and crash into him almost before its driver saw him. Such a welcome end to his trouble that would be.

A lamp was on in the little hall of No. 2 Bury Row, the front door was open and Maud was standing there waiting for him.

'You're so late, I thought something had happened to you.'

'What could have happened to me?' he asked, though he had been imagining only ten minutes before just what could have.

He was afraid she might ask him about Bertie's letter but apparently she had had one herself by the same post. Sybil had written to say that their father had had an 'apoplexy', the word people once used for what was now usually called a stroke. John Goodwin was at home, confined to bed, his face twisted and his voice hoarse but otherwise unimpaired. Would Maud please tell John, as he might like to come home and see his father?

She handed him Sybil's letter. 'They don't want me, you see.'

They sat down to their much-delayed 'tea', sausages and mash, which was John's and Hope's favourite. John knew it was his duty to go to Bristol, little as he wanted to. He realized that he had lost almost all affection for his parents. They seemed as far from him now, as remote, as that newly discovered planet called Pluto. Maud and Hope were much closer, little as he enjoyed the child's name for him, wincing each time she addressed him as Daddy. They were Mummy and Daddy, the loving couple with their seven-year-old daughter, the lie he had to live every day and increasingly hated.

'I'll go to Bristol,' he said to Maud as she served their second course, tinned peaches and condensed milk. 'But I have to go to London first. Please don't make your usual comments about a situation you don't understand. I shall go on Saturday, and the following week, when it's half-term, I'll go and see Father.'

She said nothing, perhaps afraid that she too might be expected to pay a visit to her parents. In silence she carried the dishes they had used out to the kitchen. John noticed for the first time what most men might not have noticed – was it because he was an 'invert'? – that she was wearing a new, smart jumper and new shoes with high heels. Clothes which no one would see but the other women meeting their children from school and which cost money they didn't have. He had almost given up hoping she would meet a man who might give her his name and a home. As for him, he planned next day to draw out of his Post Office savings account everything he had in it. Exactly why he couldn't have said.

Having sent a letter to Bertie saying that he would come up on Saturday, John decided to take the first London train. No reply had come, but he was used to that. Bertie only wrote when he wanted something, not when someone else did. The only letter on the doormat was addressed to him in Ethel's writing. She had not been in touch for perhaps two years, but she was evidently quite excited by no fewer than three pieces of news she had to impart: that their father was 'doing well', that their grandmother Halliwell had died aged eighty-eight and that she, Ethel, was expecting another child that, simpering, she described as 'maybe a sister for Tony'.

Maud resented Ethel's writing to John and not to her. What harm had she ever done to Ethel? Maud felt like writing to her sister and telling her that she would be less keen on writing to their brother, making him into a kind of substitute head of the family while their father was ill, if she knew the sorts of things he got up to with a man friend of his. Of course she didn't do that, more because she always remained a little afraid of John than through a softening of her attitude towards him. As angry people sometimes do, she took her resentment out on the person she lived with, and the evening before John left for London she was sullen with him, replying to the things he said in monosyllables, and finally, as they parted for the night at the top of the stairs, asking him why he bothered to come back if life with Bertie was so attractive to him.

John forbore from saying that if he didn't come back, what were she and Hope going to live on? He wrote to his mother, slept badly, got up at five because his bed and bedroom were so dreary, and, having posted his letter, was on his way to Exeter on the first bus. Alighting at Paddington, he recalled the hours he had spent in the waiting room there, a time made lovely in memory because Bertie had come and sat beside him and changed everything for the better. It was a fine day for November, the fog lifting and a mild sun breaking through. He walked up Eastbourne Terrace, asking himself what he was going to say to Bertie. What could you say to someone who intended either to impoverish you or else to destroy your life by heaping on you the worst disgrace known to society? The law used the expression 'gross indecency'. Putting it like that made John wince as he walked and squeeze his eyes shut as if it were Bertie he could see instead of the grim and sordid environs of Paddington station.

The real Bertie was there. John had feared he wouldn't be and that his whole journey might have been in vain. But his lover opened the front door to him and they went into the living room John had never before been in. A young woman was there, sweeping the floor.

Saying he hadn't expected John to come, instead of introducing her, Bertie said, 'Dot's living here now. She's got the first floor back.'

John could tell she was no candidate for his ever-watchful jealousy but just a tenant and occasional cleaner.

'God knows this place needs it,' Bertie said. 'Cut along now, Dot, there's a good girl. Chop, chop.'

She scuttled away and Bertie closed the door after her.

'Women who look like that,' he said with a laugh, 'make me glad I'm queer.'

Plunging straight into the middle of things, John said, 'I can't give you what you want, Bertie. I'm not the wealthy gentleman you seem to think. I can just about pay the rent and keep my sister and her child and that's it.'

'Why can't she work? There's always one thing a woman can do.'

It took John a moment or two to realize what he meant, an interpretation Bertie underlined by saying, 'Every woman's sitting on a fortune, is what my old dad used to say.'

John should have hit Bertie for that, he thought, for insulting his sister, but to do that he would have had to raise his hand and punch it into Bertie's jaw, and he knew his hand would have refused to obey his brain's instruction. He knew now, just from the few words they had exchanged, and from Bertie's coarse talk and repeated laughter, that to tell him of his hurt and the bitter pain the blackmailing letter had brought him would only be to court more mirth or sneering contempt. Yet as he looked at Bertie's beautiful face, the honest dark blue eyes, the gentle, even sweet expression and the curving lips he had loved to kiss, he felt the same enduring love for him as he had all those years ago when first they met in the pub in Formosa Street.

'Do you remember the Prince Alfred?' John said, meaning to say something quite different. 'Do you, Bertie? And how we sat by Paddington Basin and looked across at that island where Browning sat and wrote his poems?'

'Whoever he may be. What's the use of talking about that? You've come here to tell me you won't give me the money and I'm going to tell you that you know what I'll do if you don't, savvy?'

In answer, John pulled out of his coat pocket all the money he had withdrawn from his Post Office savings account and laid it on the dirty, pitted table, the pound notes and the ten-shilling notes, silver and copper coins, covering up the white rings left by hot dishes. As he did, he felt an enormous, almost virtuous sense of self-denial.

'I'll take back five bob,' he said. 'That'll buy us our dinner. The rest is yours.'

Bertie counted, seeming gratified by the sum. It was forty-two pounds, ten and ninepence, not quite all John had, because he had kept back, at No. 2 Bury Row, enough for the next week's house-keeping. 'That'll do for now,' Bertie said.

'It'll have to do for good.'

Shaking his head, Bertie said, 'You can spare a couple of quid a week out of your wages, or salary as you call it. Let's go. I'm getting thirsty.'

So first it was the pub called the Hero of Maida, both by common, though unspoken, consent avoiding the Prince Alfred, then going on to the enormous Crown, which some called Crocker's Folly. Today, mild and sunny now the mist was gone, the nearby canal was clear of green weed, its waters unruffled and calm. They walked along the towing path, watching the boats that were moored and the boats which passed, their hulls stacked with boxes and drums and coal sacks.

'Me and you could live on one of them boats.'

Probably Bertie wasn't serious. Boats were expensive, at least a hundred pounds, John thought, but the idea was wonderful, romantic, delightful – and impossible. He imagined the two of them looking after each other, cooking in the little galley such a boat would have, sitting side by side on deck appropriately enough in deckchairs, while on another passing boat someone was singing to a guitar.

Bertie broke into this absurd reverie. 'There's a caff over there where the boatmen go.' He turned to John, laughing. 'You know what? A lot of folks would say that a blackmailer, which is what you say I am, puts himself in danger walking on the riverbank with the bloke he's blackmailing.'

John stopped. 'What do you mean?'

'Come on, Johnny. You know. Me and you, you could murder me. Stop me speaking, savvy?'

Shaking his head, John said, 'You come on. Let's go to your café.'

Once again he had the feeling that Bertie had no idea of the depth of John's love for him. This theory of a blackmailee killing his blackmailer must have come out of one of the books Bertie read, shilling shockers with lurid covers of dead girls lying in pools of blood, only his were more like twopenny shockers. They went into the place called Teds Caff. One of the boatmen was still in his sou'wester, while his dog slept under the table between his feet. The waitress, a clean and decently dressed girl, took their order, Bertie's for pie and mash, John's for sausages, though he had no appetite and wondered if he could bring himself to take a bite out of one of these pallid objects lying on his plate in congealing brown gravy. John paid. When they came out on to the canal path once more Bertie wanted to go to another pub, but John stopped him, making him sit down on a wooden bench.

'You didn't really think I would harm you, did you?' This suggestion of Bertie's had been haunting John throughout the meal.

'You never could take a joke,' said Bertie sullenly.

'That you could be afraid of me, think I'd hurt you – it cuts me to the heart.'

'The way you go on, anyone'd think I was a girl.'

John said nothing. If two men couldn't love each other, be as close as he and Maud were supposed to be but weren't, his life was meaningless. It was pointless saying so. They began to walk once more, quite alone on the canal bank, the water still, a dull, cloudy yellow colour. Above the tall, rather sinister-looking, four-storey houses on the other side, the sky was broken into choppy clouds of varied grey. They walked along the stone coping of the waterway, passing the moored boat of the man with the dog. Its oars rested in their rowlocks. John stopped and stood to gaze at the pair of pink-footed geese that glided westwards. They reminded him of a Chinese poem he had once read about how when you see the geese flying north, if you must shoot, kill not one but both of them so that the pair will not be put asunder.

His reverie was interrupted. 'Well, which one of us is more likely to push the other one in? You or me? Why d'you think I'm standing well back? I wouldn't be where you are, with my toes hanging over the edge.'

With that, John felt a touch on his lower back and then a harder thrust as Bertie's hand pushed against his spine. He teetered on the brink, snatched at the air and fell. The water was dirty and cold. John floundered and gasped. He had tried to learn to swim when he was at school, but the lessons had for some reason stopped and he had never mastered the technique. He sank below the surface, seeing the canal bottom below him, seemingly yards below him, and cluttered with wood and metal waste. Kicking and splashing, he surfaced and cried to Bertie, 'Fetch an oar!' John was quite near the stone coping, but as he tried to grasp it, get some sort of purchase on it, his frozen hands slipped away from the granite and he sank once more.

He rose up again, his mouth and nose full of filthy water, gasping for breath. The paddle end of an oar touched the water and was pushed towards him. He tried to grab it, but as he did so, Bertie pulled it away, laughing.

'Bertie, please. I shall drown!'

Then, as if that was what he'd wanted, what he'd intended all the time, Bertie raised the oar a foot above John's head and shoved it hard against his forehead, thrusting him under the water. John knew that this time he would never come up again, all his strength was gone. Twice in the past he had imagined ways to die, had almost hoped to die. Once more his nose filled with water, then his mouth as he opened it uselessly to shout, and the icy liquid stifled and choked him. He was dimly aware of horror and of the yellow world turning black as he struggled, beating against this alien water, then he sank for the last time into the hopeless darkness.

Making sure that the old man with the dog was still in the café, Bertie put the oar back. He didn't know how to replace it in the rowlock so he threw it into the bottom of the boat. He began to walk back the way he and John had come. If he regretted anything it was that John's pocket had contained the coins he had kept back. The meal hadn't cost anything like five bob. Still, Bertie had the considerable sum of forty-two pounds, ten and ninepence John had given him.

John would be all right, Bertie told himself. He'd only given him a little tap with the oar. Swimming underwater for a few yards, he'd have come up by now, maybe gone back into the café to get dry and have a moan to Ted. If he caught a cold it served him right for talking to a bloke like he was a girl. It was more than embarrassing, Bertie thought, it was downright shame-making. He glanced back once and thought he could see a head above the water on the far side, but when he looked again he saw that it was only a child's ball, fallen from a passing boat.

The letter from a solicitor in Bristol told Maud that she had inherited five thousand pounds under her grandmother Mary Halliwell's will. Mrs Halliwell's house and the bulk of her fortune had gone to her children, including Maud's mother, with fifteen thousand to be divided equally between her three granddaughters. Nothing was to go to John. But that was not surprising, as she had always preferred the girls.

Maud could hardly believe it. She thought at first it was some sort of hoax. If John had been there she would have asked his opinion, but John still hadn't returned from his visit to London. He had taken her at her word, obviously, and stayed with that man Bertie. Daphne Crocker, Maud's neighbour at No. 4, was on the phone. Greatly daring, because she had hardly ever used one, Maud asked Daphne if she could make a long-distance call to Bristol. Daphne had to get through for her, but eventually Maud, reiterating her promise to pay Daphne, spoke to the solicitor and had her legacy confirmed.

'Ask for an advance on the money,' Daphne whispered. 'Ask him to send you a postal order.'

Maud did, and was told that would be no trouble.

'Oh, Daphne, I still can't quite believe it.'

'What will your husband say?'

Maud had told everyone that John was visiting his parents because his father was ill, and perhaps he was. 'He'll be thrilled. Of course he will.'

It was a large sum of money. She felt that it had saved her life. All she had was the money John had left behind when he went to London a fortnight before and since then she hadn't heard from him. Two letters had come for him, one of them with the name of the school on the envelope, the other she guessed, without knowing for sure, from the headmaster. Then Elspeth Dean had come. Was Mr Goodwin ill? Everyone was so worried.

Tired of prevaricating, Maud said, 'I don't know where he is. I don't know what's wrong. I'm as much in the dark as any of you.'

In her cape, her trailing coatee and long skirt, her long red hair loose about her shoulders like an extra cloak, Elspeth was unlike any other woman Maud knew. 'If you ever want someone to confide in, Mrs Goodwin, you can talk to me. You can trust me, you know.'

'I've nothing to confide.' Maud clamped her lips tight shut.

The truth was that she had too much to confide. Of course they would all think John had left his wife. Now she had the money, perhaps it would be best if they did think that. She would get sympathy and help. After all, she had never really liked the arrangement they had, it was all his idea and she had never been consulted. They were meant to be husband and wife, Mr and Mrs Goodwin, but she had often wondered how much of the truth Mrs Tremlett had guessed. That bed in the second bedroom, for instance. How often had Maud forgotten to make it look, on the days her neighbour came to clean, as if no one had slept in it? Sometimes, when calling at the village shop, she had had some strange looks from other women. One that she had been in the habit of passing the time of day with walked past her without a word. Perhaps now, if John stayed away, she could move out of here and take a nicer house in a nearby village – when, for instance, the time came for Hope to change schools.

The money came, and in the absence of John to advise her, she plucked up her courage to go into an Ashburton bank and open an account. The manager treated her with deference when he knew how much money she had to deposit with him. She called herself Mrs Goodwin, as she always had. Hope had begun asking when John was coming back. Maud could only tell the truth and say she didn't know. But she had begun to worry rather than accept, and so had Hope. Several times she came upon the child crying in her bedroom and could say nothing to reassure or comfort her. Lying awake at night, trying to think where John could possibly be if not with Bertie, she wondered if he could have had some sort of accident and, with nothing on him to show who he was, have died in a hospital or even in the street. She searched the room that had been his and found, not a letter from Bertie, but an address torn from the top of a letter. The backward-sloping handwriting was easily recognizable as his.

Not really expecting a reply, she wrote to him asking if John was with him. She had forgotten Bertie's surname and she felt awkward addressing him as Bertie instead of Mr something. But it hardly mattered. He might not even live at that address any more. His answer came two days later, almost by return of post. He addressed her as 'Mrs Goodwin' as if he really believed her to be John's wife. Apart from the handwriting and the grammatical errors, his letter might have come from a different person, not the Bertie she had met. He told her he hadn't seen John for more than a year and then only to have a cup of tea with him in a café. Nor had they 'corasponded'.

Maud decided to break her rule and go home to Bristol. Some word about John might have reached her parents rather than her. Well off and independent now, she understood that she could have taken Hope with her. Years had passed since her little girl had been rejected and surely she would now be purged of the taint of illegitimacy. But Maud was afraid to risk it. She left Hope with Gladys and her children, who were all friends of hers, and promised to be back next day. However she was received, they could put her up for one night. She wrote to her mother, leaving on the train on the day her letter would have got there.

Having money did not make Maud profligate but rather induced in her a degree of saving if not quite miserliness. She could have afforded to travel first class, but still she went third, as she and John had done when they escaped originally and came here. She had with her an overnight bag and a photograph of herself and Hope and Gillian Tranter taken in the Bury Row garden, 'on the off chance', as she put it to herself, of her mother's asking to see a picture of her granddaughter. Telling herself that she didn't care what they thought of her or how they received her, all she wanted was to know John's whereabouts, she had nevertheless dressed herself in her new red tweed costume, her coat with the fur collar and dark red court shoes. Let them see that she flourished and that their treatment of her hadn't beaten her down.

Her mother stared. She seemed hardly to know Maud, although the letter had arrived that morning.

'Well, here you are, then,' was all she said, opening the front door a little wider and stepping back for Maud to come in.

Sybil, who was not at work for some reason, kissed Maud and said she was pleased to see her; she asked why Maud hadn't brought 'the little girl'. Maud made no answer to that but accepted the tea Sybil made. Mary Goodwin had grown thin and looked ill. *They had all been ill*, Sybil said, all had severe flu, except Father, who was bad enough without that. She was still recovering from it and still off work.

'There's a lot of it about,' Sybil said. 'Quite an epidemic. Be careful you don't catch it. You won't want to give it to the little girl.'

'She has a name,' Maud said angrily.

'Hope, yes,' said her mother. 'I expect she will need it.'

Maud resolved not to lose her temper. She drank her tea, noting that she was offered nothing to eat.

'Now you're here you'd better come upstairs and see Father.'

Was she to break her rule of never speaking to him again?

He lay in bed, propped on three or four pillows, his face grey and drawn down on one side, the eye half closed, his mouth crooked and sagging open. From the opening a slimy trail of saliva dribbled.

Sybil wiped his face with a handkerchief and said in a theatrical whisper, 'It's no use talking to him. He doesn't speak.'

It was impossible to look at that face and the bewilderment in the one good eye without feeling pity. To end like that, how horrible . . .

Sybil suddenly bawled at him, 'All right, are you, Father? Nothing you want?'

Maud fancied that the distorted face winced, but it might have been her imagination.

'See you in a while, then,' Sybil yelled, and they went downstairs.

Mary Goodwin had prepared a meal while they were upstairs, a kind of cross between dinner and high tea, setting out pork pies, cold ham, sliced tomatoes and hot boiled potatoes on the dining-room table. Maud and Sybil sat down and their mother said grace. When she had finished asking the Lord to make them truly thankful, almost without taking a breath, Mary Goodwin said, 'I thought John might have come with you.'

Maud had her answer. But still she asked.

'We haven't seen him since goodness knows how long,' said Sybil. 'Mother had a letter saying he'd come and see Dad, but he never came.'

'Weeks ago, that was.' Their mother sniffed. 'He remembered my birthday last year but not this.'

'I don't know where he is,' Maud said. 'He's missing. He's disappeared.'

Her mother turned on her a look that seemed like hatred. 'He won't come here wherever he is. Thanks to you, he's cut himself off from his family. He's never even seen Ethel's children. He can spend his time and his money on your by-blow, but his legitimate nephew and niece might as well not exist.' With that, Mary pressed her napkin to her eyes and ran out of the room.

Maud realized there was no point in her staying longer. She kissed Sybil, who, though tactless, had always been nice to her and must lead a miserable existence in this house. As Maud was leaving, her sister said, 'Oh, by the way, I nearly forgot, Ronnie Clifford got married last week. She's a lady doctor. I was surprised.'

Maud wasn't surprised. He was bound to marry someone some time, and it plainly wasn't going to be her. But Sybil's words made her quickly forget the kindly feelings she had had towards her sister. 'I don't know what business it is of yours,' was her parting shot.

She walked to Temple Meads station and got on the train that was standing there, as if waiting for her. Clearly, John was missing,

John had disappeared. She asked herself what she should do, and with that thought came another. She was quite alone, had no one to turn to, no one to consult. Her mother plainly hated her; her father was nearer death than life; Sybil was useless. Anyone she told would also have to be told of the years of deception, that John was not her husband but her brother, not Hope's father but her uncle. Much as she liked Gladys and Daphne and Mrs Tremlett, she knew these people were not fit to advise her and, if they were told the truth, would turn against her.

Hope had her ninth birthday and a party, as was customary for little girls. Maud made her a dress out of white organdie but, as she remembered Mrs Imber's snub, without smocking. Would the Imbers help her? The memory of not only Mrs Imber's dismissal of her but also the older woman's refusal to let her daughter come and play with Hope was still with Maud, but since then Charmian, the Imbers' only girl, had died of tuberculosis and her mother, said to have been bowed down with grief, was a changed woman. Mr Imber, whom Maud had never met, might be prepared to give her advice, and both he and his wife, being so different from the village people, were less likely to be shocked and horrified when told of Maud and John's deception. One mild, damp day just after Christmas, she had even begun the walk along the footpath, past the church and up the drive to Dartcombe Hall, but when the house was in sight she lost her nerve and gave up. There must be someone among her acquaintances to whom she could confess the charade she and John had acted out for nearly ten years, but it wouldn't be anyone ranked so far above her as the Imbers. Oddly, her dislike of Alicia Imber increased from that day as if, instead of being innocent of any involvement in Maud's abortive quest, the chatelaine of Dartcombe Hall had turned her away from the house.

Hope continued to ask about John until Maud lost patience and told her not to speak of him again. There was no sign of him. By now he would have lost his job at the school, probably his chance of a pension one day. He must be dead. She thought quite suddenly of Elspeth Dean, who had offered her, if not a shoulder to cry on, an ear to listen to confessions. The spring term had just started. Maud was anxious, even if she was obliged to confess to weakness and shame and inadequacy, to look what she truly was now, rich and handsome. She dressed in the clothes she had worn for that wretched visit to her family, the red tweed suit, the coat with the fur collar and the red court shoes, took the bus to Ashburton and waited outside the school gates at half-past three.

The boys came out, one master, then another, then for five minutes no one. From John's description, Maud recognized the headmaster leaving, getting into his black Austin 7 that was parked just inside the gates. Everyone must have gone before Elspeth appeared, unmistakable in her green cloak and carrying her violin in its green leather case.

'Mrs Goodwin!'

Maud said nothing. She gave Elspeth her tight smile.

'What brings you here?'

'Would you please call me Maud?' was all Maud could find to say, but almost immediately words came to her, though not the words she had intended. 'My daughter will be coming out of school now. A friend is going to meet her and keep her till I come back. If we go to a café and have a cup of tea will you let me talk to you?'

'Of course. But wouldn't it be better if I came back to your house with you and we talked there?'

'Would you do that?'

'Come on. I know the Dartcombe bus times and there's one due in just ten minutes.'

They waited for it at the stop. 'I think that when I talk to you,' Maud said hesitantly, 'you may be very shocked and – well, disgusted with me. And with John. I've decided that if I'm going to talk to anyone – well, you – I must tell everything and not keep anything back. I thought I should warn you of this, so that if you think you wouldn't want to get involved because you're – well, a single woman who may not know that such things go on – oh, I don't know, but I'm just trying not to get you sort of entangled in shocking things.'

Elspeth was laughing, shaking her head and laughing so that her red hair flew out and crackled as Maud had heard such hair does.

'You don't know me, Maud, but I hope you soon will. Now here comes our bus.'

Sitting at the very back of the bus with Maud next to the window, Elspeth began to show Maud how to know her better. 'I did my training in London. I was in the music school there, thinking I could become a concert violinist, but perhaps I wasn't quite good enough for that. I had a little flat in Chelsea, a walk-up with a tiny kitchen and sharing a bathroom with four others. Somehow I gathered a lot of friends about me. We were a bohemian crowd, I'm sure you know what that means. We were musicians and actors and artists, none of us very successful, none of us well off and none of us conventional.

'On the floor below me lived two young men who were lovers. I can see by your face you know what I mean. They called themselves queer, but some people called them Uranians and some inverts. There were several couples and they lived together but they weren't married. I had someone I lived with, but we need not go into that now. It's enough to say that it didn't work out and in the end he left me. I had a little money but it was running out. I managed to get a job playing my violin in a big department store, but the truth is I couldn't bear it. I couldn't bear sitting there playing Tchaikovsky and Mozart on my violin while people laughed and chatted as if I wasn't there.

'I'm talking too much. You don't want to hear all this. I've explained the essential things, why you shouldn't mind telling me things. You won't find I'm easily shocked.'

'Why did you leave London?'

'There was nothing for me to do there and no one I much minded leaving behind. My lover was gone. I applied to various schools in the country and got this one, teaching music to boys. They're very nice to me and I love it.'

Turning to face her, Maud understood that she now saw Elspeth in a new light. Until ten minutes ago she had seen her draperies as ridiculous, her long hair Gypsyish, but now she saw a beautiful face, green eyes that were unlike the way she had used to view them, as cat-like, sharp and untrustworthy. Elspeth's eyes were soft and kind.

'I will fetch Hope,' Maud said, 'and then we'll have tea and talk.'

Maud had intended to hold back certain parts of her story. John's relations with Bertie – and possibly with others – surely there was no need to tell all that. Nor was there any need to mention her sister Ethel's refusal to know her, or Ronnie Clifford's treatment of her as if she were a street woman he had picked up somewhere. His marriage to the 'lady doctor' might be kept secret. But at some point in Elspeth's description of her London life, her absolute acceptance of what Maud's parents called 'living in sin' and of the two young men as lovers, Maud decided that if she talked she must tell everything. Anything else would be useless and a kind of insult to Elspeth.

All this thinking, something Maud was unused to, gave her a headache, and once she had made the tea, set out a big home-made ginger cake on the table and opened a new tin of Huntley & Palmers biscuits, she swallowed two aspirins. Having met Elspeth before, Hope talked to her with little sign of shyness while both of them ate large slices of cake. John wasn't mentioned in front of the child. Maureen Crocker, Daphne's daughter, was coming over to play and the two girls went up into Hope's bedroom. Maud was so certain that John, for some reason, was never coming back that she had given his room to Hope.

A dark blush mounted on her face as she began telling Elspeth the history of her life and John's from the day she'd first started walking home with Ronnie. Her face felt so hot that she put her unaccountably cold hands up to it. A fire blazed in the grate but she was still cold.

'Take it slowly,' Elspeth said. 'I think you're not used to talking about yourself.'

It was true. Maud had hardly ever done so, and never to her

mother, whom she now saw as the natural recipient for the confidences of a young girl. She warmed even more to Elspeth, but still couldn't bring herself to say much about what had happened between her and Ronnie. But she could tell of the discovery of her pregnancy, of her *mother's* discovery of it, of her parents' plan to put her into a Methodist home for unmarried mothers. As she began to tell of John's sacrifice to take care of her and to provide her and Hope with a home, she saw for the first time what he had tried to give up for her and, in failing, what he had lost.

'He brought this man here,' Maud said. 'They slept together.' The blush was beginning again. 'I didn't want it, but I couldn't stop him. I'm sure this must shock you, considering John wasn't a stranger.'

'Oh, I knew about him. I've always known.'

'You can't have!'

'I really did. I could tell. Don't look like that, Maud. That I knew doesn't mean anyone else could, and I'm sure they didn't. That's why I used to wonder why he'd got married. I didn't know you were brother and sister then, remember. It made me want to get to know you both better, but you rather froze me out. I understand that now too.'

Maud told her the rest. She was suddenly tired but her headache was gone. She looked down at her clothes, the tight, short skirt, the stiff tailoring like the garments of a secretary or a typist, she thought, the shoes of too bright a colour and too high heels. Whom was she trying to impress? All that must soon be over and a hard time coming.

'What am I to do?' she said.

'I think we must go to the police. Do you have a police house in the village?' Maud nodded. 'It will all come out now, I'm afraid. I'd say "your secret" except that that sounds a bid melodramatic. You see, John may be lying dead somewhere with no one knowing who he is or what's happened to him.'

'I thought of that.'

'There's no time like the present. Is it far?'

'Just down the road and in the next street. Must I do it now? What about Hope?'

'Ask a neighbour to keep an eye on her and the other child.'

Elspeth seemed slightly amused by Maud's change of dress, smiling but in a kindly way when she came downstairs in an obviously home-made frock and lace-up shoes, her face a picture of fear yet with a new determination.

'"We who are about to die salute you,"' said Elspeth. 'Come along. You'll feel better when it's over.'

So Maud, trembling all over, both hands clenched on the strap of her bag, went to PC Joseph Truscott's house, interrupted him at tea with his wife and sons, and told him John Goodwin was missing, had been missing for nearly two months. She told him too, the tears falling from her eyes, that he was not her husband but her brother, leaving out, on Elspeth's instructions, any mention of what Maud called, to herself but not to him or Elspeth, his taste for activities of 'gross indecency'.

PC Truscott thanked her in his slow and stolid way. He would 'let them in London know'. She should be let know if anything came of it. No surprise was shown, though Elspeth felt great haste was shown in hurrying them off the premises. She thought but didn't say to Maud that the moment they were out of sight Truscott would be sharing all this information with his fascinated wife. How long before the whole village knew?

20

Since first she came to Dartcombe Maud's had been a sheltered life. She had never realized this herself. The painful incidents in it, Mrs Imber's rebuffs, Bertie's visit, Rosemary's and Sybil's visits, stayed with her, festering. There they would be for ever. They were high spots in her existence, if high spots can be bad and troubling. But this interview with PC Truscott surpassed everything. It seemed to her that she had been obliged to tell him things no one should ever know and which would ruin for ever her reputation and her life in the little world she had made for herself.

Weeping bitterly when they were home again, she sobbed to Elspeth that she couldn't be alone here in Bury Row with these terrible revelations – as she put it – hanging over her. Elspeth's promise that things would be better once Maud had confessed to the policeman couldn't have been further from the truth. She felt worse now than she had when she'd found out she was pregnant with Hope. This was the worst day of her life and she blamed John for it.

The hesitation was momentary. 'I'll stay. Of course I will. You'll have to lend me a nightgown and a toothbrush.'

Maud threw her arms around Elspeth's neck. Then, a changed woman, her tears dried, Maud went to cook something for supper. When John left all those weeks ago, he had taken his toothbrush with him, so Maud gave Elspeth hers, first carefully boiling it in a pan of water. She offered to give Elspeth her bed, but this was refused in favour of the green velvet sofa in front of the dying fire. Hope was enthralled by Elspeth, her long red hair, which the little girl was allowed to plait, her cape and the contents of her handbag, combined comb and brush, a lipstick called Tangee, which looked transparent in its case but turned red on the lips, photographs of their new guest's mother and brother and sister. For the first time, Hope forgot John and failed to ask when he was coming back.

Nor did Mrs Tremlett ask when she came in the following morning to see if everything was all right – it was so unlike Maud to go out in the evening leaving Hope with her.

'Quite all right,' Maud said, understanding that even if the news was bound to circulate in Dartcombe it hadn't yet reached her neighbour.

The sofa was still disarranged with blanket and eiderdown. Elspeth had gone into the kitchen to wash. 'An overnight visitor, I see,' Mrs Tremlett said.

'Just a friend from John's school.' As soon as the words were out Maud wondered if she had said too much, but Mrs Tremlett seemed to accept it without question.

The milk no longer arrived in a jug from the churn but in bottles. Maud hesitated before going out of the front door to fetch it. No one was about in Bury Row when she picked up the single milk bottle, but as she returned Daphne Crocker came out of No. 4, looked her in the eyes and turned back, slamming the door behind her. It had begun.

'Don't leave me,' Maud said again when Elspeth came out of the kitchen in Maud's dressing gown.

'I must. I'll go back to Ashburton and fetch some things – including a toothbrush. When I've locked up I'll come straight back and I'll fetch the shopping so you won't have to go out if you don't want to.'

'I shall never want to again,' said Maud dolefully.

'All right, but I shall have to go back to school. It won't be as bad as you think. You've made a great drama out of it, but these people are only ordinary country people. They're not fiends, they're not witch-hunters. Maybe some of them will turn their backs on you, but does that matter so much? My mother says you need to have a broad back in this world.'

'Only I haven't,' said Maud, not liking to be told she had made a drama, as if taking things seriously hadn't been justified.

Elspeth brought clothes to change into, but less than half the number Maud would have packed for herself. Elspeth did the shopping by herself, took Hope to school, though the child was quite old enough to go on her own, saw the policeman again and managed to get him to tell her that a body had been found, a man had drowned in a canal in London. More than that he wouldn't divulge, saying he would prefer to tell anything that had to be told to Maud herself. But Maud didn't want to speak to him, didn't want to listen to what he might have to say. She received some curious looks from neighbours, and women who had passed the time of day with her in the past no longer spoke. Two days later Elspeth went back to Ashburton, but with many promises to return at any time Maud might want her.

Plucking up her courage required the sort of effort of will Maud had never been good at. But one fine morning in early spring, when the garden and the lane were growing green and the blackthorn had burst into its tiny white flowers, the weather raised her spirits, as it does everyone's. She would go out. If she met a neighbour who turned away from her, she would plant herself in front of the woman and force her to listen while she explained. Mrs Tremlett hadn't been near her since she commented on Maud's overnight visitor; Gladys followed her mother's example in everything, so she too hadn't been seen. Mrs Paine in the village shop was coldly polite to Maud but that was all, and after a single visit Maud hadn't gone there again. But now she felt that everything could be explained, and she would do it even if it meant confessing Hope's illegitimacy. Maud still had to learn that while to resolve is easy, to enact that resolution takes rehearsal and practice and the kind of will she didn't possess.

John was probably dead. He was very likely the drowned man they had pulled out of the canal. She didn't know and didn't want to know. She asked herself if she felt any sorrow for her brother and told herself she didn't. He had forfeited any grieving for him she might have had by his shameful behaviour. Now she had money she could forget him, begin again with Hope, perhaps in a new place. Then, after Elspeth had been gone a fortnight and Maud had managed to avoid seeing the looks she got in the street and being ignored, another letter came with a Bristol postmark. This time, though, the address was in Ethel's handwriting.

She remembered the only other time Ethel had written, and that was to John. *Dear Maud . . .* How strange that people always began letters like that; even when they would never call you 'dear' to your face, even when they had never met you, were writing a business letter or one that held a series of insults. You were always 'dear' to correspondents.

Father has asked me to write to you and tell you what follows. As you must understand, he is unable to perform this task himself. The police came to Mother and Father and then to us to tell us about the truly horrible discovery they made in a canal in London. Someone was needed for the dreadful task of identifying the body they found. Father could not possibly do such a thing so they asked my husband. Being a very courageous and resolute man, Herbert agreed.

He has just returned from London, where he looked at the remains and identified them as our brother, John. Herbert may have to go back to attend the inquest. This is involving us in great expense. I must say I think that if you had reported John missing earlier than you did and had gone to London to see the body yourself you would have saved your sister and brother-in-law, apart from the financial consideration, a great deal of pain that will endure for a long time.

You should realize that your expenses are minimal. You are now a rich woman with no one but yourself to spend your money on. Living in the country has not changed you, Maud. You are the same childlike creature you were when you ran away and broke Father's heart all those years ago.

Your affectionate sister,
Ethel

Maud was learning that the widely held belief that the people whose judgement you don't value can't hurt you is not true, or not true in her case. Ethel's censure caused Maud disproportionate distress. She was particularly indignant at the suggestion she was living on her own, as if Hope had never been born or should be treated as non-existent.

Instead of going out as she had planned, Maud went back to bed. It was the start of a habit of a retreat from life, escaping from trouble into oblivion. Although she had slept well the night before, she fell asleep almost immediately and was still asleep when Hope came home from school at half-past three, and when she opened Maud's bedroom door she worried that her mother must be ill. Maud got up and scolded her for making a fuss. Hope had given few signs that things had changed for her since the man who might have been her father or else her uncle had disappeared. She had become a much quieter child who was pleasant and affectionate to her mother, but noticeably never confided in her. How she might be getting on at school, what she was learning, who her friends were apart from George Tranter and Maureen Crocker, Maud was told nothing about. So the abusive epithet must have gone deep with Hope for her to ask that evening, 'What's a bastard, Mummy? Trevor Pratt called me a bastard.'

Maud burst into tears. Instead of explaining, all she could say was, 'It's just a bad word, Hope. You don't have to know what it means.'

But the insult to her daughter decided her. They must leave Dartcombe. She must rent or even buy a house in Ashburton or another village. She decided she would be incapable of doing this herself, but Elspeth could do it for her. Elspeth had said she would return any time she was wanted, and she was wanted now. She could find estate agents (or whatever they were called), she could write to removal people – wasn't there a firm called Pickford's? Elspeth would know – she could advise her on what needed to be bought for the new house. She would see about Hope's leaving the village school here. Elspeth could be to her what John had been and could now no longer be.

The spring term was halfway through for Elspeth. Maud wrote to her, begging her to come. Maud's own needs had become paramount to her. Perhaps they had always been. That Elspeth might have a life of her own, with friends and occupations of her own, hardly occurred to Maud, but Elspeth recognized Maud's helplessness. One of the worst things that could happen to a young girl had happened to her, but having a child without a husband, instead of strengthening her, had made her more dependent on others. When Elspeth arrived in Bury Row on the Friday afternoon, she found Maud in bed, with Hope sitting beside her and a tray of tea things on the eiderdown between them.

Now her friend had come, Maud said she would get up, but getting up didn't mean putting on clothes and she came downstairs in her dressing gown. Maud soon made it clear to Elspeth that she intended to do nothing towards finding and buying a house except paying for it, nothing towards furnishing it or choosing it somewhere convenient for the school Hope would go to after (and if) she had passed the entrance exam taken at the age of eleven. These were to be Elspeth's jobs. Maud complained about suffering from that invisible and unprovable illness, recurrent headaches, but when a visit to the doctor was suggested she said it was well known that nothing could be done to cure migraines.

Elspeth had long thought it strange that Maud possessed no wireless. Electricity had come to Dartcombe three years before and central lights hung in all the rooms. But the only way for national and international news to come into the house was by a newspaper bought in the village shop, where Maud no longer went. Elspeth's own wireless was too cumbersome to be brought with her. She suggested that having this now nearly indispensable adjunct to a household might improve Maud's quality of life, even restore her happiness, and Maud rather reluctantly agreed. Elspeth went into Ashburton the next day and bought a wireless in a veneered wood-grain case which the shopkeeper delivered that afternoon. She also visited an estate agent, listing her friend's requirements: a house, not a cottage, a big garden, at least three bedrooms. Maud had no idea how much she should pay, and knowing the amount she had inherited and invested, Elspeth suggested she could afford up to four hundred pounds.

If Maud gave much thought to poor dead John, she said nothing about him to Elspeth. He was gone and she had forgotten him. Elspeth thought that now Maud had money of her own, John's value in her life as a provider was in the past and whatever affection she had had for him when first they lived together, all that was over now. She never spoke of him, but Elspeth believed that he was there in the back of her mind as a vague threat, someone who, beyond death, might yet affect her through the kind of life he had led.

It was a cold, wet spring, a horrible April. But Elspeth had found a house for Maud, and Maud, persuaded to visit it, liked what she saw and agreed to the price of three hundred and seventy-five pounds. The house was mid-Victorian, red brick, double-fronted with a slate roof. The garden was walled with fruit trees and shrubs but no flowers except when Maud first saw it, when the trees were a mass of white and pink blossoms swept by gales and rain. It belonged to a man of about forty who lived in a fine Georgian house on the edge of Ottery St Jude and owned several properties in the village.

Elspeth had come to stay over Easter and Maud took it for granted she would be with her every weekend. In the evenings the two women listened to the wireless and heard about the war in Spain and the prospect of a war with Germany. Maud had never before taken any interest in international events, but Elspeth was politically minded and took the side of the Republicans while Maud favoured Franco. But even this was a departure for Maud, who barely knew that England had had three kings in one year in 1936 or that Edward VIII had abdicated.

It was Elspeth who had to tell Mrs Tremlett that Maud wished to terminate her tenancy. Such news as hers couldn't be kept secret for more than a day or two in a village such as Dartcombe, and Maud's neighbour already knew that she and Hope would be leaving.

'I know most of the people here have it in for her, but I have never been like that,' said Mrs Tremlett. 'Poor thing, she was only a child when she had a child.'

Gratified, Elspeth hastened to tell Maud of these kind words, but Maud only said that how she lived was no business of her neighbours and Elspeth should wait and see when Mrs Tremlett tried to charge her for damage to the interior of No. 2 Bury Row.

'You haven't damaged it, have you?'

'Of course I haven't, but you try telling them that.'

But other residents of Bury Row no longer acknowledged Maud's existence and shut themselves up in their houses when the Pickford's van came to take the furniture to Ottery St Jude. On their first evening in The Larches the man who had sold Maud the house walked up from River House, bringing with him a bottle of champagne, something Maud had never before tasted and Elspeth had tried only once. He told the two women he was a writer of fiction and a journalist who wrote for the *News Chronicle*. Elspeth asked him if he thought war was coming and, if so, whether they would be safe in the Devon countryside.

'I think the Germans will bomb Plymouth,' Gabriel Harding said. 'It will be an important target for them because of the dockyard. But I'm sure you'll be safe here, though we may all get refugees – if that's the word – from Plymouth taking shelter with us.'

Maud seemed horrified at the prospect, and Elspeth noted their visitor's tolerant yet amused eyes on her. After he had gone they went back to tidying up, making beds and putting away kitchen utensils and the food they had brought. While Maud was spreading the new pink eiderdown on her double bed – she had passed the old one on to the spare bed – she asked Elspeth if she would give up her tiny, two-room flat in Ashburton and come to live with her. Remembering her friends in the town, a man who was becoming more than a friend, her job and the five-mile distance from Ottery St Jude, Elspeth said she would think about it. In bed that night, just before sleep came, she thought about the writer, a widower as she had learned, a comfortably off, nice-looking man. Had that glance he gave Maud meant not that he believed her ignorant and selfish but rather that he admired her? Certainly, she was a beautiful woman. If he was looking for a wife . . . But Elspeth fell asleep.

When school, for both Elspeth and Hope, broke up at the end of July, the former had still not made up her mind whether to accept Maud's invitation. In some ways it was attractive. Elspeth would pay her way, but Maud had by now told her repeatedly that she wouldn't want rent for the two or three rooms she would put at her friend's disposal. Maud also suggested that she might buy a car. Both could drive it and Elspeth could use it to go to school.

'Like the headmaster,' said Maud, as if this would be a temptation.

What would happen to her, Elspeth wondered, if their new neighbour – he had asked them to call him Guy, as everyone did – fell in love with Maud, if he hadn't already fallen in love with Maud, married her and took her and Hope to live with him at River House? Elspeth would be without a home and with no means of getting one. Guy was a frequent caller at The Larches. He brought them fruit, strawberries and raspberries and redcurrants, from his kitchen garden. He had his own pew in St Jude's Church and asked them to use it, which Maud sometimes did with Hope. Elspeth, an atheist who called herself a humanist, said she attended enough assemblies at school without the need to do so on Sundays, and Maud and Hope were welcomed on their own. This only confirmed Elspeth's belief that Guy was choosing Maud for the second Mrs Harding.

In August, when Elspeth had been staying for three weeks at The Larches, something happened which changed all that. A note addressed to 'Miss Elspeth Dean' was put through the letter box early in the morning, before either woman was up. Hope found it and laid it beside Elspeth's plate on the breakfast table. The postmark was noted, and Elspeth wondered who in Ottery St Jude, where she knew hardly anyone, could be writing to her. She knew by now Maud was not much interested in other people. After watching Elspeth open the envelope, Maud, indifferent, went out to the kitchen to make a fresh pot of tea. Guy had written:

Dear Miss Dean

I have two tickets for a concert of Mozart and Vivaldi in Torquay on the evening of Saturday week. It would give me much pleasure if you would accompany me to Torquay. The concert begins at seven p.m. If you do me the honour of accepting we would leave here at five-thirty and I would call for you in my car.

Apart from business communications in respect of job interviews, it was the most formal letter Elspeth had ever received. Her first question to herself was, Why had he chosen her over Maud? Only, surely, because he knew she was a music teacher and the function was a concert. Her second, whispered in front of the mirror in the bedroom, was, Why do you make so little of yourself? She undid the chignon on the back of her head and let the mass of red hair fall about her shoulders. The man in Ashburton she supposed she would marry one day, a teacher like herself but in a different school, disliked the colour and preferred her to wear a hat. So might this man, she thought. What did it matter?

She put off telling Maud, then thought how cowardly she was being and came straight out with it.

'I wonder why he's asked you,' Maud said. 'He could have anyone. Good-looking, plenty of money, that house, he's quite a catch.'

'He's asked me to a concert, Maud, not to marry him.'

'Goodness, no. I should think not.'

'Anyway, I shan't go.'

His car was a black Armstrong-Siddeley with comfortable leather seats. Being driven anywhere in a car was a treat to Elspeth. They glided smoothly along the narrow lanes, where the hedges in August were overhung with wild clematis and the reddening berries of the wayfaring tree, while Guy asked her about her music, the instrument she played, her pupils, her favourite composers. When the sea came into view in a steep V between the hills they stopped for a while and Guy said it always reminded him of the Amalfi Coast and was just as beautiful. Elspeth said she had never been abroad, then wished she hadn't said it because it sounded like angling for an invitation – as if such a thing were possible.

Vivaldi's *Four Seasons* came first, the Mozart being saved up for after the interval, and because it was warm, even after sunset, they walked out on to a broad balcony from which the sea could again be seen. Guy saw someone he knew and introduced her to Elspeth as Alicia Imber, a friend of his. Elspeth immediately recognized the name as that of a woman who had been rude and patronizing to Maud, or so Maud said. But Alicia was charming to Elspeth and said she hoped to see her again, though Elspeth found it embarrassing when Alicia said Guy must bring her over to Dartcombe Hall for tea.

'She's a good friend of mine,' he said to Elspeth when they went back into the concert hall. 'A widow now. Her husband was the dearest man. She has two sons, Christian and Julian, and she had a daughter called Charmian. The poor child died of tuberculosis.'

'Some say that's the worst thing that can happen to anyone,' said Elspeth, 'to lose a child.'

'I can believe it.' He hesitated. 'Would you come with me if I drove over there one day? I know how much Alicia would like it.'

Elspeth felt she was blushing but she managed to speak firmly. 'Of course. I'd like to.'

The Mozart transported Elspeth. It was rare for her to hear live music apart from that which she – sometimes with the school orchestra – made herself. She was aware of her companion's eyes once or twice turned to her face, appreciating perhaps her rapt expression. On the return journey she found herself, perhaps too effusively, she thought, thanking him over and over for the concert, but he seemed to like her enthusiasm.

Next day, persuading herself that her decision had nothing to do with Guy and the concert and his invitation to a small party he was giving on the following Wednesday, she told Maud that she would give up her flat in Ashburton and come to live at The Larches.

21

War was averted for just a year, though how short the postponement would be had not been known or even imagined when Neville Chamberlain had returned in triumph from Munich in September 1938. He carried with him a sheet of paper signed by Hitler and expressing the wish that the English and the Germans were 'never to go to war again'. All over the country the usually phlegmatic English gathered in the streets, cheering and dancing, drinking and congratulating each other. At River House in Ottery St Jude, Guy's housekeeper, Mrs Grendon, had asked him if he planned to have a party, but he said celebrations were premature. Hitler was not to be trusted, and after Czechoslovakia, who knew which country he would invade next?

If the residents of Ottery St Jude knew that Maud had never been married and Hope was illegitimate, no attempt was apparently made to ostracize her. Not then. Not yet. Maybe they accepted her because of the frequency with which Guy visited The Larches, giving as it were his seal of approval to the woman who had bought the house from him. Another reason was possibly that she was known to be well off, in possession of a private income derived from an inheritance. Unmarried mothers with nameless children were usually poor, obliged to work at menial jobs such as a maid or charwoman. Not that Maud made friends in the village. She was thought to be stand-offish with airs above her station.

Elspeth's decision to move into The Larches, and before the autumn term began, was what Maud had wanted, and if she failed to greet the news with an outburst of delight, this was probably because she never showed much enthusiasm for anything. Going to bed for the day was becoming, if not a habit, an indulgence of hers when anything even mildly unpleasant happened, even rain falling in the morning. For all that, her already handsome looks improved as her twenties progressed, and she was even better-dressed now she could afford more expensive clothes. Her neighbours stared when she walked to the post office in a smart tailored suit with a fox fur and a pillbox hat, while Elspeth continued to dress in a jumper and skirt and the only coat she possessed. But Maud believed that men are attracted by smart clothes. While John was alive she could never think of marrying because she was supposed to be married to him. She could never think of being appealing to men because she was a married woman. Things were different now. She had no wish to be married, but she would have liked men to want to marry her.

She appeared not to notice the friendship or something more that was growing between Guy and Elspeth. Plainly, she rather disliked Guy, whom she continued to call by his surname in spite of being asked not to. Yet Elspeth noticed – she doubted if Guy did – that Maud dressed with the greatest care in her newest garments when he was expected to call, even going to the village hairdresser that morning. Elspeth was aware too, much to her dismay, that Maud believed Guy was attracted to her, was perhaps in love with her, even when he called to take her friend out. Maud even explained that these outings were all to musical events (though they were not) because music bored her while Elspeth liked it and indeed taught it.

'I told him I'd fall asleep if I had to sit through a – what's it called? An oratorio, is it?' Maud told Elspeth.

She and Guy had been to hear *Messiah* in Exeter Cathedral, a source of wonder to Maud. Christmas came and this time Guy did have a party. Maud refused to go, saying she had always hated the season and longed to have a quiet time at home by herself. And 'by herself', increasingly frequent, seemed less and less to include Hope. Elspeth took Hope to the party, where she met the Imber boys, Julian, who had just started at Oxford, and Christian, who was home for the holidays from Stowe. When Maud heard that Alicia Imber had been there she was furious.

'Don't think you can bring that woman here,' she shouted at

Elspeth. 'You don't know how she insulted me.' Elspeth had been told many times. 'My daughter wasn't good enough for that child of hers who died, that Charmian, if you've ever heard such a ridiculous name.'

Elspeth said quietly that she wouldn't dream of bringing anyone to The Larches without asking Maud first. 'It's your house, Maud.'

'I'm glad you realize that.'

Elspeth took the bus into Ashburton every weekday morning and sometimes back again. But Guy had begun meeting her in the Armstrong-Siddeley after school and, instead of dropping her at Maud's gate, driving her back to River House or taking her out to dinner. Maud seemed to have no objection to Elspeth's going out two or three evenings a week, and Elspeth wondered why Maud had wanted her to share the house. An efficient daily woman called Mrs Newcombe kept The Larches clean, did all the washing and ironing, and even cooked if Maud had taken to her bed. But she seldom spoke and, when she did, offered no opinions. She never seemed to gossip. Hope often spent the evenings in her mother's bedroom, doing her homework and listening with Maud to the wireless. The newspapers carried frightening stories about 'storm clouds gathering over Europe', and extracts from Hitler's rants, but the BBC's broadcasts were anodyne, avoiding European news. Maud enjoyed the comedians and the serials.

One Saturday evening in April – it was Guy's forty-second birthday – he and Elspeth drove over to Dartcombe to have tea with Alicia Imber. Elspeth expected to be taken back to The Larches, but instead Guy drove her up to River House, asking her if she remembered the champagne he had brought over when Maud moved into her new home. Of course she did. Elspeth thought she remembered every occasion spent with Guy.

'I'm hoping you and I are going to have another bottle tonight,' he said.

'You're hoping? You mean you're going to have to buy it or find where it is?'

He laughed. 'I mean the circumstances may not be propitious but I'm hoping they will be.'

She had to be content with that. As to the circumstances, she had no idea what they might be. At River House they went into the drawing room, where, to her astonishment, he went down on one knee (with ease) and said, 'Elspeth Dean, I love you very much. Will you marry me?'

She was surprised but not stunned or made awkward. She had never dared allow herself to hope for this but she didn't hesitate. 'I will. I love you too. I think I have from the start.'

He had held her hand but never kissed her before. It was a very satisfactory kiss. The champagne then appeared. Guy was the only person she knew who possessed a refrigerator and the bottle was ice-cold, frosted with water drops. Mrs Grendon, the housekeeper, was called in, and Susan, the little maid-of-all-work, to share it.

'To celebrate my engagement,' Guy said, raising his glass, his other arm round Elspeth's waist. 'Miss Dean has done me the honour of promising to be my wife.'

Until she became engaged to him Elspeth had read only one of Guy's books, and that from the Ashburton public library before she had even met him. She had enjoyed it but could not find any more of his work and had never been able to bring herself to ask. When he drove her home that evening she took with her all the remaining five, signed by him and inscribed to 'my beloved Elspeth'.

Maud had to be told. Priding herself on knowing the unwisdom of putting off the evil day, for she was sure that it would be an evil day, Elspeth nevertheless waited until she and Maud were alone and Hope had gone to see the newborn puppies at Greystock's farm.

Turning round slowly to face Elspeth, Maud said, 'You mean he has proposed to you?'

'Yes, he has. Of course I mean that.'

'But why?'

Not knowing how to answer, Elspeth said something very unlike her: 'What a question, Maud.'

'I don't suppose it will come to anything,' Maud said, as if Elspeth had spoken of some holiday planned for the distant future.

Maud made no comment on the diamond which appeared on the third finger of Elspeth's hand in the following week and grew quiet when Guy called to take Elspeth out and invited Maud to congratulate him. She said, 'Congratulations,' in an ungracious way and was waiting up for her friend when she was brought home at eleven that night.

'I can't understand why you came to live here with me if you were going to go away the moment some man asked you.'

'Not "some man", Maud. Please don't say that.'

Maud began to cry and sobbed even more when Elspeth sat beside her and took her in her arms. She clung to Elspeth, whimpering that it wasn't fair to leave her alone in this place where she knew no one.

'You know me,' Elspeth said. 'I'll be living less than half a mile away. We shall see each other all the time.'

Maud spent the next day in bed, saying she felt unwell. Going upstairs to see how she was, Elspeth was told Maud wanted to know nothing about the wedding, when or where it was to be, because she had no intention of attending. In her opinion, Elspeth had treated her badly, pretending to come here as a companion to Maud while in fact bent only on catching a husband. Elspeth managed neither to take offence nor to produce excuses, but said only that Maud would feel differently when she got used to her friend's changed status.

Elspeth and Guy were married in St Jude's Church in the beginning of June 1939. Only Guy's sister, Patricia, her husband, Alicia Imber and two friends of Elspeth's from Ashburton were present. After lunch at River House they left to spend their wedding night in Weymouth. That evening after dinner, feeling like Tess of the d'Urbervilles, Elspeth told her husband she wasn't a virgin.

Unlike Angel Clare, Guy started laughing. 'Funny you should say that, because nor am I.'

Her lover – the only one – had been a musician she had met while studying in London. Thinking she should tell Guy about him, she began rather hesitantly, but her husband said she 'really need not' as it wasn't his business and anyway it was a long time ago.

Next morning they took the ferry to St Malo and three trains across Europe for their honeymoon on the Amalfi Coast.

True to her word, Maud had failed to attend the wedding, and she stopped Hope going. The first postcard that came from Elspeth Maud put into the coke boiler unread, but by the arrival of the second one she was so miserable and sorry for herself that she read it and wept over it. Elspeth had written that instead of remaining away for a month they were returning early in spite of having 'such a blissful time'. The coast was the most beautiful place she had ever seen, the sun shone all day and at night the sky was full of stars, but in other ways Fascist Italy was uncomfortable, and if war was coming their place was in England. If they delayed they might not be able to get back. Maud decided she would give Elspeth and Guy the cold shoulder in a dignified way but would gradually 'come round'. They should see that she was not angry but hurt by what they had done, which she now saw as purposeful deceit.

Maud began counting the events in her life which she calculated had soured her and made her what she now was, a sullen woman with a huge share of self-pity. It had begun of course with the conception, then the birth, of Hope. Next had come John's horrible and ugly ideas of what constituted happiness for him; then his disappearance and death; and lastly the tendency of everyone, it seemed, to desert and abandon her. Even her daughter, once the dearest person in the world to her, was showing in her eyes more affection for Elspeth and her husband than for Maud.

Evacuation from London and the other big cities was not confined to schoolchildren and their mothers. Between the end of June and the beginning of September 3.5 million people moved from areas thought to be dangerous to safe ones. A cousin of Guy's that he hadn't seen or spoken to for twenty years drove up to River House in her Daimler and presented herself on the doorstep, begging for 'sanctuary'. The rector and his wife found themselves harbouring the parents of children who were at boarding school with their daughter. The Fox and Hounds, never before dignified with the name of hotel, took in two families from Plymouth willing to pay inflated prices for rooms from which the landlord turned out his own children into the attics.

Unenthusiastic about taking in London evacuees – stories about lice-ridden, filthy and half-starved children were rife – Guy and Elspeth nevertheless went to Ashburton station and, with the approval of the billeting officer, carried off a young woman and her pair of wide-eyed, frightened waifs wearing armlets and labels and carrying their gas masks. At River House, their mother being too shy to speak, Elspeth took Arthur and Rose into the garden to play with her new puppy, Rover. While the spaniel went off to chase rabbits, the children stared in silence at the River Dart and the woods and hills beyond, at a pair of swans gliding down the stream and the dragonflies, whose iridescent wings skimmed the water. They held their pinched faces up to the sun and Arthur said, 'Have we died and gone to heaven, miss?'

Local authorities in the reception areas had carried out house-to-house checks on possible billets. A man called on Maud, but she told him she had no room, citing Mrs Newcombe, Elspeth and the long-dead John as residents at The Larches, as well as herself and Hope. She was later to wish she had taken a mother and child or two, for they would have been welcome compared to the evacuee who in fact turned up. This man's arrival, after Christmas, was to begin the damage to her character for the second time, and through him, ultimately, her reputation, such as it was, was ruined.

The school-leaving age was to have been raised from fourteen on 1 September 1939, but it never happened – and was not to happen for eight years – for that was the day Hitler marched into Poland. Great Britain had threatened the German dictator with dire consequences if such an act took place, but their warning was not heeded and on 3 September Neville Chamberlain broadcast to the nation that Britain was now at war with Germany.

People were terrified of bombing, especially in London – and later on with good cause – but it was to be a long time before bombs fell. England settled down into an uneasy period that nevertheless seemed a compromise between peace and war. Some of the children were taken back to London, but not Arthur and Rose, whose no-longer-shy mother begged Guy and Elspeth to keep them while she returned alone. Apparently Elspeth was worried about what her husband 'got up to' in her absence. Although Elspeth had already come to love the children, she was glad to see Mrs Cramphorn go. She had done her best to stop her children from taking baths, reading books and eating vegetables. Besides, Elspeth was expecting her first child the following summer and was finding it hard to stop herself from listening when Mrs Cramphorn constantly dilated on the horrors of childbirth and their lifelong consequences. Not for a full year would Arthur and Rose go back to London, into the care of relatives, their mother having disappeared.

Social life in the country remained largely unchanged. Cinemas and such theatres as there were had been closed on the outbreak of war but later on reopened. In London the dance halls were packed, but cinemas closed at six and League football, stopped for a while, resumed on a reduced level, a relief to the promoters of football pools, the most popular form of gambling in Britain. Christmas passed quietly at River House. Rather surprising Elspeth and her husband, Maud consented to bring Hope for Christmas dinner, but changed her mind when she was told Alicia Imber and her sons would also be there. She intended to send Hope on her own and her daughter was about to leave when Guy arrived in his car to fetch her. Maud spent Christmas alone, listening to the wireless and eating slices of the fruitcake she had made.

January and February were the coldest since 1895. The Thames froze hard for eight miles of its length and there were huge falls of snow. Mainline trains were hours late, but not the train bringing a young man travelling on his own from Paddington to Ashburton. He caught a bus to Dartcombe, where he found No. 2 Bury Row occupied by strangers who had no idea where Mrs Goodwin (an exaggerated emphasis was placed on that 'Mrs') had gone. Mrs Tremlett knew. She had met him once before and, bearing him no ill will, gave him Maud's current address.

'She came into money. She's quite the lady now, by all accounts.'

'The Larches, Ottery St Jude,' he repeated, writing it down.

'It's five miles at least,' said Mrs Tremlett, 'and there's no way of getting there but by Shanks's pony.'

He had never heard the expression before but he guessed what it meant. Carrying his heavy knapsack on his back, he would have to walk through what remained of the snow. His clothes were inadequate: an old, nearly threadbare coat that had once been his father's, cotton trousers and shirt. It was March and still cold, though the hours of darkness began later. British Summer Time had been changed. Fields lay under a dappling of half-melted snow, while the hedges and trees remained as black as midwinter, a pale bluish light that seemed unnatural lying over the landscape. He set off to walk, knowing that the soles of his shoes were worn so thin that his bare feet inside them would soon be soaked.

In the distance, shrouded in grey mist, Dartmoor lay bleakly on the horizon. Darkness came slowly and it grew colder. The glitter on fences and gateposts told him of frost. All signposts and place-names had been removed for the duration of the war, so he had no idea whether the village he was entering, one cottage, then two, then a row of them, was Ottery St Jude or not. And all these little stone houses were in darkness, the blackout applying in the countryside as well as in town. His feet were so cold and numb that he wondered if you could get frostbite in England as well as in foreign parts. As the dark closed in, he had to peer at each gate and sometimes go right up to a front door to check on the cottage name. Most had only numbers. The Larches wasn't to be found. Maybe he had further miles to walk.

He remembered Mrs Tremlett calling Maud 'quite the lady' and talking of her coming into money. Perhaps she now lived in a big house. Perhaps she now had a husband, which was a less welcome thought. But as he was picturing some burly farmer coming to the door, he found himself in a patch of deeper darkness and saw that he was in the shade of several trees which, though leafless, were something like the shape of Christmas trees. Again he went up a path to a front door. He had found what he was looking for. Barely readable but still beyond doubt when he brought his eyes within a couple of inches of the letters was the name The Larches. He put his finger to the bell push and heard the shrill sound ringing through the house.

22

Maud heard the bell ring. Of course she wasn't going to answer it. Few people called on her, none after dark that she could recall. Someone must have mistaken the house, she thought, easy to do in the blackout.

It rang again and Hope called out, 'Mummy, that's the front door.'

'Yes, I know.' Maud spoke so softly that the child couldn't hear.

She expected whoever it was to give up and go away, but instead a violent racket began, the bell ringing and the front door shaking with the blows rained on it, as if one finger were on the bell push and the other hand beating on the wood panels.

Hope, who was in the dining room reading, dropped her book and rushed into where her mother had just turned off the wireless and was standing transfixed. 'Is it an air raid, Mummy? What shall we do?'

Maud stood inside the front door. 'Who is it?'

'It's all right,' a man's voice said. 'I won't hurt you.'

She recognized the voice. Her first thought was to retreat into the house, hide in the living room and stuff her fingers in her ears. But his renewed hammering made her think he might break the door down. She undid the two bolts and opened the door. 'Bertie.' She even remembered his surname now. 'Bertie Webber.'

'I'm frozen.' He stepped inside and held out his hand to her. 'I had to walk from where you was living before.'

She ignored the hand. 'What are you doing here?'

'I'm an evacuee, Maudie. I'm scared to stop in London.'

'You'd better come in for a minute. You can't stay. And don't call me Maudie.'

He looked about him, taking in Maud's new prosperity, as he

made his way ahead of her into the living room. Hope was there, staring at him with large, round eyes. 'My, my, you haven't half grown.

'Nice place you've got here.'

'Yes,' said Maud. 'I like it.'

She expected him to ask about John, but he didn't. 'You got anything to eat in the house? I'm starved. Preferably to drink, in fact. I could do with a double Scotch, since you didn't ask.'

Bertie had already sat down. Maud sat opposite him with one arm round Hope, holding her close as if the child were under threat. 'This place is bigger than Dartcombe. There's a public house and a hotel where you could get a room – if they've got any left. The people who've come from Plymouth have taken most of the rooms.'

'If they'd got twenty I couldn't take one. I've no money. I used all I'd got on my train fare and it was a single fare. I'm not planning on going back.'

'Why aren't you in the forces?'

'Just like a woman. That's what they all say. I've not been called up yet, that's why. I hope it happens soon. My job's gone and my lodger's gone. I've not got a bean, Maudie.'

She went into the kitchen and came back with a mug of tea, two thick slices of bread and a pot of plum jam. She wasn't going to give him her butter or cheese ration. It had begun to rain. She could hear it drumming on the porch roof. 'You can stop here one night, but that's it. I can't have a single man staying here. There'll be talk. The people round here are just waiting for the chance.'

He was wolfing down bread and jam. 'You're a doll.'

She told him to have a bath before he slept in her nice, clean sheets. 'Five inches of water, that's all we're supposed to have.'

Humiliated, he simply nodded, but he had the bath. Proud of the home she now had, she showed him to the bedroom he was to sleep in and preened herself when she saw the awe in his eyes. After he had gone to bed, she lifted the blackout curtain over the front door, went into the porch and stared through the rain at the dripping larches and the empty road, as if she expected to see droves of curious and censorious people on the lookout for breaches of morality on her part. In her bedroom, the door closed and locked, she wondered why he hadn't asked about John. Because he knew what had happened to him? Or because he had forgotten his existence?

She fried Bertie an egg for his breakfast next morning. Whatever food shortages there might be, eggs were always plentiful in the country. Still without a telephone, she sent Hope in mackintosh and rubber boots up to River House with a note for Elspeth asking her, and if possible her husband too, to come to The Larches urgently. Something unforeseen and 'awful' had happened.

Elspeth was six months pregnant and the ground was slippery with slush and water. Guy was afraid for her if she went out on foot. Being annoyed with Maud was no new state for him. He would have liked the friendship between her and his wife to end, but he tried never to show his animosity to Elspeth. If she wanted to go to The Larches he would drive her there, taking it slowly because of the state of the lanes. Hope, who had added to the cryptic note that a man she didn't know had come to stay, was sent back with the message that they would be with her mother within the hour.

Maud was almost hysterical while she waited for them, subjected as she was to descriptions of Bertie's destitute condition, what with his house decaying around him, the roof leaking, his poverty and his utter friendlessness. She alone was left of the crowds of people he used to call his friends, and she was rich and comfortable and well housed, with plenty of room.

To get rid of Bertie the only way she knew would work, Maud gave him two half-crowns and ten shillings and, once it was open, sent him to the Fox and Hounds, with instructions not on any account to say he was staying with her. He had barely got to the corner of the street when Elspeth and Guy arrived.

'Who is this man, Maud?' Guy asked, while his wife held Maud in her arms, hugging her and patting her back. 'And where is he now?'

'Gone to the public house.' Maud failed to add that she had sent him there. 'He was a friend of John's. He stayed with us once and now he wants to come back because he's not safe in London.'

'Safer than he'd be in the army, I dare say,' said Guy.

Maud said he hadn't yet been called up.

'How old is he?'

'John would be thirty-six if he were alive and Bertie's a couple of years younger.'

'In that case he'll get his call-up papers in June, when the compulsory enlistment age goes up, and you'll be rid of him.'

Maud burst into tears, rocking back and forth and clutching Hope. She couldn't have him stay here that long. A single man and a single woman under the same roof for four months. What would people say?

'*Ma, il mondo?*' sang Guy, making Elspeth frown.

Maud sobbed all the louder. Without knowing that it meant 'What would the world say?' she saw this operatic rendering of her own question as deliberate mockery. But once she knew Bertie would be obliged to join the army in June she began to feel better. Getting into the car, Elspeth said to Guy, 'That's the first time I've ever heard you say something unkind.'

'Is it really? I'll try not to do it again.'

Bertie stayed and Maud took to her bed more often. She didn't know if Guy was aware of Bertie's relationship with John. Elspeth knew the truth, but had she told her husband? It wasn't only that Maud didn't know, she didn't want to know. It was better that way. It was her philosophy of life. She had a small plaster ornament in her living room of the three wise monkeys, who see no evil, hear no evil and speak no evil. Maud often said she 'aped' that, proud of her pun. She forbore to say, and perhaps she was unaware of it, that she saw, heard and spoke little good either.

Hope disliked Bertie. He either ignored or teased her, telling her that he had seen her 'making eyes' at boys in the village, that she would soon be looking for a husband and that she had no business to be so tall at her age and have legs like Betty Grable. Hope started spending the weekends at River House, taking Rover for walks and, once the university was down for the long vacation, dreaming and hoping for a visit from the Imber boys.

The weather that summer was magnificent, the temperature reaching ninety degrees in June, but the war was going badly for the Allies. Brussels had fallen to the Germans and by nightfall on 20 May they had reached the Channel coast. The British Expeditionary Force, Belgian troops and Frenchmen were surrounded in a pocket inland from Dunkirk. On the 26th, when the evacuation from Dunkirk had begun, hundreds of small boats from England had gone out to fetch the troops home.

With the one o'clock news on the wireless in her bedroom – and Guy present at her bedside, much to the doctor's amusement and the nurse's dismay, an unheard-of departure from convention in 1940 – Elspeth gave birth to her son, Adam. The baby was a healthy and vigorous screamer, weighing eight pounds, and his mother, determined to feed him herself, put him to the breast at once.

'Because we don't know if we'll be able to get baby milk or any milk at all when the Germans come.'

The people of England believed that the German army would follow the rescued BEF across the Channel and the much-feared invasion would begin. 'We shall fight in the fields and in the streets, we shall fight in the hills; we shall never surrender,' said Churchill, addressing the Commons. But, inexplicably, Hitler failed to invade and his troops turned southwards to the heart of France.

As Maud had predicted, Bertie's presence in her house gave rise to gossip and disapproval. Worry over the fear of invasion, the erecting of roadblocks and makeshift barriers in the country lanes, the building of gun emplacements in the fields, while occupying minds, still left room for speculation as to the identity of this man who was living with Mrs Goodwin. It reached the ears of Thomas Cole, a member of the newly formed Home Guard, but his duty, rather than curiosity, sent him to The Larches one evening. Part of the blackout curtain had come down from a window and branches of the larch trees were inadequate to screen the blaze of light. Maud had taken to her bed, as she increasingly did these days, and Bertie answered the door. Thomas Cole went in, pinned up the curtain himself and, noting that the man was drunk but reasonably steady on his feet, asked him for his name.

'What's it to you?'

'There's a war on, or hadn't you noticed?' said Mr Cole. 'I'm in the Home Guard and it's our business to know the names of everybody in this village.'

Confused from the beer and whisky chasers he had drunk in the Fox and Hounds, Bertie supposed that the Home Guard was another name for the police. 'Albert Edward Webber. I live at 43 Bourne Terrace, Paddington, London.' And after a hiccup: 'But I'm kipping here now with my friend Mrs Goodwin.'

It was not the wisest way to describe the situation to a stern moralist and Baptist lay preacher such as Mr Cole. He delivered his prepared lecture on behaviour that assisted the enemy in its declared purpose to conquer and subdue Great Britain, said that he would be keeping his eye on The Larches in future and made to leave.

Hearing the raised voices downstairs, Maud, who had been in bed listening to the wireless, put on her clothes and came downstairs. She would have worn a dressing gown had she not felt that such an obviously bedroom garment could only give support to the view that Bertie was her lover. But although Mr Cole was still in the house he was on his way out and did no more than exchange a glance with her.

'You're drunk,' she said to Bertie. 'You'd better get it into your head that I'm giving you no more money.'

'If you've got it I can take it. I'm a man and I'm stronger than a weak little bitch like you.'

'I'm sending for the police in the morning and d'you know what I'm going to tell them? That your call-up papers will be on the doormat at that hovel of yours in Paddington. If you don't go back and get them you'll go to prison.' Maud had no idea what the punishment for avoiding 'joining up' would be, but prison sounded good. It was the worst penalty she could think of short of hanging.

'You wouldn't do that, Maudie.'

'Try me,' she replied unwisely.

Bertie lurched towards her, his fists up, but he tripped over the rug and fell sprawling. Maud poked at him with her foot in its furry slipper. 'From tomorrow, I'm not keeping any money in this house. I'm taking it to my friend at River House to look after for me. This is your last chance, Albert Edward Webber –' she had heard him giving Mr Cole his name and address – 'before I fetch the police. Tomorrow I give you your train fare to London and you go home and join up.' She quoted his favourite version of 'Do you understand?': 'Savvy?'

Maud would not have needed to call the police even if Bertie had not gone, for Mr Cole had his own access to the law and had already written the letter that would set retribution on Bertie's track. Mrs Cole had been Deborah Joan Goshawk before her marriage, a London girl and a Baptist who had been spending a week's holiday in Teignmouth with other chapel members when she met the man who was to become her husband. Her brother was that Detective Sergeant George Goshawk, now Inspector and a famous scourge of criminals, one who had solved several hitherto unsolved crimes. Sergeant Goshawk and his wife had stayed with the Coles in the past; the detective had never met Maud but had heard the gossip about her and that a man who might have been her husband or her brother had disappeared. The name John Goodwin had stuck in his mind and he had sometimes thought that here was a mystery he would like to solve. Thomas Cole wrote to his brother-in-law George Goshawk at his address in Clapham that evening and posted the letter on the following day.

23

The Battle of Britain began on 10 July 1940, the first battle fought over British soil since Culloden, some two hundred years before. The aim was to destroy Fighter Command, this achievement to be followed by invasion. Neither of these attempts succeeded and the German aircraft were finally routed. Churchill made his famous speech about never before 'was so much owed by so many to so few'. One fighter pilot was said to have remarked that this must refer to mess bills.

But the German aircraft had retaliated and for the first time Greater London was seriously bombed. The southern suburbs suffered, and while George Goshawk's house near Clapham Common escaped anything more damaging than broken windows and tiles blown off the roof, houses in the neighbourhood were destroyed, reduced to heaps of rubble. A versatile man, Inspector Goshawk set about mending his windows himself, while his children scoured the streets for shrapnel to add to their growing collection.

Goshawk was an ardent patriot. But he hadn't allowed the war to deflect him from his principal job as hunter of those he termed 'villains'. He specialized particularly in men and women who had, he believed, escaped justice through what judges and magistrates and coroners called lack of evidence. John Goodwin had been a victim in such a case and his name had lingered for years in Goshawk's memory. Out of curiosity only, Goshawk had attended the adjourned inquest (which took place on his day off) and been struck by one fact that emerged. Though terribly disfigured by its long immersion in water, the body bore signs on its forehead of a blow made before death. The doctor giving evidence was asked what in his opinion had caused this severe abrasion but said he would not care to guess. The coroner asked him if it could have been caused when Goodwin's head hit the stone coping bordering the canal and the doctor said he supposed it could. The verdict of death by misadventure seemed to Goshawk to take a lot for granted, but he did nothing about it until he was alerted to the case by the letter from his brother-in-law. Whatever Goshawk did would have to be done in his own time, as he rightly guessed that his immediate superior would have nothing to do with the case.

'A coroner's court is good enough for me, George,' said Detective Superintendent Horlick, 'and should be for you.'

So it had been early in the war that Goshawk set out along the south bank of the Grand Union Canal. He had a week off, had sent his wife and children off to Bournemouth for a holiday with her sister and, using his 'own time', began the walk along the canal towing path from Fermoy Road in the east to Kensal Green Cemetery in the west. Goodwin's body had been found in the water near Kensal Road, where the canal passes under Ladbroke Grove. The district was not the kind of area, Goshawk decided, to which a young man would come on his own for a walk or with a friend (a girl?) for a picnic, but a sluggish, dirty waterway between clusters of soot-blackened warehouses and the backs of shabby, four-storey houses whose rear walls came down to the canal's edge without intervening gardens.

Walking back the way he had come, Goshawk took it more slowly. He noted rowing boats tied up alongside jetties that led to tumbledown cottages, but at this point no smart houseboats. Looking northwards, he could see beyond the dirty alleys and throughways a red bus moving along the Harrow Road. The water here was coated in green weed, the covering it made broken only where a pair of geese or a coot swam doggedly along, heading to the grassy spaces and sheltering trees of the great cemetery. As far as he could tell, no shops or pubs or any pleasant diversions were available to the visitor, and then, rounding a shallow bend in the towing path, he came upon a small café tucked between an abandoned, boarded-up cottage and the blackened timbers of some sort of windowless factory. This kind of place was commonly called 'a pull-up for Car men', meaning the drivers of lorries, but no lorries were here or roads to drive them along, only boats and boatmen. The name above the window was Teds Caff, the apostrophe missing from the first word and the second misspelt. Goshawk, a stickler for such things, noticed the mistakes with pain.

Inside, to his surprise, it was clean, the four tables covered with red-and-white-check cloths. Goshawk asked for a cup of tea, milk but no sugar, and when it came, brought by Ted himself, the detective asked him if he had heard about the body of a man dredged up out of the canal.

'Nasty, that,' said Ted. 'Didn't do my business no good either.'

Amused by its proprietor calling Teds Caff a business, Goshawk asked him if he could recall ever having seen the dead man before.

'Well, I wouldn't,' Ted said. 'Most days I'm not here. I'm the boss, see? It's my daughter as is here most days, waiting tables like. What's it to you, anyway?'

Goshawk produced his warrant card and the man's manner immediately became more affable, not to say fawning.

'Anything I can do to help, you've only got to ask.'

'First, I'd like to know if you ever saw this man.' Goshawk produced the poor-quality sepia snapshot of John with Sybil and Ethel taken in the Goodwins' Bristol garden that Mary Goodwin had given to the police.

'Dunno. Might be anyone. You'd have to ask my daughter.' Ted added, 'She got married at Christmas, though,' as if matrimony might adversely affect a woman's memory. 'I can tell you one funny thing that's come back to me. There's an old boy used to come in here for his dinner. Not every day, mind, but as often as not. He had a dog with him, big black bruiser. I'll tell you how he made his living. He lived up there just before you get to the cemetery, had a bit of garden and a greenhouse he said he put up himself. Used to grow vegetables and bring them down the canal in his boat to deliver to the houseboats in the Basin. Folks'd put in orders and he'd bring the stuff next day, put it through their window in a box. Then he come back here and have his dinner, leaving a bit for the dog.

'Well, I don't know when this happened, long time ago, years maybe. He had his dinner and the dog had his and off he went, but he was back in a minute, shouting the place down about his oar.'

'His what?'

'His oar, the thing he rowed the boat with. Or one of them. He was shouting the place down that someone must have had a lend of his oar without a by-your-leave and when he'd bring it back, he'd chucked it in the bottom of the boat instead of putting it in that thing, what d'you call it?'

'A rowlock,' said Goshawk.

'That's him. Now, there was no harm done, but for days afterwards, maybe a week, he went on about that oar, who'd taken it and what for, who'd chucked it back in his boat and so on and so forth, making a right hullabaloo, saying he'd have the law on whoever it was, but I don't reckon he did.'

'No,' Goshawk said, while wondering if it would ever have reached Ted's ears if the man had. 'You heard all this?'

'Me? No, not me. Whatever gave you that idea? It was my daughter, my Reenie, her what lives in Elkstone Road.'

'The old man, what's his name?'

'You mean what *was* his name. He's dead now. That was another funny thing. His dog found him and set up howling till someone came. But the dog died next day too.'

Ted launched himself into what threatened to be a long account of all the animals he had known who had died when their owners did, leading him to all the married couples among his relatives and neighbours who had died within days of one another, but just as he was starting on Uncle William and Auntie Rhoda, Goshawk made his excuses and left.

He had been wasting his time. The incident with the oar was probably the only piece of excitement which had come Ted's way in years and, such as it was, it hadn't even happened to him but to his daughter. He had never even encountered Goodwin, never seen him. Wondering if anyone would remember that far back, Goshawk called at those houses which backed directly on to the canal, their footings in the water, but he was right about the tenants' memories. Either they had forgotten or else those who might have remembered had moved away. Only one elderly woman said she could recall a couple of 'young lads larking about' on the opposite bank and one of them falling in. It had stuck in her memory. This seemed promising until she said that the reason she remembered was that the one who fell in was 'a darkie' and you saw few of them about.

Goshawk wasn't the kind of man to give up. Unrewarding as Ted had been, it might be a good idea to go back to the café and get Reenie's address. When he could make the time. But returning to the canal bank some two weeks later, after there had been more bombing of west London, he found the windows of Teds Caff boarded up and a heavy padlock on the door. Whether this closure was the result of bombing was impossible to say, but Ted was gone. Another week went by before Goshawk could make time – his own time, of course – to go looking for Reenie in Elkstone Road. With no young police constable to help him, he began on the first of those house-to-house calls that had been such a frequent chore of his youth.

His task was made all the more difficult because many of the houses were divided into rooms or flats, and he had knocked on nearly thirty doors before he found Ted's daughter. She was living with her husband, who was at work in a glass-bottle factory, in two rooms and a scullery, the lower half of a house in Elkstone Road. The district was poor but not a slum, and Reenie Davis, though she looked malnourished and downtrodden, was clean and neatly dressed.

Her father was all right, she said, but he had been bombed out of his house in the Harrow Road and gone to live with his sister in Basingstoke. She showed what Goshawk called 'the sentimentality of the working class' when he asked about the old man whose dog died with him. No, she never even knew what the man was called, but it was a crying shame him dying like that, all alone but for his dog, it brought tears to your eyes. Reenie suited the action to the word and gave a little sob.

The young man in the photograph? She might have seen him and she might not, she couldn't say. She remembered the incident of the oar put back in the wrong place, the poor old man shouting and yelling and the dog running up and down and barking, but she couldn't have said when it happened. A lot of fuss about nothing, if you asked her. Now, if he'd mentioned another young man who often came into Teds Caff, she could have told the inspector about him. He was so good-looking, he looked like Leslie Howard, but she wouldn't want her husband to hear her talk like that, he was that jealous.

'This other young man, the handsome one,' said Goshawk, 'did he ever come in the café with anyone else?'

'Of course he did, but only men. All the girls were after him, but he steered clear of them. Didn't want to get tied down, if you ask me.'

Goshawk referred to the photograph. 'Did you ever see him with this man?'

Reenie couldn't say. She might have. She couldn't remember everyone who came in. 'Only the good-looking ones, eh?' said Goshawk, and she giggled.

'I can tell you where he lives. It's Bourne Terrace, off the Harrow Road. I know what you're thinking, but I'm a married woman. It's my auntie lives down there, that's how I know.'

None of this was much help to Goshawk. He went to Bourne Terrace but it told him nothing. What did he expect this grim, dirty street to tell him? He had no reason to suppose, anyway, that the good-looking young man had any connection with drowned John Goodwin. He called at houses on both sides of the canal, but so many streets had been devastated by bombing that his quest inevitably came to nothing. For the time being, he had to leave it. A big murder case in Clapham near where he himself lived occupied all his time and attention.

It was bombs falling near Paddington station, where Goshawk's sergeant lived in one of the houses that escaped the destruction, that brought John Goodwin's death again to mind. Goshawk took a walk along Bourne Terrace, which was relatively unscathed but for a damaged house here and there, to come out into a scene of terrible devastation, a whole district flattened but for remnants of little houses sliced in half by bombs, here and there an exposed wall with a fireplace still in it and patterned paper on the part that remained. He wondered if Reenie's aunt had survived and, come to that, the handsome young man. What he should do, he told himself, what he should have done two years before, had such an action not been forbidden, was to have a couple of detective constables conduct a house-to-house enquiry in Bourne Terrace. Perhaps he should do it himself on a day off, just as he had performed a similar exercise in Elkstone Road. For what purpose, though?

He had no name, no photograph, no date and no evidence, but something had haunted him across those years, a question he had forgotten to ask Reenie. He went back to her home after a while, doubting if she would still be there. But she was, and to his surprise she recognized him. Her husband, she said, was in the army, he'd been called up in the over-thirty-four intake.

'There's been a lot of bombing here,' Goshawk said. 'Was your auntie all right?'

'Fancy you remembering! Well, *she* was, but her house took a direct hit. Auntie was in the Anderson shelter in the garden, and who d'you think was in there with her? A girl that's called Dot and that young chap I told you about, the good-looking one. They was all in there and they was all OK. His place wasn't touched.'

Goshawk went home, where he reread his brother-in-law's letter. Albert Edward Webber of 43 Bourne Terrace, Paddington. He had been living in Devon, it appeared, living with a woman who was either John Goodwin's widow or his sister.

24

Maud no longer read a newspaper, and though she listened to her wireless set, it was never to news bulletins. Coming home from school one day in late November, Hope told her mother she had heard that Bristol had been heavily bombed on the night of the 24th. Although Hope had never met any of them, she knew that her mother's parents and sisters lived there.

'I don't know why you're telling me,' Maud said. 'They're nothing to me.'

She was far more concerned and shocked by the news brought to her by Guy that Bertie had been sent for trial to the Central Criminal Court for the wilful murder of her brother, John. And he had stayed here, in her house! She had given him money! Because of him, everyone thought she was a loose woman! As for her parents, she had almost forgotten their existence, and when she had a letter from Sybil two days later to tell her that their father had died on the night of the bombing, she threw it away without replying. Nor did she go to the funeral, though Sybil had written again to tell her when and where it was. And when Elspeth showed that she was shocked by her refusal to go, Maud told Elspeth how she had changed since her marriage from the unconventional, bohemian creature she used to be.

Patiently bearing her mother's moods, on a day in the school holidays just before Christmas, Hope turned. Maud hadn't taken to her bed but had been silent all morning. Heavy rain was falling and Hope had had her usual recourse to books. She had been reading for three hours when suddenly she laid down her book and said, 'What happened to Daddy?'

Maud was startled because Hope had given up calling him Daddy a year before he went away. 'Your uncle, you mean.'

'Well, I never really knew, did I?'

'He was your uncle, my brother. He died.'

'If you won't tell me I'll ask Elspeth. She knew him.'

'All you need to know is that he went to London and drowned in a canal. You weren't particularly fond of him, were you?'

Hope made no answer. 'You've never told me who my real father is. You've never told me anything.'

'Don't speak to me like that, Hope. You should have respect for your mother.'

They had both been invited to River House for Christmas and this time Maud agreed to go. She had made sure that Alicia Imber would not be there. Hope asked if she could stay on over Boxing Day and the next day when she heard that the Imber boys were coming.

'If Mrs Harding will have you,' Maud said. She expected Hope to call her friend that, though Hope never did. She was fast learning to disobey her mother because in her opinion Maud made such ridiculous rules. 'Those boys are men now. They won't have time for a little girl like you.'

There was some truth in that. Hope had just become eleven, while Christian had reached seventeen. He had a car of his own now and drove his brother to River House, where the two of them took part in grown-up conversation and drank sherry along with the adults. Hope played with baby Adam while longing to be alone with Christian, Julian making a third if need be (if absolutely need be). When they had gone she too went home. She felt she had lost her only friends, for the children she had known in Dartcombe had been missing from her life for several years now. At school she liked a lot of girls and they seemed to like her. Most of them lived in Ashburton and she had gone home to tea with some of them. One good thing about having a mother who was a 'semi-invalid', as Hope was instructed to tell people, was that Maud noticed less and less whether Hope was at home or not, but asking a friend back to tea – even if she got the tea ready herself – was not allowed. The two girls would make a noise while Maud was having her afternoon sleep. She was now twenty-seven years old, but she led Hope to believe she was twenty-nine. To reveal her age at all to her daughter – any age – was hateful to her, but even worse would be to let her know that Maud had been only fifteen when the child was born. Nearly eighteen was respectable – let her believe that.

Much as Maud wanted nothing to do with her family, her upbringing died hard. She had taught Hope the difference between right and wrong, or what Maud thought was the difference. One thing she had never told Hope was where babies came from, but she was already anxious to keep her daughter aloof from the dangers of men's company so gave her some limited sex education. As Hope was to tell a friend many years later, it was 'how babies came out but not how they got in'. The girls at school took the opposite line. Childbirth interested them not at all, though they were saturated in biology lessons with diagrams of the female reproductive system and encouraged to watch pet rabbits giving birth. Fertilization was another matter. Those confident enough to instruct the others correctly called sexual intercourse 'fucking', in their innocence having no idea that this was the worst of all possible 'swear words', unspeakable in society, never heard or uttered by most of their parents and unprintable for years to come. The process it defined was described by an embarrassed teacher as getting married, loving your husband very much, and sleeping beside him 'in a special kind of loving embrace'. If Hope wondered what married people did, a couple such as Elspeth and Guy, for instance, her curiosity was soon satisfied by one of the confident girls, who gave her a graphic account, very different from the 'loving embrace' version.

In March Bristol suffered again. Maud made no attempt to find out what had happened to her mother, Sybil and Ethel and her family. Plymouth had so far escaped the bombs but suffered a two-night blitz on the 20th and 21st, flattening the centre of the city and damaging suburbs. St Andrew's Church, Plymouth's Anglican cathedral, was almost destroyed. Afterwards, for years, it bore on an arch left standing the single Latin word *Resurgam*, 'I will rise again'.

Thirty thousand people were made homeless in Plymouth. One young woman, married to a serviceman, abandoned her house on Mutley Plain and, with her new baby in a sling strapped to her chest and her two-year-old in a pram, walked halfway across the destroyed city to wait for a train that would take her to Ashburton. She had once been a pupil of Elspeth's and had heard that she lived in Ottery St Jude. With another long walk ahead of her in the bitter cold, not until the dawn of the next day did she reach River House. Elspeth was pregnant with her second child, but she took Pauline Moran and her children in. Of course she did. She never thought twice about it.

News of their arrival soon reached The Larches. Hope brought it to her mother, not in bed at that particular time, but reclining on the old sofa, which was now reupholstered.

'We ought to have taken them. Elspeth's going to have her baby soon and they've only got Mrs Grendon to help. Susan's left and gone into the munitions factory. We've got two spare rooms, we ought to have taken them.'

'Please don't be silly,' said Maud. 'That sort of thing isn't for you to decide. I'm the mistress of this house, in case you'd forgotten.'

'Then I shall go up to River House and help whenever I can.'

'So long as you don't forget your homework comes first.'

Hope was growing into a tall and good-looking girl. She wore her long fair hair not in two plaits, as was the fashion, but a single one, a thick golden pigtail. Her eyes were a clear dark blue, her features classically regular, if the lips were a little too full for perfect beauty. She had become what Maud called (secretly to herself) the 'spitting image' of Ronnie Clifford. Like most children, Hope had loved her mother dearly when she was younger. John Goodwin had never meant much to her nor she to him. But he had been there, he had been some sort of a companion, someone to talk to. These days her mother never spoke to her unless Hope spoke first. Sometimes she thought Maud wouldn't notice if she walked out one day and never came back. Her love for her mother was receding fast and turning to contempt. What kind of a woman pretended to be ill when she was in fact well and strong? What kind of a *person* had no friends, rejected all offers of friendship and had even begun to turn away from the one woman who had never deserted her in the face of all kinds of rebuffs?

Elspeth gave birth to her daughter, Dinah, after a long labour and a painful delivery, and had to stay in bed for a week after. Brave and resourceful, Pauline Moran had got her children out of Plymouth, had kept them warm in blankets, had walked for many miles with them, breast-feeding the baby on the way, but once at River House she had suffered a violent reaction, become feeble and frightened, unable to perform even the simplest household tasks. Hope took over. It was Easter, so there was no school, and she moved in.

'But, darling, you can't do this,' Elspeth said. 'It's not right at your age.'

'A lot of nursemaids in Victorian times were no older than me and they managed fine.'

Hope too managed fine. Mrs Grendon cleaned and changed beds and did the laundry. Guy showed an unexpected talent for cooking, much to his housekeeper's disapproval. He even began making bread, the wholemeal kind the government said everyone should eat. For two years now they had been growing vegetables in what used to be the flower gardens, keeping chickens and ducks and even a pig, which became a pet because no one had the heart – let alone the ability – to slaughter it when the time came. Hope looked after the babies, four of them, none more than two years and two months old. In January the meat ration had fallen to a new low level and stayed there, but Guy managed meals for Elspeth with eggs and vegetables, and Hope ran upstairs with them, sitting beside her while Elspeth fed Dinah, thinking but not saying, I shall do that myself one day.

'She is like another daughter to me,' Elspeth said to her husband.

When Hope finally went home to prepare for a return to school next day, Maud said she might have brought some eggs with her, the Hardings must have dozens, and when did they expect their first strawberries to ripen?

The sewing machine John had bought her Maud had used for only a few months. The rebuff she had received from Mrs Imber remained with her always and the sewing machine symbolized it. Every time she looked at it, even under its cover, she remembered Mrs Imber's words or constructed words Maud imagined the woman had said. The real words had been swallowed up in a series of insults. Maud's life since Hope was born had become so sheltered and protected that she had never learned to take criticism and perhaps profit from it. She had never understood that what she did might be less than perfect, or that any woman in her situation, if she wants to live a contented life, must show the society she moves in that in spite of her past she is worthy of respect. She dealt with even the smallest problem by taking to her bed and brought up her child by inflicting precepts on her while giving her no example to follow.

Noblesse oblige, Mrs Imber had said to her, Maud had taught herself to remember, meaning that upper-class people owed it to themselves to be condescending to what she had heard John call the proletariat. The work she had done, making that dress for the child who had died, hadn't been up to Mrs Imber's standards. The woman had refused to allow her daughter to come to play with Hope. From making Maud indignant, this rejection had rankled over the years until it had now reached a peak of bitterness and resentment. In her memory Alicia Imber's words had been so distorted that Maud now remembered her saying that the smocking on the dress was poor and far below the standard she expected; she wouldn't 'dream' of allowing Charmian to come to play with a lower-class child such as Hope.

'I hope you'll never mention those people in this house,' Maud said to Hope. 'Don't you realize how grossly that woman insulted me?'

'It wasn't Christian and Julian who said those things to you.'

'If you went to church like you should you'd know that the

sins of the fathers are visited upon the children, and that means mothers too. Or in other words, those boys are chips off the old block.'

Maud never went to church herself. The congregation was composed entirely of residents of Ottery St Jude, the occasional guest of one of them and now the influx from Plymouth. Setting foot inside St Jude's on a Sunday morning or evening would mean talking to her neighbours or even getting to know them. Hope never went. When the rector called – he said he was 'looking in' – Maud told him she had gone back to being a Methodist. She was still shocked when her daughter said she was an atheist. Hope lost her belief in God when He did nothing to stop the bombing of Plymouth but let the Germans make thirty thousand people homeless and left refugees from the stricken city, mothers with small babies, to wander about Dartmoor in the bitter cold of the night.

'You've been listening to that Pauline,' was Maud's only comment.

Alicia Imber married again. Her new husband was the widowed father of a boy Christian and Julian had been at school with. The big wedding was at All Saints, Dartcombe. The Hardings were of course invited and, to her surprise, Maud with Hope.

'Not that I would dream of going,' said Maud. 'Fancy marrying a man called Brown, it's almost as bad as Smith.'

'I'd like to go. You could wear your pink dress.'

Maud had used all her annual allowance of clothing coupons on it, fearing, as the rumour had it, that a range of hideous garments called Utility, with no trimmings, pleats or cuffs, would appear in the shop. A year was to pass before this happened, but she was taking no chances. The dress had a full skirt and a tight bodice with tiny buttons from neck to waist. Twenty-five pearl buttons, she noted. Maud sometimes put it on when she was alone and wore silk stockings and high-heeled shoes with it. Once or twice Hope had come home and found Maud dressed like that, with one of the best china teacups on a tray and the silver teapot.

The first time this happened Hope was relieved that her mother, as she saw it, had at last had a friend to tea.

'No, I've been quite alone. Can't you see there's only one cup?'

But in the late summer of 1941 Maud had a visitor, unexpected of course, as anyone coming to The Larches must be. Maud's first thought on seeing her sister Sybil on the doorstep, even before either of them spoke, was how much Sybil had aged. Still a couple of years under forty, she had the lined face and round shoulders of an elderly woman. Quite a lot of grey was in her hair.

Maud was wearing the pink dress and the high heels and this she thought a lucky chance. 'What brings you here?' she said, but because she was pleased with her appearance in contrast to Sybil's, rather more graciously than usual.

'It's so long since I was last here. Mother would have come with me but she's not well. She wanted to know how you were getting on. But I see you're expecting company.'

'Oh, no. I hope I don't only dress properly for visitors.'

'You always were one for nice clothes,' said Sybil, and then, her gaze travelling from Maud's hair, done in fashionable 'Victory rolls', down across the pink silk to her feet in black patent shoes, 'You look lovely, Maud, really beautiful.'

Enormously pleased, Maud said an enthusiastic, 'Well, thank you, Sybil. One has to do one's best, don't you think, hard though it is.'

Tea was over and the seed cake, home-made but not expected ever to be cut, had been half eaten when Hope arrived home. Sybil made the requisite remarks about how she had grown and how was she getting on at school. Youngish people ought to remember how much they hated this comment and this enquiry when they had themselves been young only a few years before, but it never deterred them from forcing such challenges on adolescents. As Maud knew Sybil would as soon as she saw her, Sybil asked Maud to come to see their mother.

'I suppose you've forgotten what happened when I did come.'

'Can't you be more tolerant? Can't you be more forgiving?'

'I never forget and I never forgive,' said Maud.

She had forgotten Hope was within earshot. 'You've never forgiven Mrs Imber, have you, Mother?'

Maud said, 'Go upstairs, Hope, and get on with your homework.'

'OK, I will. I just want to say that I'll be going to the wedding. Elspeth says I can go with them.'

'We'll see about that, and don't say OK.'

In the evening, after Sybil had gone to catch her train back to Bristol, Maud went upstairs and changed out of the pink frock, not for some other daytime garment, but into nightdress and dressing gown. She walked into Hope's bedroom and told her that if she went to 'that woman's' wedding she need not think she could come back to The Larches. This turned out to be an empty threat, even though Hope passed an almost sleepless night worrying about it. Where was she to go? What was she to do? Elspeth told her it wouldn't happen and Elspeth was right. Anyway, she always had a bed at River House. Hope had a lovely time at the wedding in a dress of Elspeth's, as her own wardrobe was rather sparse. She particularly enjoyed seeing Christian take his mother up the aisle and give her away to Mr Brown. England was passing through one of its food-deprived times of the war, and despite plenty of spirits, sherry and wine at the reception, little was available to eat, skimpy brown-bread-and-tomato sandwiches – there was a bumper crop of tomatoes that summer – hard-boiled eggs and gooseberry fool.

Guy drove Hope home to The Larches and waited ten minutes outside in case Maud turned her out. But Maud was in high good humour. A young farmer who had been bringing her eggs and cream and an occasional chicken unasked, had called and asked her to marry him. After enquiring how he dared, Maud answered him with a bald no. Young Mr Greystock was unwise enough to ask why not, and Maud said she would never marry. The truth was, she knew that if she said yes to him or to anyone else, in the banns she would be called 'a spinster' instead of 'a widow of this parish', as if it were still possible to deceive the village as to her status. Jack Greystock said she didn't mean that and he would try again. The following week he brought the eggs and cream as usual and a rabbit too and a guinea fowl. It thrilled Maud that she had given the man what she called his 'comeuppance' and she even asked Hope how the wedding had gone.

Hope said quietly that it was nice. She often used this phrase to her mother, about anything. It could be applied to: How was school? How was Elspeth? What did you have to eat? Was it cold? Was it hot? But Maud questioned her less and less. Maud wasn't interested in the answers she might get, for she never made an enquiry of any importance.

As to Jack Greystock, she wouldn't say she liked him, but she tolerated him because he seemed never to have heard the gossip about her in the village, or if he had, he didn't care. She put everyone she knew to this test: did they look down on her because of her ruined reputation?

25

Reading an account of Bertie Webber's trial in the morning paper, Guy walked down to The Larches to tell Maud the outcome, that Bertie had been condemned to death for the murder of John Goodwin. Guy and his wife were strongly opposed to capital punishment, but both felt Maud would be in favour of it, would rejoice at the verdict.

She wasn't pleased to see Guy. She was never pleased to see anyone. Hope let him in and called out to her mother that Guy was downstairs.

'You should call him Mr Harding,' Maud replied, but she came downstairs, stood a yard or two from Guy and said, 'Hello,' and that most frosty of greetings, 'What brings you here?'

'Perhaps we could sit down.'

He didn't know Maud well if he expected some transport of joy or excitement at what he was about to tell her. Her joyous days, her excited days, were past. Their passing had begun with those two episodes in the fields with Ronnie Clifford. She was capable of rage, petulance or sullenness but not of spontaneous pleasure. She listened to Guy in silence, asked no questions and said when he came to the end, 'Well, I suppose that's something to be thankful for.'

Elspeth had told him to invite Maud to lunch. He had shot a rabbit that morning and they always had vegetables. Apparently, his wife thought Maud would need the comfort of company when reminded of her brother's dreadful death. Elspeth should have known Maud better, but, like her husband, she did not. Of course Maud wouldn't come to lunch, she had too much to do at home, though what that too much was she didn't specify. The house appeared clean and tidy, the sewing machine, which she had brought with her from Dartcombe, hidden as always under its cover.

Maud was never heard to speak of her brother again. How her mother and Sybil and Ethel reacted to his murderer's conviction she never enquired. Hope was never told about it, though John had been her uncle and for years she believed him to be her father, but of course she found out. She was an inveterate reader of newspapers and, denied one at home, often bought a newspaper on her way to school. If she never mentioned the trial or its consequence to Maud, Bertie's fate marked a watershed in her relations with her mother. The days when she sat in her mother's bedroom to do her homework, when she sat and listened to the wireless with Maud, when she confided in her mother about her friends at school, all those were over. Too many subjects were banned by Maud as topics of conversation: Christian and Julian Imber as well as their mother, grandmother and aunts in Bristol, young Mr Greystock and, it seemed, the entire population of Dartcombe. John had joined the list, and when Hope told Maud what she had read in the papers, Maud rounded on her, shouting that Bertie must never be mentioned.

'I never want to hear that man's name in this house again, do you hear me?'

Hope started spending even more time with the Hardings. She was always welcome, and not only because of the help she gave with the children. In the autumn it seemed that there was to be no more serious bombing of Plymouth, and Pauline Moran and her son and daughter went home to the house that had needed only the glass in three of its windows replaced. Hope had made one good friend at school, a serious 'best friend' called Rosemary Langley. Before the deep rift caused by Maud's taking exception to Hope reading about Bertie, Hope had told her mother about Rosemary, unwisely asking if she could ask her to tea. Maud, of course, had a previous Rosemary in her life, and one she now hated for no reason she could even have given to herself, but it was enough for her to forbid Hope ever to see this new friend again and not to answer her if she spoke to her at school.

Though Hope was sometimes saddened by what she saw as

losing her mother when she had already lost the man she thought of as her father, she was (as she put it to herself, laughing rather bitterly) a big girl now. Ronnie Clifford had been over six feet tall, a Nordic god of a young man, and his daughter was the tallest girl in her class, blonde and beautiful. While it may not be true that suffering refines the nature, hardship and neglect may certainly build character, and those particular kinds of adversity had done so for Hope. Thinking it over carefully, she had concluded that she could defy her mother if her mother was unreasonable, and what could Maud do about it? Turn her out of the house? Bar the door against her? Hope doubted if Maud would ever go as far as that. Besides, Hope always had her refuge at River House.

A strange thing happened in the early spring. A parcel arrived for Maud, postmarked Dartcombe. A past mistress of the art of avoiding anything that might prove unpleasant, she considered simply not opening it. But leaving it alone or throwing it away was beyond her. She handled it, turning it over and over, trying to feel what its contents might be through the thick brown-paper wrapping, shaking it and holding it to her ear to find out if it rattled. Finally, curiosity got the better of her and she tore off string, sealing wax and paper.

Inside was a battered and stained cardboard box. Again Maud hesitated, waited, looked at it and felt it. She shook the box. Something inside it slid an inch or two, then shifted back again. The box was a little too big for its contents. She left it on the table while she took the brown-paper wrapping to the rubbish bin. As if the box had eyes, it seemed to follow her round the room as she came back, sat down, got up again, pushed the box so that it was almost hidden behind the bowl of hyacinths. Hours passed before she opened it.

When she did it was on an impulse, a sudden burst of energy typical of her. She had the power to briefly suspend all thought and all fear, though both would quickly return. She had had her lunch, a single egg scrambled and served on toast, which she ate seated alone at the dining table, accompanying it with a glass of water. The table was cleared of plate and glass, the utensils washed up. It was time to change for the afternoon. She put on the latest new dress, high heels, powdered her nose and applied bright red lipstick, returned to the living room and sat down, her eyes now fixed on what almost hid the parcel, the hyacinth bowl. The impulse came then. She jumped up with a spurt so fierce that it wrenched from her a cry of 'Ah!' and grabbed the box, a blow from her elbow snapping off the stem of one of the hyacinths.

Now she had the box in her hands again, hesitation was past. She pulled off the lid and clenched her hands. Inside was what looked like a large piece of yellowish folded cloth. She touched it, then lifted it out and shook it. It was a bedsheet. Single-bed size, once white, hemstitched at both ends, it was stained with brownish patches and green streaks. She looked at the cloth label attached to one of the shorter sides and recognized the maker's name. It was one of Mrs Tremlett's, left for their use in the house in Bury Row. Underneath it, still in the box, was a note written on lined paper torn from a notebook. The signature was G. Tranter. There was no 'Dear Maud' but only the words, 'This was dug up out of the garden by Mr Hoddle of 2 Bury Row. Mother says she does not want it.'

This was a sheet, Maud now understood, from the single bed John had slept in all the time the people of Dartcombe had thought he was sharing her bed. 'Mother', of course, was Mrs Tremlett and the sheet was marked with her initials. So she knew, had perhaps always known. Bertie had slept there too, lying beside John after he got up from the sofa and crept up the stairs. Now Bertie was going to be hanged and she was glad. She would have liked to see capital punishment extended to Ronnie Clifford and his wife, to Mrs Tremlett and her daughter, Mrs Imber now Brown and all the Imbers. The sheet was too big to go in the boiler and be burned. Maud would make a bonfire in the garden tomorrow or the next day or the next and watch the flames consume it.

Ten days before he was to be executed Bertie Webber killed himself in his cell. In American prisons a condemned man on death row is watched night and day, but no such careful watch was kept on Bertie. He made a rope and noose out of his trousers and shirt, placed the noose round his neck and hanged himself from the bars on the small window high up in the wall, but not too high for John Goodwin's killer to reach when standing on the stool that was the only piece of furniture apart from the pallet bed and a bucket. When he had checked with his hands that the noose was in place he stood for a moment or two with his head resting on the rope and thought about John. What a fool! What a soppy fool! The way his mouth went slack and his eyes went swimmy. Good riddance to bad rubbish, thought Bertie, and he kicked away the stool.

No one associated with Bertie – the prison governor, the warders who had most to do with him, the two prison visitors who saw him – suspected his intention. He always seemed a cheerful, happy-go-lucky man and indifferent to his fate.

Only the prison chaplain had reason to be apprehensive. Bertie had no religious faith and had no interest in acquiring any. But he seemed to understand shame and regret at the last. 'He loved me like a woman,' Bertie said. 'What a fool! I wish I never done it.'

Young, innocent and shocked, the chaplain passed these words on to Guy, who knew him. 'I can tell you what he said. We're not Romans, it wasn't like the confessional.'

Nothing appeared in the papers but two lines about the inquest, where a verdict was returned of suicide or *felo de se*.

Guy and Elspeth were debating whether to tell Maud, fearing that she would shut her ears to them – literally perhaps covering her ears with her hands as she sometimes did – but Detective Inspector Goshawk forestalled them. He made the train journey to Ashburton and took the bus to Ottery St Jude specially to bring her the news.

The front door of The Larches was opened by Enid Biddle, the sixteen-year-old who had taken Mrs Newcombe's place and whom Maud, in time-honoured Goodwin fashion, called 'the maid'. Small, thin and perpetually frightened, Enid showed George Goshawk into the living room and told him, in a Devon accent so thick that he barely understood her, to sit on the sofa. Maud wasn't in bed. Dressed in her best new frock, covered by a voluminous white apron, she was in the kitchen, using her sugar ration and eggs from Jack Greystock to make a Victoria sponge that she would eat herself, a single slice a day for the next week. In pink high-heeled shoes, she had just opened the oven door and inserted the tin of almost liquid yellow mixture when Edith came to the kitchen and timidly told her a gentleman had come. Maud took off her apron.

Telling herself, but in silence, that a policeman wasn't a gentleman, Maud nodded to him and used that phrase which was becoming habitual with her and would do for anyone. 'What brings you here?'

Goshawk asked if he might sit down and suggested that she should too. Maud did so with an ill grace, and, using euphemistic terms and a gentle tone because she was a woman, he told her what Bertie Webber had done. She said nothing for a moment, then, 'I can't say I'm sorry.'

'I don't suppose you are, Mrs Goodwin.' He gave her that courtesy title, the kind of honorific given to a cook or a housekeeper because the work she did merited respect. Not that this applied to John Goodwin's sister, whom he had previously called miss.

He had come a long way, spending hours on the journey and paying his own fare, but she offered him no tea or even a glass of water. 'Is that all, then?'

'Quite all.'

'Then if you don't mind, I've got things to do.'

He had thought he could no longer be affected by rudeness, but this time he was. He had brought her brother's killer to justice and been considerate enough to tell her the news of his death before, he hoped, anyone else could. But he said nothing of any of that.

'I'll say good day, then,' he said. Before he had gone three steps from the front door, she had shut it behind him. He set off on the long journey back to London.

The things Maud told Inspector Goshawk she had to do were look once more at the letters which kept coming for her, or rather, the envelopes that she often didn't open. Her name and address were in capital letters and sometimes misspelt, and, according to their postmarks, all came from towns and villages in South Devon. The people who wrote the insults and what Maud called 'bad words' knew all about Bertie staying with her and about his suicide. After Goshawk had gone, she opened one of the envelopes she had so far only looked at in the vain hope perhaps that its contents were kind and favourable to her, but this one too was abusive.

How many 'fancy men' had she had? it enquired. Maybe it didn't matter to her once she had fornicated with her own brother, but this one, a murderer, was what the anonymous letter writer called 'the last straw'. Up till then Maud had kept all the letters, with a vague brave resolve to show them to a policeman one day. But this one really was the last straw. None of the others had accused her of sexual relations with John. It was his fault, she thought, he started it. Everything that was bad began with that. If she could no longer see the letters she might forget them. She opened the door on the kitchen range and pushed all the letters inside.

Enid Biddle was given the afternoon off and after Maud had watched her depart she took the sheet out into the garden, piled firewood on top of the newspapers Hope had left in the house and deposited the sheet on top. Then she poured on paraffin and threw in a lighted match. It was so satisfying to see the sheet burn that she wished she had saved all the anonymous letters and their envelopes and watched them burn too.

26

Hope returned home to The Larches that evening, though not intending to stay, and Guy and Elspeth came with her. Guy was prepared to tell Maud about Bertie and his dreadful end, but she interrupted him before he had finished the first sentence, said she knew what had happened and had no wish to talk about it. But to their surprise she produced a bottle of sherry. It was hard not to see this, poured into the best and seldom-used glasses, as a celebration.

In their estimation, as it had been in George Goshawk's, though he had said nothing, Maud had never looked so well or, in Guy's rather old-fashioned word when used of a woman, so handsome. She was now a beautiful woman and must surely be aware of it, otherwise why dress with such care and paint her face so elaborately. It was a time – perhaps the first time in history – when ordinary women, not actresses or street women but working-class women and factory girls as well as the middle classes, wore make-up as a matter of course, powder and rouge and scarlet lipstick, coloured eyeshadow and eyebrow pencil. Elspeth had never succumbed to the trend and Hope hadn't begun, but Maud never set foot outside her front door without what Guy called her 'war paint'. But whom was it for? Herself, it must be, Elspeth said, for Maud was now entirely without friends, unless Elspeth and Guy could be called friends, and this was their first encounter for a long while. Maud wanted no one. Jack Greystock had proposed twice more and been refused again, but he continued to bring gifts of food.

Maud kissed her daughter when they parted and told her it was kind of Mr and Mrs Harding to have her and not to wear out her welcome. It was the last time Maud saw Hope for several weeks, which embarrassed Elspeth, who feared for the girl. She who had been adored by her mother when she was a baby and young child was now almost rejected, a burden and a nuisance when she was in the house. Elspeth tried to talk to Maud about it, the two of them on their own, but Maud only said, 'If you don't want her why don't you say straight out?'

'Of course I want her, Maud. I love her. She has become part of our family, but I think she needs you.' Elspeth didn't add that Hope was afraid that if she came back to The Larches more often than she did, Maud would tell her she wasn't wanted. It was a real fear. Hope told Elspeth, in the frankest confidence she had ever made to her, that if her mother refused to let her in it would break her heart. Without the Hardings and their children, Hope would have been a lonely adolescent, unable to understand what she had done to make her mother reject her.

'I suppose she has come to blame her for existing.' Elspeth said that while once Maud had felt that Hope had transformed her life, bringing her her best happiness, Maud now saw Hope as having ruined it. Without her, where might Maud have been now? A university graduate, a teacher perhaps, married to a wealthy man and with a family of children.

'But does she really feel like that?' Guy asked.

'Who knows?' Elspeth said. 'She will never say. Would it have been different if John had lived?'

'Only if she could have accepted him for what he was.'

'She would never have done that.'

They were quiet times in the countryside, those later years of the war. For Hope there was school and a few friends, including the Rosemary Maud had refused to have in the house but Elspeth welcomed. For Maud one thing only had changed, and this was enormous. Hope was nearly fifteen, the age at which her mother had conceived and given birth to her. Something Maud said to her frightened Hope more than anything Maud had ever said to her before.

'You should cut off that hair of yours.' Not 'your hair' but 'that hair of yours'. 'You should let it go back to its natural colour too. You've been bleaching it, I can tell.' A few hours later, she peered into Hope's eyes and said, 'You can't see very well, can you? You get that from my mother, she was short-sighted. We shall have to see about glasses for you.'

Hope told Elspeth, and Elspeth, who tried never to criticize Maud to her daughter, told Hope to take no notice but she could have an eye test if she liked. When they were alone Elspeth said to Guy that she wondered if Maud had said that because she feared competition from Hope, who had quickly become so beautiful. 'And I've wondered,' Guy said, 'if Hope reminds her too much of the father. If, say, she sees the child's father every time she looks at her. Of course, we've no idea what he looks like.'

Alicia Brown invited Hope to come to stay at Dartcombe Hall in the summer holidays and again the following spring. Christian, down from Oxford for the last time, had a first in modern history and was going into the navy. Hope was nearly as tall as he and undeniably beautiful, but to Alicia she was still a little girl, lucky enough to have been taken up – practically adopted – by those kind Hardings, and because of her nice manners and helpfulness, a welcome guest in her own house. Her son was a man now and would look on Hope as a child. Alicia was unaware of the kisses Christian gave Hope and she gave him in the twilight garden before he left for his ship at Portsmouth.

That summer Hope passed her School Certificate examination with two 'distinctions', four 'credits' and two passes. These successes meant she could proceed into the sixth form and prepare to take her Higher Certificate in two years' time. If Maud noticed her child's achievement she made no comment on it to Hope herself. But she must have been aware that while her daughter had seemed to follow in her mother's footsteps, she was now well past the age when Maud herself had come to the end of her childhood, her youth and her education by becoming pregnant. Hope was set to go on to higher education and, while at Reading or Exeter, perhaps meet some suitable young man, very different from Ronnie Clifford.

But if Maud thought in these terms she talked about it to no one. It was now years since she had had any contact with her family in Bristol, if they were still in Bristol, if her mother was still alive. That Sybil was still in what Maud called 'the land of the living' she knew, for a card came regularly at Christmas with her sister's Christian name signed under a sentimental verse. Maud herself had sent Christmas cards while John was still with her, no more than half a dozen, but still they were sent and signed by both of them as if they had really been husband and wife.

27

After a few months the anonymous letters ceased. Some neighbours and people in the village still turned away their heads when they passed Maud in the street, some women still turned their backs. But Elspeth Harding remained loyal to her, a good friend, and Jack Grey-stock the farmer was still her admirer.

The events that happen in families happened, beginning with a death, Mary Goodwin's. The news was brought to Maud in a cold letter from her sister Ethel, who told her when and where the funeral was to be. Maud's usual reaction to news of someone she had heard nothing of for a long time was to remind herself of the injuries, real or imagined, that man or that woman had done her in the past. In the case of her mother, these were many. Resentment replaced indignation in her mind and sullenness resentment. They need not any of them think that she would turn up at that funeral. Her bad temper vented itself on Hope, now seventeen and with a place awaiting her at the University of Reading. Hope had also had a letter, but hers was from Christian Imber, now applying himself to the study of law in London. It was the most recent of many letters, all of which she kept from her mother, knowing that any mention of them would bring denunciations of the whole Imber-Brown family from Maud.

But Maud had picked up this letter from the doormat before Hope could forestall her – shades of the days of John and Bertie – and recognized Christian's hand. 'I'm surprised he bothers with you, considering all the beautiful girls he must meet in London.' Did Maud never see her lovely daughter? Or did she see too much? 'Unless he's unlike the rest of his family, he can't be doing it out of kindness.'

Hope made no comment on this. She was going to spend the coming weekend in London with Christian in a hotel in Kensington, her preparations including equipping herself with a wedding ring and telling Maud she would be staying with Rosemary's family in the Cornish village of Lostwithiel. Maud had romantic plans of her own, or rather plans for the denial yet again of romance. Jack Greystock was coming for a glass of sherry at six o'clock, his excuse for the visit (and hers) to bring her half a dozen eggs, a capon and two jars of his mother's damson jam. He asked her to marry him about twice a year and she calculated that the six months was up. They had become as near to being friends as Maud would allow with anyone apart from Elspeth, but once Jack had handed over what he called the 'provisions' and she had thanked him, they had little to say to each other. They drank their sherry and each had a second glass. He said he was in love with her, but Maud doubted it. What was he in love *with*? Her looks, of course. She looked in the glass and saw that at thirty-three she was better-looking than ever, her face and figure the sort of ideal that would be particularly attractive to a Devonshire yokel (the way she thought of him) – blonde, blue-eyed, regular-featured, with an hourglass figure, high-insteped feet and shapely legs.

He had a lot of money. The farmhouse was commodious and well cared for. That would have amounted to nothing from her point of view if his mother had lived with him. But she lived in a big and pretty thatched cottage some hundred yards away, where she made her jams and scalded her clotted cream and pickled her eggs. Maud was comfortable, but she was well aware that she had a fixed income which might not look so flourishing in ten or twenty years' time. She sat silent and patient, waiting for Jack to ask her to marry him, prefacing the proposal as he always did with, 'You know I'm crazy about you, don't you?' delivered in a stiff, steady voice, as if he had had to learn the words by heart.

But he didn't ask. This time there was no proposal. He neither said he was crazy about her nor asked her to marry him. Maybe the six months wasn't quite up. Maud tried to check it out after he had gone. Now it was September and last time he had proposed had been March. She knew it was March because Elspeth's birthday was in March and it had been the day after her birthday. Perhaps he was never going to propose again. Maud led such a routine-driven, steady life that she disliked anything happening to disturb this regularity, though if he had proposed she had intended to disturb it herself. She had been going to say that she didn't know but she would like to think about it.

Denied this chance, she got out the file where she kept bank statements; studying them, she wondered with increasing fear why her financial situation had throughout those years since John's death seemed so satisfactory. Now, though it was unchanged, she saw poverty returning and a destitute old age. Jack Greystock was her only hope.

Did she want to marry him? She wanted more money and freedom from worry. Something had to occur in her life that would push her over the edge into accepting him. She knew that, she knew herself well enough for that. But nothing much was likely to happen to her, it was so long now since anything had.

Hope had behaved badly. She knew she was behaving badly and she did it on purpose, refusing to take the obvious step to prevent it. It was revenge on her mother for neglecting her. The odd part of it was, perhaps, that until she knew what had happened she failed to realize the similarity it would have to Maud's own experience. No one was told except Christian. Neither of them quite foresaw the extent of Maud's rage when Hope told her. If Christian had had the slightest idea of how Maud could react – if he had been aware, for instance, of how she had leapt from her seat and screamed at her sister when a suggestion was made of the then favourite Hope's exclusion from a family gathering – he would have taken care to be present at Hope's disclosure, not a few miles away making his own confession at Alicia Brown's house in Dartcombe.

It would hardly have occurred to Hope to let her mother

discover the fact for herself, walking into her bedroom while her daughter was dressing, as Mary Goodwin had done. For the first time in a fortnight she had slept the previous night in her bedroom at The Larches and she came down next morning at a little after nine.

'You're very late,' said Maud. She was sitting at the table, observing her customary habit of eating quarter-slices of toast with her left hand while using her right for the sipping of tea. 'You're here so seldom that I suppose you'd forgotten we're early risers in this house.'

'I didn't think you'd mind.'

'I suppose I have to put up with it.'

The tea was cold. Hope was used to drinking coffee at breakfast at River House, but she made a second pot of tea and brought her mother some in a fresh cup and one for herself. Maud thanked her in a preoccupied tone. She wasn't looking at a newspaper – there wasn't one – or reading a book, as her daughter had been told not to do at table, but thinking, as she did a lot these days, about Jack Greystock and what was to be done about him. He must long ago have heard the rumours about her past, the circulating tales of Bertie Webber and the speculations as to what her true relation to John had been, not to mention her having given birth at only fifteen – or had they only reached him between his last proposal and the due date of the one that never came? She was so preoccupied with these thoughts that she was barely aware that Hope was speaking to her.

'Yes, what did you say?'

'I said I had something to tell you.'

If it had occurred to Maud that her daughter hardly ever called her Mother these days, let alone Mummy, which had once been usual and sweet to her ears, or by any name, she never remarked on it. 'Yes, all right, what is it?'

'When someone's going to give you a shock, have you noticed how they ask you if you're sitting down? It's as if they think maybe you'll faint or collapse or something.'

'I really don't know what you're talking about.' Maud stood up, as if she had known what Hope meant but was determined to defy it. 'What is this something you've got to tell me?'

'You're not sitting down, but never mind. I want to tell you something that's bound to give you a shock.' Hope took a deep breath. 'I'm pregnant.'

Maud sat down. She sat heavily like a woman twice her weight. 'I beg your pardon?'

'I really did say that. I'm pregnant. I'm going to have a baby.'

Maud behaved exactly as she had when Sybil had told her that if she came to see her father she should leave the child behind. She jumped up, let out a loud scream and shouted, 'I don't believe it. It's not true. You're lying. You want to kill me.'

Hope also had got to her feet and Maud, who had never before done violence to anyone, threw herself on her. Slapping her face and seizing her by the shoulders, Maud began to shake her, shouting all the while that her daughter was lying, that she was making it up. But Hope was taller and much stronger than her mother. She grasped Maud's hands and forced her arms down by her sides, turning her face away until she felt Maud grow limp and weak and collapse into her chair in gushes of tears.

'Well, I'm going to have a baby,' said Hope, 'just like you had me, only I'm two years older than you were. You see I do know your real age. And I don't want to hurt your feelings, but I think I've got more sense than you.'

The almost mechanical response to that was, 'How dare you speak to me like that?'

'Well, as you see, I do dare. Christian Imber is the father, by the way.'

'What do you mean, "by the way"?'

'I thought you might want to know that vital fact. Children are quite keen on knowing who their fathers are, in case that fact has escaped your notice.'

This time Maud said nothing about Hope's lack of respect, but she seemed to have forgotten the treatment she had received from her own parents in a like situation. 'You can't stay here,' she shouted. 'I've had enough disgrace, none of it my own fault, and I'm not having you bring more on me. I knew those Imbers would ruin me, I knew it the first day I met that woman.'

Hope had sat down. She had moved from her chair on to the sofa and put her feet up. She was waiting for her mother to tell her that although she hated Christian (as an Imber), he would have to marry her. If anyone had told her she would one day enjoy getting revenge on her mother, Hope would never have believed it. She hadn't thought she was that sort of person, but perhaps she was. But Maud said nothing of that. She ran upstairs, encountered the open-mouthed Enid Biddle plying the carpet sweeper on the landing and stormed into her bedroom. When Maud came down again she was wearing the last outfit she had bought before clothes rationing began and a hat Hope had never before seen. She didn't ask her mother where she was going. Hope knew and knew, too, that it would be pointless to try to stop her.

It was a warm day, but Maud arrived at the front door of River House in a pale blue tailored suit, a maroon felt hat and maroon suede shoes with high heels. She was so dressed up that Elspeth, in answering the door, thought for a moment that one of them had mistaken the date and Maud had come to lunch or even a party. The illusion lasted only seconds, for Maud, marching in, began shouting that Elspeth and Guy – she addressed them as Mr and Mrs Harding – had led her daughter astray, corrupted her morals and contrived that Hope and Christian share a bed in their house. Where else could 'the deed' have been done? No doubt, Maud had forgotten the meadows behind the Bristol home of her parents. When Guy appeared and asked what was going on, she called him a 'pimp', a word the Hardings were amazed she even knew.

Her rant continued for some time, growing more and more hysterical, until she had taken herself into the drawing room and begun picking up small ornaments, books and cushions and hurling them across the room. Fortunately, all but a rather nice little piece of

Royal Copenhagen were unbreakable. When Elspeth made a mild effort to restrain Maud, she struck out, landing a glancing blow on Elspeth's cheek. Guy stepped in and got Maud on to a sofa, forcing her to sit down. Rage broke into cries and sobs, which subsided when Guy held a small glass of brandy to her lips. It was rather late in the day, a good half-hour after all this had begun, that Maud was in a fit state, though tear-stained and hiccuping, to understand that neither of the Hardings had the least idea what she had been talking (or, rather, screaming) about.

After she had been given tea and comforted, Guy drove her home. Maud made no apology to him for her abuse. She never did apologize to anyone. Once he had left, her intention was to go to bed, but she had something important to do first. There was no sign of Hope. What had happened was the trigger that would set off a change in Maud's life. Writing materials were fetched out, a sheet of the headed paper she had scarcely ever used, the fountain pen Elspeth had given her for a birthday present, and an envelope to which she affixed a stamp from a book of them Hope must have bought and left behind. She sat down, first addressed the envelope to 'John Greystock Esq.' – if they called him Jack he must be John, mustn't he? – 'Windstone Farm, Ottery St Jude, Devon', then wrote, taking it slowly and carefully:

Dear Mr Greystock

After much careful thought, I have decided that I can accept your proposal. Perhaps you would call and we can discuss arrangements for our forthcoming marriage. I would like our nuptials to take place as soon as is convenient.

With kindest regards,
Yours sincerely,
Maud Goodwin

Reading it, Maud found nothing unusual in this letter. Calling a prospective husband 'Mr' with his surname would have been acceptable in 1847 but hardly a hundred years later. Still, she liked it and wouldn't have considered changing it. Jack had not renewed his proposal, but this she chose to ignore. *He* had not yet accepted *her* and perhaps would not, but this she hardly considered. As to the banns and the description of her as a spinster, perhaps they could get married in a register office, where she had an idea no reference to her status or whatever it was called would be made.

She was quite pleased with what she had written and took it to the pillar box at once. It was still early when she returned home, but she went upstairs, had a long, hot bath and retired to bed. Nothing unusual in that. When had the hour or the position of the sun affected her bedtime? Not for years.

28

When Hope came back Christian was with her. Judging from her own experience, Maud had made up her mind that the father of her daughter's child would never be seen again. Even if he wanted to 'stand by her' his mother would stop him. But here he was, on her doorstep, Hope having rung the doorbell instead of using her key. Maud got up to answer the door.

She had decided she wasn't going to speak to him, she wouldn't even look at him.

Hope said, 'When I told you this morning I thought there was one question you were bound to ask me, but you didn't.'

'Oh, yes, and what was that, then?'

Hope and Christian both came in, walked into the living room.

'If you're not going to we'll tell you,' said Hope. She looked at Christian and he smiled at her.

'Perhaps it's best if I tell your mother, Hope.'

The words were scarcely out when Maud screamed, 'Don't you dare speak to me. I never asked you in here. You can get out!'

'I was only going to say,' he said, 'that we've just been to see Mr Morgan and he'll marry us in three weeks' time.'

Maud was speechless. It never crossed her mind to apologize. She wouldn't have known how to. She stared at him, she stared at Hope, then threw her arms round her, an unfamiliar embrace from which Hope escaped and retreated a little. For her mother's happiness Hope felt only distaste and a touch of dismay at the triumphant and almost virtuous note Christian had put into his announcement. Ever since she had known of her pregnancy and told him, she had wished she had the courage not to get married but to do the modern thing that some people even in 1947 were doing and live with him 'in sin'. She had even told him so, but wistfully, soon yielding to his insistence that they marry. She hadn't been strong enough to hold out against him and (it would soon follow) his mother and her mother and everybody else they knew.

Goodbye to university, she had thought, and it was no good his saying she could go there later or in two or three years' time. She knew that would never happen now. Her reputation would be saved and the child would be legitimate. That was all. Without really knowing what being in love was like, she knew she wasn't in love with Christian.

Her mother brought out a bottle of sherry and three glasses, and if anyone thought alcohol wasn't good for Hope as an expectant mother, no one said so.

For the first time in her life Maud proposed a toast: 'To mother and baby.'

Hope stared. She could hardly believe her eyes and ears.

It had been a good and satisfactory day. On the whole. But Maud soon put out of her mind the screaming fits and destruction of other people's possessions. If she even remembered them at all. Hope was getting married to a wealthy man and would live in comfort a long way away. Nothing to worry about there. She too would have a rich husband, and she pictured the engagement and wedding rings he would give her, the dress she could have made for her wedding. But, no, no church wedding for her where the word 'spinster' would be mentioned. Still, she could have a lovely afternoon dress and hat. She might even make things up with Ethel and renew her affection for Sybil so that they could come. She would have to think about the Hardings, whether she could break her rule and forgive them for leading Hope into immoral behaviour, something she was now sure they had done, in spite of their denials. A long time yet to go before sunset, she fell asleep with the yellow light on her face.

29

Hope and Christian were married on a fine Saturday in November at St Jude's Church. Christian's mother and stepfather were there and his brother, Julian, and Hope's mother, Maud. The Hardings came with their children and a large number of Imber and Brown relatives. But no members of the Goodwin family were invited, and if Sybil Goodwin or Ethel Burrows read the wedding notice in the *Western Morning News*, they gave no sign of having done so to Maud or Hope. Rosemary Clifford, now Rosemary Lindsay and on her second marriage, wrote to Maud, sending best wishes to the young couple, passing on her brother Ronnie's greetings to his daughter and enclosing a cheque from him for twenty pounds. Maud threw letter and cheque into the fire, a rare occasion when an angry gesture of hers was justified.

Christian bought a little house in a pretty street in Chelsea and in a nursing home in Sloane Avenue Hope's son was born the following June. But long before that another wedding had taken place in Ottery St Jude. Jack Greystock had finally given up proposing to Maud when her letter came, had given up months before, and received the letter with a kind of wonder. It made him smile but he also greatly admired it. A poorly educated man himself, though not illiterate, he marvelled at the expressions she used. 'Nuptials', for instance, was a word he had never heard before. He thought long and hard about the letter, considered showing it to his mother but decided against it. It was Maud herself that he thought about, not best pleased that she had taken it upon herself to propose to him without waiting for him to come again to her, but on the whole this scarcely bothered him.

Maud was undeniably good-looking, lovely figure, good legs. She looked healthy. She had money, a private income, and he knew that rather than renting it, she owned The Larches. The daughter, who might have been a nuisance hanging about the place, was about to get married herself and apparently intended to live in London. Her existence showed him that Maud was a fertile woman who would bear him children. He would accept her proposal, but keep her waiting a few days. During those few days, which stretched into a week, Maud suffered the agonies that would have been hers had she truly been in love with Jack Greystock. He would never reply, her money would run out, his mother would forbid the marriage, one by one everyone she knew would desert her. Her daughter was soon going, her only friends would be sure to abandon her once Hope had left. The illness she was convincing herself she had when she'd told Hope she was a 'semi-invalid' was taking the form of recurrent headaches, a pain in her back, a temperature that came on in the evenings.

All these symptoms, or whatever they were, went away when Jack Greystock arrived on her doorstep. He walked in, put his arms round her and kissed her. Maud submitted, she thought she had better. After all, there would be plenty more of it if they were to be husband and wife and she must get used to it. Ronnie Clifford and the springtime meadows were a world away.

Genial and cheerful when everything was going his way, Jack told her without being asked that he had never believed a word of that village gossip, but he was adamant on the subject of a register office wedding. Of course they would be married in church, no question about it.

'Don't let me hear any more nonsense like that,' said Jack, no longer genial but taking a hectoring tone.

Maud whimpered but let him hear no more nonsense like that. The vicar, an innocent, unsuspicious man, took it for granted she was a widow and that was how she was referred to in the banns: 'Maud Jean Goodwin, widow of this parish'. She could hardly believe her luck and was cheerful for the rest of the day. But in the years to come she sometimes wondered if that single word, the wrong word in the right place, would make her marriage illegal; if perhaps the time came when Jack wanted to escape matrimony, or, come to that, she did, they could get out of it by telling the vicar she had really been a spinster.

The wedding was quiet, attended only by Jack's mother and some village people, his friends, not Maud's. But the Hardings came and Mr and Mrs Christian Imber came. Jack took Maud on honeymoon for a long weekend to Sidmouth, where she began sharing a bed with a man, something that had never happened to her before, and experienced something else that had only happened twice, sexual intercourse. She remembered something she had forgotten for years, the teacher telling Hope and the other girls that sex between husband and wife was a 'special kind of loving embrace'. She had no intention of passing that one on to Jack. He never said much, but told her again and again that he was crazy about her. It became a kind of mantra, accompanying every sexual advance. He never used contraception as he hoped for several children, and she didn't know how to.

If Hope's marriage, entered into so young, seemed happy enough, with four children arriving in twelve years – they jogged along, as Christian put it, pointing out that few people divorced in the 1950s – Maud's was something of an ordeal. While Jack kept her in a higher level of comfort than she had been used to, he behaved as if the Married Women's Property Act, now more than seventy years old, had never been passed. Taking it for granted that everything she possessed should be transferred to him, he nevertheless refused her a joint account on the grounds that women knew nothing about handling money. Jack was a sadist in a small way. It amused him to make Maud afraid of him, justifying his intimidating behaviour by reminding himself that his wife hadn't been a pillar of virtue when he married her. There was the illegitimate child for one thing, then the funny business of pretending her brother was her husband, not to mention that murderer who had lived in her house. A spot of bullying was only what she deserved.

He was a big man with a loud voice, and her feeble shows of defiance resulting in his, 'That's enough of that, my girl,' his hands clenched into fists, reduced her to a sullen silence. He never struck her but often thrust his face close to hers, his jaw jutting, as he reminded her that in making her wedding vows she had promised to obey him. The children he wanted never came. If he blamed her he never said so, though his mother sometimes reproached her, accusing her of 'doing something to interfere with nature'. But the Greystocks lived well. Windstone Farm was a land of plenty while for years the country suffered post-war privation. Their harvest supper was a great event in Ottery St Jude. Maud did most of the cooking for it – the best cakes on display were hers – as she did for the dinners Jack liked to give frequently for his numerous friends and their wives. These were the only times perhaps when Jack and Maud gave the impression of being a happy couple, as Jack boasted about her housewifely skills and showed her off in a new dress he had chosen and bought for her.

Hope and Christian sometimes came to stay with their troop of children, allotting a few days to Windstone Farm, twice as many to Alicia Brown and her husband down in the village, and a weekend to Guy and Elspeth. Jack made no secret that the Imbers' visits were a nuisance to him, but they showed him one thing, that children were tiring creatures to have about the house and not having any of his own might be a blessing. After the family had left he and Maud always found themselves closer for a few hours than at any other time, their accord deriving from a shared dislike of the Browns, Jack's because Geoffrey Brown had once snubbed him at the County Show and Maud's from the mythical *noblesse oblige*. Always quite abstemious, Maud celebrated her family's departure with a glass of sherry, while Jack had tumblers of whisky and water. Without realizing it, she had replaced her forebears with her descendants, so that Hope and Christian had taken the place of Mary and John Goodwin and their children those of Sybil and Ethel, people to be resented and ultimately disliked.

Time passed and Maud gradually separated herself from Elspeth and Guy. As Jack put it, Maud had eggs and milk and game 'coming out of her ears', and no need of charity from the likes of the Hardings, snobs as any friends of the Browns must be. Maud was in

Ashburton one Friday morning, shopping for a pair of shoes. Clothes rationing was long past; Jack had given her the money and told her it was all right with him for her to splash out a bit. A car drew up at the kerb and Ronnie Clifford got out of it. The great changes that come to a man's or a woman's appearance over the years had not yet taken place in either of them and she recognized him at once. He may have known her, and she thought he had by the deep flush that coloured his face. Her stare fetched from him an 'Oh, hello', but the word which should have come after it was absent. He had forgotten her name.

In silence she walked away into the shoe shop.

2011

I

I had never lived quite alone before. I had always shared or had a neighbour living just across the corridor. Dinmont House was quite a place to be alone in, so large, so high-ceilinged and, if in a street of houses, isolated inside its ivy-covered walls. Just as I had been when walking along the canal towpath and the cyclist nearly knocked me over, I was aware of my special vulnerability and of my baby's. Fay had known that and had asked me if I would like to stay with them for the next four months and beyond if I liked. I was grateful but I refused. She pressed me, almost nagged me, which was most unlike her. After I had failed to answer my phone a few times but let it go to message and then failed to call back, she came round – in both senses. I was determined not to stay with them, but I gave in enough to agree that in future if she rang me more than three times without getting an answer, she and Malcolm would drive over. I think she understood that I felt I had to be here for Andrew when he came back. If he ever did.

I never gave a thought to James's ghost or to power cuts. The former wasn't possible and the latter was something I could cope with. Sara came with her baby, Ashling, and Damian came with his fiancée and their baby. Fay and Malcolm often came. People talk about loneliness as if any sort of company puts an end to it: the cleaning lady coming in for two hours or someone calling himself a friend but whom you've never really liked. Anyone will do, apparently. I was lonely but I was lonely for Andrew. Not even for James, though I appreciated his phone calls and his attentive emails. I kept in mind what he had said about never again lying to Andrew, and I wondered if this extended to his telling my brother each time he was in touch with me or had his promise been to tell the truth but not the whole truth? While Andrew had lived here days had gone by when we didn't see each other, but I wasn't lonely then. I knew I would see him tomorrow and if not tomorrow, the next day.

Another source of anxiety was the thesis, and I had begun thinking that maybe they were going to reject it out of hand when I heard I had a date for my viva. I was to defend it on a day in October. I went along to confront the two women and a man, expecting to be told that many changes needed to be made, but when I walked in I was greeted as Dr Easton, to my great surprise. Mostly, after that, it was praise and congratulations, and only when I was about to leave did they mention, as if in passing, that 'one or two little things' needed attention.

I knew the trial of Kevin Drake was in November and though I had forgotten the precise date, I had this curious feeling that after Andrew had given his evidence and it was all over, things would somehow come right. But how they would resolve themselves I didn't know. Thinking along these lines would always lead me to the enormity of what I done, because it was what *I* had done, not so much what James had done. I could have said no, I should at any rate have *acted* no. And it would have been easy. It could have been done pleasantly and with a smile, with a shake of the head and a gentle removal of myself. Now, when I revisited the event, I could hardly imagine why I had done it. I wasn't in love with James, I wasn't passionate about him, madly attracted, nothing like that. These inquisitions always ended with my telling myself that if I hadn't done it I would not have been carrying Tess, not had Tess inside me, moving herself about in a cheerful determined way.

Last winter the weather had been bitterly cold, heavy frosts and snow falling in November. We even had that rarity, a white Christmas, that so many people seem to enjoy. This year it is mild, even warm, like September. Flowers are coming out that shouldn't bloom till April and yesterday I saw a swallow that should have gone off to a southern country but was deceived by the mildness and stayed behind. I worried about that swallow, though I never saw it again, and I wondered if it had died. But the cold we expected never came.

It was mild, but it still got light late in the mornings and dark early in the evenings. Fay often came in on her way home from work and once or twice it was warm enough to sit in the drawing room with the French windows open on to a winter garden where the leaves were still on the trees but falling gently. On one of those evenings, after Fay had gone and I had bolted the front door, the doorbell rang. This happened seldom, just as the landline rang seldom. Callers (in both cases) used their mobile phones, either in preference to the landline or on the doorstep. The doorbell ringing was so unusual, especially since I was alone in the house, that at first I didn't know what it was. Then I did and decided not to answer it.

Its ringing again, insistently this time, brought to mind Maud in *The Child's Child* hearing the bell but not answering it when Bertie had walked all those miles on a cold, wet night. In the end she did because Hope made her. But I had no little girl yet to impel me. I wasn't going to answer that door, not I, a lone woman in a big house at eight in the evening. Instead, I went into the study and looked out of the window. A man and a girl were walking away down the path, but they both turned round when I opened the window.

Their appearance registered strongly with me, and it was well it did. They were young, she several years younger than my graduate students, he nineteen or twenty. He wore those clothes that have become a uniform for men the tabloids call 'youths', black leather jacket, blue sweatshirt, jeans, while she wore a skirt that came half-way down plump, naked thighs that were red from the cold. It might be a mild night but it was November. Her hair was the colour of custard, too orange a blonde to be natural, his invisible because he had shaved his head. In the light from the study window I could see the acne pits and scars on his face.

Of course I didn't take all this in before I spoke to them and they to me, but while they were speaking, while he was asking me if my brother was at home. Not if he lived at Dinmont House, but if he was in.

'Mr Andrew Easton,' was how he put it in that London street talk that is often quite hard to understand. 'Is he like in now?'

The girl was nodding her head.

They were not threatening, they were not aggressive, but I felt I must be careful. I must be cautious and non-committal. Tess moved, gently waving a hand or a foot. 'He doesn't live here any more. He moved out a long while ago.'

'Where's he gone to?' This was the girl murdering the English language, so that I had to ask her to repeat what she had said.

'I don't know,' I said. 'I barely knew him.'

What could they want? I didn't know. They seemed harmless, too young and ignorant and – well, too lost to be any sort of menace. And when I denied Andrew I felt like St Peter, though comparing myself to biblical characters isn't my style. 'Sorry I can't help,' I said, and closed the window.

They looked back to watch me watching them go.

I wrote to Toby Greenwell, telling him I had liked *The Child's Child* and thought it publishable. No one now could possibly object to the clinical details and frank references to homosexual love. I attended to the improvements I had been told the thesis needed. But all the time half my mind was on the boy with the acne and the improbably blonde girl who had come to the door. I couldn't forget them. I wished I hadn't thought of that phrase about murdering English. Murdering anything or anyone. Why did it bother me? I didn't know, but I dreamt of seeing someone I didn't know, someone I had never before seen, a Middle Eastern man lying dead on the pavement in his own blood, surrounded by fiendish, Brueghel-like people.

All the time we had been apart I had never contacted James but left it to him to get in touch with me, as he did quite regularly, but he and Andrew had gone away for a week's holiday that would come to an end a week or so before the trial. Their being away didn't preclude James's being in touch, he could have emailed or phoned or even texted, but he hadn't done so during their last short break. What stopped me speaking to him was my certainty that any – well, communication James got that came from me, that came from anyone, Andrew would know about. Belatedly, I wished I had asked that boy and girl for their names. Then I could have given them to the police. But for what reason? They had done nothing, they had only asked where my brother lived. I still wondered why they should want to know where he lived.

James called me when he and Andrew came back. Just to find out how I was. I told him about the boy and the girl, and James told me that it was nothing, nothing had happened. That nothingness was true for my encounter with them too. They had told me nothing and I had told them nothing except that Andrew no longer lived at Dinmont House, which was true. James almost dismissed it, but I knew he disliked anything about the coming trial being discussed and this wasn't even, as far as we knew, about the trial. Talking about Martin Greenwell's book would be a distraction from that for him, and I wanted to discuss it with him. I wanted to talk to him about what he knew of his great-uncle and if he had met a fate similar to John Goodwin's. My mind going back to the boy and the girl, I thought that they might have had some entirely different reason for wanting to contact Andrew, though I was bound to say to myself that I couldn't imagine what that would be.

Fay told me that the trial was due in a week's time. After the incident with the shaven-headed boy and the blonde girl I would be glad when it was all over. I tried to put it out of my mind and more or less succeeded. Then I woke up in the middle of the night to ask myself if the shaven-headed man could be Gary Summers, the one who was with Kevin Drake at the time of the murder but of whom Andrew and James couldn't be sure enough to identify. No photographs of him had been in the papers and I knew his name only from Andrew.

Four days before the trial was due to begin I was out, meeting Louise for lunch in Hampstead High Street. It was a fine, bright day but rather cold, and baby William was almost invisible inside his furry brown all-in-one garment that made him look like a plump puppy. Next time we met, I would have baby Tess with me, similarly wrapped up, for it would still be winter and probably much colder. She, too, my daughter, would be related to James's great-uncle, a great-great-niece, something I had never thought of before. Louise's news was that she and Damian were getting married, and I thought to myself that this marriage would legitimize William, though I doubted if anyone cared much about that or even noticed it. It was just that I tended to think along these lines since the thesis.

Louise came back with me to Dinmont House for an hour or so. We had tea, I saw her to the tube station and I began the fairly long walk back up the hill. It gets dark so early at this time of the year and the sun having long gone behind the gathering clouds, it was dusk before I came within sight of Dinmont House. Our street, which is rather more like a country lane, is always quiet and apparently deserted. The people who live in its few houses come and go in their cars, which are parked inside garages. If there is on-street parking, no one uses it. So I was surprised to see a man standing by our front gate and, when he saw me, he moved a little down the road. The street is full of big trees with leopard-skin trunks, planes I suppose, and he stood under one of them, his head turned away, until I had opened our gate and walked halfway up the path towards the front door.

He must have moved fast and silently. I had reached the porch, glazed in and with a kind of glass hood over it, when I turned my head and saw him closing on me. It's an unpleasant sensation to turn and, expecting to see someone in the distance, find instead within inches of your face another, unknown, face, especially perhaps one with a scarf tied round it under the hood. I cried out,

'What do you want?' – a useless manoeuvre as no one was within two or three hundred yards.

'You know what I want.' He clamped his hand over my mouth. I tried to duck, but the pressure of that hand on my face was too great. 'If you do what I tell you, I won't hurt you.'

I suppose they all say that. At any rate they all say it in films and on TV. I thought of Tess, and as I did I felt her move gently. I looked at my attacker. He was a big man, not the shaven-headed boy.

'Give me your bag.'

A pregnant woman is the most vulnerable of human beings. Anything I could do – kicking him, kneeing him, stamping on his foot – would ultimately result in injury to me and therefore to her. I gave him my bag. He took the keys out of it, opened the door and pushed me inside ahead of him.

'Christ. A hundred people could live in here and you'd still have space.'

He couldn't have got an answer from me and maybe he didn't expect one. His voice was educated, more or less, rather like those of my students, who had spoken like the blonde girl when they were small but whose diction had got some polish in their teenage years. I thought of them and momentarily of Maud, asking myself why I had never wondered what kind of accent she had had.

He took away his hand and pushed me from him. I had to catch hold of Verity's sofa to stop myself falling.

'You know what I want to know.'

'Do I?' I said, ashamed of my suddenly squeaky voice.

He looked at me from the top of my head down to where my waist had been and a bit lower. 'You'd better.' In those two words were somehow the worst kind of threat to Tess. Death to her if not to me.

I made a little sound, a tiny noise of fear and protest.

'Tell me where Andrew Easton lives. That poof, that queen.'

My reaction was strange. My face burned and I felt myself blush as I muttered that I didn't know.

'Of course you know. He's your brother.' He was holding my bag. He put the keys back in it, took out my mobile and pressed the contact icon. I knew he was doing this because he told me so. He began a sort of running commentary on his actions. 'I'm looking for your brother's address.'

'It's not there.'

Some people add a home address to where there's space for it, but I never did. Come to that, there was no space there for Andrew, whom I'd always thought of as living here. The man didn't seem to know James's name. He told me to sit down and, when I moved to the sofa, shouted at me not to sit there but on the only upright chair in the study. When he felt in the pockets of the padded jacket he wore and brought out a coil of rope, it should have been obvious to me what he wanted it for, but it wasn't. To torture me, I thought, to whip me. But it was to tie me up. Though not in the study.

'Get up, and bring the chair.' I hesitated, flinching a little, but I did get up. 'Do it. Do as I say.'

He was carrying the rope, leaving me to carry the chair. He took a cigarette from a packet, and for some reason this frightened me more than anything else that had happened so far. As he raised the scarf to free his mouth, I thought of the cigarettes used to torture people in the thrillers I'd read on holiday or on flights, stubbed on the palms of hands or worse.

'Sit on the chair,' he said when we'd reached the dining room, the furthest room from the front door, but I didn't. I stepped backwards, holding it like a shield. The next thing I knew, he had struck me hard across the face. The way Maud had slapped her daughter but as no one had ever slapped me before. I gasped and sat on the chair. It was all I could do not to appeal to him to not hurt me. I could resist struggling, and that was easy, my eyes on the glowing cigarette tip.

Someone says of Maud in *The Child's Child* that she had led a sheltered life. But haven't most of us done that in the Western world? More now than in Maud's day? I had never been hit, nor had I ever had any physical violence done to me. To withstand it, you need practice, you need to have got to some extent accustomed to it. I tried hard to stay rigid and not to tremble, but I failed. My whole body was shaking as he tied my legs to the chair legs and my hands behind me to the chair back. My dome of a stomach was raised up now and vulnerable, but in a way the discomfort helped with the fear.

He lit another cigarette. I could hear my mobile ringing, but of course neither he nor I thought of answering it. I noticed he was wearing heavy boots, not trainers, and holding the cigarette a few inches from my chin, he raised one leg and placed his foot on a stool. Perhaps it wasn't a threat, but it seemed like one.

'Where does he live?'

I was in such fear that, insane as it sounds, I had forgotten James's address. I knew it perfectly well, though I had never been there. Something saved me then. I looked up at shelves full of Verity's books, the books that were everywhere, even in this room, and my eye caught the novels of Paul Scott. That was when I blessed Verity all over again for having so much reading matter.

'Paul. Paultons Square.' The number came to me without difficulty.

I was so enormously relieved at remembering, at the foot being withdrawn and the cigarette stubbed out (albeit on the arm of a chair), that I forgot for a moment what I had done. The enormity of what I had done.

'If you've told me a lie . . .'

'I haven't, I haven't.'

'I'm not taking any chances.'

Louise had left her scarf behind, draped over the back of a dining chair. He picked it off and gagged me with it. I knew how it was done. I'd seen it on TV. You have to bite the scarf so that it's half in your mouth before it's tightly tied. I submitted, I had no choice. The choice had been made before I said Paultons Square.

'If he doesn't live there, I shall come back.'

The gag didn't hurt and I could breathe all right but I was uncomfortable. Tess was moving vigorously, as she always did at this time of the evening. If I was deprived of air would she be? He was an expert tier-upper, I knew that each time I shifted and wriggled, but instead of loosening on my hands the rope seemed to grow tighter. The phone rang again. How long before it rang again or how many times would it have to ring before someone got frightened for me and came over?

Some places I'd lived in I would only have had to get myself on to the floor, though still attached to the chair, and pushing myself along up to the dividing wall between this flat and the next, drum as hard as I could with my feet, the chair as a means of making the noise greater, before someone would have heard and been aware something was wrong. But this house was large and isolated. Many yards separated it from its nearest neighbour. Besides, getting myself on to the floor would mean throwing myself and my baby on to a hard surface. Would that matter? Would it perhaps provoke labour, even though my due date was three months off?

I didn't even know where the phone was, where he had left it. Not that it would have helped me if I had. The clock on the dining-room mantelpiece had said ten-past six when I had first come in. It now said quarter to nine. When you've been gagged, one of the orifices through which you inhale air has been blocked. My mouth was useless for breathing, but my nostrils were still usable. But once I'd thought of that I began to worry that something might block my nose. A sneeze could do that if I wasn't able to blow my nose afterwards, and once I'd thought of it I seemed to feel a tickle behind the septum and then a kind of stuffiness I was sure hadn't been there before.

I am making myself sound a terrible solipsist, for I had scarcely given a thought to Andrew's fate, but I did then. His address had been needed so that they could kill him, I had no doubt of that. The clock told me it was nine-fifteen. However the man had travelled to Paultons Square, he had had ample time to get there by now, to collect others or one other and go to find Andrew. I prayed that he and James might be out, but if they were they must still come home some time. The phone rang again at ten to ten. This time it must be James, calling to tell me they had found Andrew. My nose hadn't blocked. My mouth ached and throbbed and the gag was wet with saliva, but all I could think of was that I had betrayed my brother for the second time.

2

It wasn't a time for crying. I remembered what Fay had said about our crying from emotion, not because we are unhappy, but still I cried. I think my tears were from fear. He might come back, he had said he would if I had given him the wrong address. I hadn't, I hadn't had the courage to do that. Had he taken my keys? I could see my handbag on the table, miles away it seemed, far out of reach even if I had any reach. The keys might still be in it, but even if they were they would have been of no use to me. It was ten o'clock and the phone was ringing again. It stopped and I was thinking of a Stephen King thriller I had read in which someone was far more horribly tied up than I but who managed just the same with incredible ingenuity and over a long time to cut his bonds and free himself. I was thinking about that when suddenly the front doorbell rang.

Frightened as I was, I nevertheless realized it couldn't be him. He almost certainly had my keys. It must be someone who expected me to answer the door. The bell rang again.

This time I leaned over as far as I could and let myself fall on to my right side, shaking with fear for Tess. On the floor, which was uncarpeted, I managed to slide and so propel myself along out into the hall and once there I made the only vocal sound I could, a kind of wordless, strangled bray through the gag. That front door is solid hardwood, but not apparently oak, which would have resisted more. Malcolm is a big man, and he and Fay had a policeman with them. I suppose the two men broke it down between them with their feet. The door fell, splintered, but nowhere near where I lay. That's one of the advantages of a really big house, there's room for a lot of manoeuvring even if you're trussed up like a chicken.

When I was free with no harm done – Tess was lurching about like a little boat in a storm – I told them what had happened. The policeman wanted to know if I would be able to identify the man, but I said I didn't think so and told him about the scarf under his hood. 'I'd know his voice again,' I said, and then I asked my mother why she and Malcolm had come, what had brought them to Dinmont House at that particular time, far too late for them to be paying a social call.

'I said we'd come. Don't say you'd forgotten.'

I had, but I remembered then.

'If I phoned three times and got no answer we'd come over.'

'Oh, yes. Yes.'

'You'll have to come back with me now,' said my mother, 'while your front door gets boarded up.'

So I picked up my handbag from the table and saw that I was right and my keys had gone. I went back with Fay, while Malcolm and the policeman went off to try to find Andrew. Fay had seen him only the day before, when he had been well and happy but not willing to talk about me, though she had raised the subject. We each drank some whisky, I remembering this was the last thing I should be doing and pouring it away after the first sip. We wouldn't sleep, we were sure of that, but Fay, who is more of an optimist than I am, kept saying that now the police knew about it Andrew would be all right.

But he wasn't. Summers and two other friends of Kevin Drake's found him, in of all innocuous places, coming out of the cinema in the Fulham Road. James had been with him but wasn't at that precise moment, having gone back to retrieve his mobile, which he thought had fallen down the back of the seat he had been sitting in. In the midst of a jostling crowd, hardly noticed, three knives went into Andrew's chest and back.

My attacker, who turned out indeed to be Gary Summers, had had several hours' start on us. It was some days before I knew what had happened. Summers had gone straight to Paultons Square, made his way into the block where James lived and in the foyer checked the number of the flat from the postboxes. You were supposed to get the porter to call up to the flat for you, but Summers avoided the lift and went up the stairs. Finding no one at home in James's flat, he turned away to come face to face with the girl who lived opposite. Yes, she had seen them go out, she knew them quite well, and James had told her they were going to the cinema. She volunteered the information, unasked, that they'd be out of there by nine-thirty and then they'd go and have a meal. She even told Summers the name of the restaurant they often ate at. As it happened, he wasn't going to need that information.

It was in the newspapers and on TV, but three days later no arrests had been made. I couldn't identify Summers, and the men that were with him remained anonymous. But it was, thank God, not murder but attempted murder. Andrew was operated on twice, lay in what hospitals (or maybe only the media) call a 'critical condition' for three days. Fay was with him most of the time and I for quite a lot of it, but they wouldn't allow poor James in. What, after all, was James but a friend?

'I wish we'd had a civil partnership,' he said to me, 'and then I could have counted as his next of kin.'

The knife thrusts had missed Andrew's heart, but one of them had destroyed his spleen. 'Who needs a spleen?' he said when he was recovering. 'I don't even know what it does.'

Did he know I sat beside his bed along with Fay and, as soon as he was allowed to, James? I never asked, and when I knew he was himself again and sitting up and talking, I went into his room in fear and trembling, sure he would turn away and cover his face in the bedclothes. That didn't happen. He was talking to Fay, saying (in typical Andrew fashion) that she would suggest that the trial be postponed for months whereas . . .

He looked up when I came in. Holding out his arms, he said, 'Mind my wounds. Hi, Sis.'

Acknowledgements

I am indebted to *The People's War: Britain 1939–1945* by Angus Calder, published by Jonathan Cape, for information on the Second World War, particularly the ways in which the war affected the British public.

Ruth Rendell

BARBARA VINE

THE BIRTHDAY PRESENT

Tory MP Ivor Tesham has unconventional tastes. And in bored housewife Hebe Furnal he finds someone to share and enact his sexual fantasies. However, one day it all goes terribly wrong. Ivor plans a special liaison for Hebe's birthday – a daring sexual adventure. But dangerous games have unforeseen costs and consequences. And when there is an accidental death, scandal and ruin cannot be far behind . . .

How long can a secret stay a secret?
How long will friends protect a reputation?
And how long before guilt catches up with you?

'Gripping, packed with menace . . . the most sinister birthday present ever' *Independent*

'The pre-eminent genius of the psychological thriller' *Herald*

'Gripping, compelling' *Mail on Sunday*

'Vintage Vine' *Literary Review*

BARBARA VINE

A DARK-ADAPTED EYE

Like most families, they had their secrets . . .

And they hid them under a genteelly respectable veneer. No onlooker would guess that prim Vera Hillyard and her beautiful, adored younger sister, Eden, were locked in a dark and bitter combat over one of those secrets. England in the fifties was not kind to women who erred, so they had to use every means necessary to keep the truth hidden behind closed doors - even murder.

'Compulsively readable... a carefully devised plot unfolded with the most cunning art. Wilkie Collins and Dickens would have admired it' *Sunday Times*

'Brilliantly plotted. Vine is not afraid to walk down the mean streets of the mind and can build up an almost tangible atmosphere of menace and unease' *Daily Telegraph*

'It is no secret that Barbara Vine is the distinguished crime writer Ruth Rendell and in *A Dark-Adapted Eye* we have Ms Rendell at the height of her powers. This is a rich, compelx and beautifully crafted novel, which combines excitement with psychological subtlety. I salute a deeply satisfying achievement' P.D. James

BARBARA VINE

KING SOLOMON'S CARPET

Jarvis Stringer lives in a crumbling schoolhouse overlooking a tube line, compiling his obsessive, secret history of London's Underground. His presence and his strange house draw a band of misfits into his orbit: young Alice, who has run away from her husband and baby; Tom, the busker who rescues her; truant Jasper who gets his kicks on the tube; and mysterious Axel, whose dark secret later casts a shadow over all of their lives.

Dispossessed and outcast, those who come to inhabit Jarvis's schoolhouse are gradually brought closer together in violent and unforeseen ways by London's forbidding and dangerous Undergound . . .

'I longed to know what would happen next. Towards the end the tension fairly gets you by the throat' *Sunday Express*

'Vine arouses a genuine fear that all that is normal is in danger of being lost' *Sunday Times*

He just wanted a decent book to read ...

Not too much to ask, is it? It was in 1935 when Allen Lane, Managing Director of Bodley Head Publishers, stood on a platform at Exeter railway station looking for something good to read on his journey back to London. His choice was limited to popular magazines and poor-quality paperbacks – the same choice faced every day by the vast majority of readers, few of whom could afford hardbacks. Lane's disappointment and subsequent anger at the range of books generally available led him to found a company – and change the world.

'We believed in the existence in this country of a vast reading public for intelligent books at a low price, and staked everything on it'
Sir Allen Lane, 1902–1970, founder of Penguin Books

The quality paperback had arrived – and not just in bookshops. Lane was adamant that his Penguins should appear in chain stores and tobacconists, and should cost no more than a packet of cigarettes.

Reading habits (and cigarette prices) have changed since 1935, but Penguin still believes in publishing the best books for everybody to enjoy. We still believe that good design costs no more than bad design, and we still believe that quality books published passionately and responsibly make the world a better place.

So wherever you see the little bird – whether it's on a piece of prize-winning literary fiction or a celebrity autobiography, political tour de force or historical masterpiece, a serial-killer thriller, reference book, world classic or a piece of pure escapism – you can bet that it represents the very best that the genre has to offer.

Whatever you like to read – trust Penguin.